THE HOLLIDAY INN

By

D. C. Cook

By D. C. Cook

The Locker Letter
Chasing Gold (unpublished)
Chasing You

This is a work of fiction. Names, characters, places, and incidents either are the product of the author's imagination or are used fictitiously. Any resemblance to actual persons, living or dead, events, or locales is entirely coincidental.

Copyright © 2022 by D. C. Cook

All rights reserved. No part of this book may be reproduced or used in any manner without written permission of the copyright owner except for the use of quotations from the book for review.

For more information

dccookbooks@gmail.com

First paperback edition November 2022

Book design by Kyleigh Poultney

ISBN 9798846127685 (paperback)

www.abooksnook.ca

Dedicated to every older sibling who feels they are responsible to keep their siblings together. I see you.

Chapter One
Molly

"Do you really have to go out tonight?" Molly chased her parents down the hall. "The inn is fully booked," she complained; running the front desk wasn't her strong suit.

"You'll be okay, Molly. It's only a couple of hours, and most people are capable of taking care of themselves." Her father, Edward, put a hand under her chin, giving her a reassuring smile.

"Can I at least have a friend over?" she grumbled, pulling her face out of his hand. It was bad enough they were making her watch the inn alone on a Friday night while Amelia was going over to Hilary's house; she had been invited to go. The least they could do was make babysitting the inn a little more tolerable. If she couldn't go to Hilary's house, they could come to the inn. It was rude to cancel plans at the last minute, but she had to, she always had to. She was the only Holliday child around to watch the inn when her parents went out.

"If you can watch the front desk with a

friend, then sure. No boys in your room." Her mother, Dorothy, waved a finger at her.

Yeah, as if that's who I want in my room. Dorothy knew Molly wasn't interested in boys, but sometimes she seemed to forget. "Whatever. Hilary's mum will probably say no. She hates driving in the snow in the dark. A Friday night, and I'm stuck taking care of guests." Molly huffed, leaning against the desk and resisting the urge to stomp her foot. She sent Hilary a text anyway; she responded with exactly what Molly expected.

`Sorry, you know how Mum is about snow.`

"Thank you for understanding." Her father kissed her head and followed Dorothy out the door.

Just because she understood didn't mean she liked it. In fact, she hated it. The inn was their job, their hard work, time, and energy. Not Molly's. She shouldn't have to be forced to take care of something she was born into. She didn't ask for it—for any of it.

She flopped on the chair at the front desk and crossed her arms over her chest. She wished they'd retire and sell the inn. It wasn't fair that she had to give up her Friday night so they could go play bingo or go to the cinema. It was a half-hour drive from the inn in the mountains to town; that was an hour round trip, not including whatever time they chose to spend there, and it was already 6:30.

Hilary invited Molly to a video call. She

THE HOLLIDAY INN

graciously accepted.

"This has to be the worst Friday night," Molly said when she joined the call.

"You say that every time you have to watch the inn," Hilary noted. "We miss you."

Molly sighed. "Why can't you just come here? This place is like a palace, we could pretend to be queens or something stupid to get us through the night."

Hilary looked at Amelia. "I wish we could. But you know how Mum is about the snow. And to drive there and back, she'd be sure to get stuck. Why are your parents going out?"

"It's their monthly date night or something. Dad's not afraid of a little snow."

If Molly was there they'd be painting together, though she was almost certain they were going to paint without her. She couldn't decide if she was hurt or jealous, so she settled on both. Not that she couldn't paint by herself, but it was much more fun with her friends.

No guests entered the lobby until nine. Molly plastered on her most believable fake smile and asked the returning guests what they thought of the town. "Magical," they always said. It took all of her willpower to not groan at the excessive use of the word. It should be magical though; Holly Grove was known for Christmas. The entire month of December, Holly Grove, England was the town to be for the most Christmas spirit.

Molly and her family have lived in Holly Grove their whole lives, and whilst it did get repetitive, she did love hearing the guests' experiences, especially those who had never been there before. They always came in with an extra twinkle in their eyes, an extra pep in their step. It almost made giving up her Friday night worth it. Almost.

"What are you doing here on a Friday night?" a middle-aged woman asked while coming up to the front desk, luggage in hand. A young boy about her age, fifteen or so, stood with her. "Surely, there's something else you could be doing." She had a thick southern US accent.

Molly mustered up her best customer service voice and turned the corners of her mouth up in the least sarcastic way she could manage. "Yes, ma'am, but my parents wanted to go out before the Christmas rush began. Are you checking in?"

"Oh yes, darlin', we ran late. I called Dorothy about it."

Molly searched around the desk for a message. Her mother didn't believe in making notes on the computer, even though that'd be way easier to locate. She finally found a sticky note attached to the desk calendar. "Tammy?"

"That's me. My son, Jacob." She smiled and showed off the boy.

"Hello." Molly kept her composure and awkwardly waved. "Let me just pull you up on the computer and we'll get your key to you." She smiled again. This customer service thing was exhausting. How much did she have to pretend to be happy to be here before it become noticeably forced? She turned her attention to the computer and dropped the act.

After a few clicks, they were checked in. "Okay, you're on the third floor." Molly turned behind her and unlocked the key cabinet. "Here is your key, room three-ten. I'll be at the front desk until ten, after that you're on your own."

"Thanks, dear. Come on, Jacob."

Molly waved them off and he grinned, which she returned out of the obligation of customer service.

Time ticked on slowly whilst she scrolled aimlessly through social media. Lots of people were posting pictures and videos from a classmate's house party. It was almost like she was there, but only seeing the highlights. Molly wasn't getting any of the gossip, nor what everyone was wearing. Not that she cared what people wore to a house party in December unless it was themed. She wasn't particularly interested in attending house parties anyway; she'd much rather spend her time with Hilary and Amelia, painting, or alone watching anime.

Finally, ten o'clock came and her parents would be walking through the door any minute. She decided to wait instead of going to the house. They liked to check on the inn a final time to make sure everything was fine before going home.

The door opened, but it was guests coming

in for the night. Molly offered them a polite greeting as they walked past her to get to the stairs.

At 10:30 she figured they were tired from their trip and went straight to the house instead. She closed the desk, locking everything, and brought the cash box to the safe in the office, also behind the front desk, and locked that door. She changed out of her shoes into her winter boots and put on the rest of her winter wear before bracing for the cold.

She made the short two-minute walk, which felt longer in the snow, to the house, but there was only Mum's new car in the driveway. Molly thought it was strange that they took Dad's truck that seemed a little too old to be functional.

"Hello?" she called into the single-level home after unlocking the door. Dorothy and Edward had it built this way for the kids, so they would have eyes on them at all times. Every door to each room was visible from where Molly stood. "Mum? Dad?" But the house was dark, and no one answered.

After undressing from the cold, Molly pressed her mother's contact on her phone, letting it ring until it went to voice mail.

She sighed. "Hey, Mum, I'm glad you guys are having a good time, but could you call me back, so I know when to expect you?" She hung up and went to her room. A room she used to share.

She sighed again as she jumped on her bed.

THE HOLLIDAY INN

The house had become so lonely so quickly. She closed her eyes, wishing that everyone would come back.

❄ ❄ ❄

She woke up to banging on the front door. The sun wasn't up yet and didn't look like it had any plans to be for another hour at least. The winter air stung her face as she opened the door.

"Can I help you?" she asked, only just registering it was a police officer.

"Do you know an Edward Holliday?"

She nodded, though he knew the answer; she knew for a fact that he did. The officer had come to the inn for Christmas parties for years. Darwin, his name was. He was familiar with her family; the whole town knew them.

"He's my father. What's this about?" She shivered as the cold December air made itself comfortable in the kitchen. "Come in."

The police car sat where her father's truck was usually parked. Her mother's car sat alone, like it was waiting for Mum to return. She made tea while Darwin took off his coat. She didn't want to believe that something had happened. Her father was always such a careful driver. She complained about it all the time that just because he was old didn't mean he had to drive like it.

"Molly," he said like they were old friends.

"Don't." She bowed her head. "The sun is

barely up, how can you say anything that isn't good news?"

He looked at her like she was a wounded puppy. "We found your father's car in the ditch on the way toward the inn. We found a phone, but it's locked." He pulled it out of his jacket. "We weren't able to identify the woman with him."

"It's Mum." She took the phone with shaky hands and put in the passcode. "They left together."

"I thought it was, but I had to ask."

She found the voice mail inbox and played back her voice mail asking them to call her back. Tears stung her eyes. Everything was becoming real. "Are they okay?"

"They were severely injured. We're not sure how long they've been sitting out there. It looked like they had some frostbite, too. They are at Saint Jane's hospital in surgery."

"Um..."

"We'll need you to come in to positively identify them."

"Everyone knows them."

"I know, but it's policy."

Molly stood at the kitchen counter in silence, letting all the information sink in. Darwin didn't say anything. Her father was one of his good friends. This news had to be extremely difficult to give.

"Do you have anyone you can call to stay with you? Declan, Ainsley, maybe—"

"Yeah." She cut him off. The more family

that got involved, the more complicated and angrier everyone would be. This wasn't a time for anger, for past mistakes or past trauma. No, when her family was involved, there was always drama. She needed to only pick a couple of people until there is a final outcome.

"I can't leave until you call someone. You're a minor under the law. I know you know how to take care of yourself, but don't you want someone with you at a time like this?" He set his teacup down.

"Fine." Molly pulled out her phone and clicked on Declan's name in her contacts. It'd been so long since they'd talked that it would've been harder to find him in the messages.

"Molly?" His voice was groggy. "Why are you calling so early? Wait, why are you calling?" Of course, she had woke him up, the sun was barely shining over the mountains. It might as well be midnight.

"Mum and Dad have been in a car accident. All I know is they're in surgery." She tried to keep her voice from cracking, but inside she was ready to crumble. Her own voice was foreign to her ears. This couldn't be happening to her. She took a breath to steady herself.

"I'll see you in four hours," he said. The rustling on his end meant he was getting out of bed to come to her now. "Did you call Ainsley?"

"Not yet, can you do that?" She wanted to see her sister more than anything, but seeing those two again, she didn't know how they'd get through it.

"Of course."

"They want me to go to the hospital to identify them." She leaned over the sink like she'd seen her mother do many times before when talking on the phone. She would sigh and rub her forehead. Molly did the same, it brought on an odd sense of calmness. She did it again.

"I can meet you at the hospital."

"Sure, I think the police have to stay with me until you arrive." She glanced over at Darwin, hating that he had to stay with her; all he did was remind her of her father.

"Four hours." His tone reassuring, but Molly felt anything but reassured.

"Bye." She turned her attention to Darwin. He looked so out of place in the house. She'd only ever seen him at the inn in his casual attire. He wasn't the same person that met her dad for poker. He wasn't the same person who laughed at her dad's terrible jokes, nearly spilling his spiked egg nog on the sitting room floor of the inn. No. He was now the man who gave her the worst news. She wasn't sure if she could ever forgive him for that.

Chapter Two
Declan

Dating during the holidays was always tricky for Declan. Some girls wanted him to join their families for their traditions, others weren't even sure if he was worth bringing home to Mum and Dad. He never thought he gave off the vibes of a player; he thought himself to be very respectable and respectful to women. Either way, he found it in his best interest to avoid dating from December until March. At least that's what he told himself. Truth was, he had a problem with women: he was in love with someone already.

But when the hot nerd from IT asked him to grab a drink after work, he wasn't able to say no. He never dated for anything serious since moving to London, he was always kind and did have good intentions, but no one compared to the one that got away.

"How long have you been in London?" Jamie asked.

"'Round five years. I moved here when I was eighteen. You?" Declan sipped on his whisky neat.

"Lived here all my life." She paused as she piled nachos in her mouth. She was a bit petite for his tastes, but she was warm and inviting.

Everyone at the company wanted to date her; she chose him, and he almost had to oblige. If only to rub it in his co-workers' faces. He was glad she was nice and not full of herself.

"What brought you to London at eighteen?"

"I'm from a small town, I needed to branch out, do something for myself, in a place where no one knew who I was. There was—" He stopped himself before diving immediately into his family drama. There was an essence about her that invited him to talk like he was unable to control himself. "There's just a lot of unresolved issues." Which was quite an understatement.

"I hear that. My parents retired and moved to Alaska. Alaska! Who the hell moves to Alaska? Don't normal people retire to Florida or something more cliche?" She chuckled, her shoulders moving slightly; he wasn't proud that his first thought was what her shoulders looked like without her shirt. "So, I'm usually left to my own devices around this time of year." She ran her hand down her long blonde ponytail and flicked it behind her.

He nodded. Here's where she invited herself into his plans or wants to do something just the two of them. He braced himself, thinking of the best way to get out of it this time. He'd be leaving for Holly Grove on December 24 and returning on the 26th, just as he'd always done. He wasn't about to invite a girl he'd only just met to Christmas with his parents.

THE HOLLIDAY INN

"Oh. Oh no, I'm not trying to guilt you into anything. The holidays are only weeks away. That wouldn't be fair."

He let out the breath he'd been holding. "Right." He eyed her. Was this the perfect girl? She seemed to know his thoughts, either a blessing or a curse. And she was easy on the eyes. Too easy. The type of pretty you see on television: blonde hair, blue eyes that seemed to sparkle, a body that probably took a lot of working out to achieve. He couldn't stop looking, it was probably creepy at this point. He cleared his throat and turned away to face the bar. "So, why did you ask *me* for drinks?"

"Being the new girl, let alone attractive, people are always all over me, asking me out. It's hard to make friends when everyone is all over you. But you weren't. I thought if anyone was worth getting to know it'd be the person who wasn't treating me like a shiny toy."

"You invited me here as friends?" he asked, raising his eyebrows, unsure if he was relieved or disappointed.

One corner of her mouth turned up. "No, are you blind?" She playfully punched his arm. "I've been trying to flirt with you all night. But you seem a bit stand-offish."

"Right, sorry." He let out a light laugh. "Normally I don't date this close to the holidays; girls can get a bit weird." He finished his drink and bit into a nacho, all while Jamie watched him, waiting for him to go on. He sighed, giving in. "No one I see is worthy of taking home, not since..."

"There it is," she said with a smile, surprisingly. "You're still on an ex." Her smile lingered; it was the last thing he expected from someone on a first date. "How long?"

Declan laughed, embarrassed. "Five years, but in all honesty, I've been ready to find someone else for a while now. I'm so used to being on my own that not everyone can match how I feel when I spend time by myself."

Jamie nodded. "It's hard to forget your first love. Took me a long time too."

Something in the interaction changed him. Maybe it was how easy he felt around her, maybe he was just scratching an itch, trying to forget his first love. "Do you want to come back to my flat for tea?"

"Absolutely." Jamie put her empty glass down and hopped off her bar seat. She followed him to his car, and he took her back to his place. He hadn't thought about taking her home when he agreed to see her outside of work. But he was comfortable.

A cup of tea and a glass of wine later, and the next thing he knew he was woken up by the ringing of his phone. *What time is it?* he thought, holding his head. No hangover, but a mild headache, nonetheless.

"Molly?" he asked after checking the caller ID. "Why are you calling so early? Wait, why are you calling?" He tried to keep his voice low, so as not to wake up Jamie beside him.

"Mum and Dad have been in a car accident.

THE HOLLIDAY INN

All I know is they're in surgery." Her voice cracked. She'd be alone with Mum and Dad in the hospital, there would be no one around to take care of her.

"I'll see you in four hours," he said. Jamie shifted. He watched her as he got out of bed to get dressed. He held the phone between his shoulder and his ear as he jumped into his skinny jeans. "Did you call Ainsley?"

"Not yet, can you do that?" He could feel she was scared, trying not to cry, poor kid.

"Of course."

"They want me to go to the hospital and positively identify them."

"I can meet you at the hospital." He understood why he was her first call, why she didn't want to call Ainsley herself. He wondered if she would call anyone else. Maybe she just wanted them two there, to not worry anyone unless needed. Their family was a lot. A lot of drama.

"Sure, I think the police have to stay with me until you arrive."

"Four hours," he assured her.

"Bye."

He tossed the phone on the bed, only for him to pick it back up and call Ainsley.

"Where's the fire?" Jamie sat up, the sheet falling off her chest. He cursed himself for having to leave. But if he didn't go take care of his sister, he didn't think anyone would.

"Holly Grove." He threw clothes in a suitcase while the phone rang in his ear, waiting for Ainsley to answer.

"Where?" Jamie tilted her head to the side. "I've never had a one-night stand so desperate to leave that they would leave their own home."

He couldn't help but chuckle. "Trust me, I wouldn't leave you if I didn't have to."

"Bloody hell, Declan," Ainsley answered, her voice groggy and tone sharp. "You know it's midnight in New York, right?"

He looked at Jamie. "Mum and Dad have been in an accident. I'm on my way to Molly now."

Jamie began to get dressed.

Ainsley immediately changed her tone. "Oh god, that poor child. I'll catch the next flight." She hung up, and he sent a text to Molly. This would be the first time the three of them were together again in years.

"I'm sorry." Jamie wrapped her warm body around him. "I'll be here when you get back. Who is Molly?"

"My younger sister. She's fifteen. She's going to need someone to care for her and help her with the inn. And I just got off the phone with my eldest sister, Ainsley." He ran his hands through his hair, weight already falling onto his shoulders. "This is going to be a mess." He walked her to the door. "We'll do this again when I get back."

"This?" She motioned into his apartment touching his chest; heat rose into his face. "I know what you mean, Declan." Then she kissed him like he was her boyfriend and left. He wasn't far behind her.

Declan would be lying if he said he didn't want to go back home, but he never felt there was a reason, and he loved his job in London.

He couldn't stop thinking about Molly and what she must be feeling. This had to be the hardest on her. She was still living with them, saw them every day, and knew them more than the rest of the siblings. He'd gone home last Christmas, but Ainsley hadn't been home in a few years. He would be surprised if she stayed longer than a week.

Sucking in a breath, he let the early December air fill his lungs. Now that he had Jamie waiting for him, he hardly recognized what his life was now, but it didn't matter. He knew it would all fly out the window the moment he set foot in Holly Grove, the moment he saw her. He wouldn't, couldn't do that to himself.

❄ ❄ ❄

Declan met Molly at the hospital; their parents lying in their hospital beds as if they were just sleeping. Neither of the siblings were oblivious to the possibility of what the outcome could be, but neither of them wanted to discuss it; it remained the elephant in the room.

"I've identified them," she said, staring at them. "I know the reality of the situation, but they look like they're sleeping. I've seen them in this position countless times, minus the machines and tubes, of course."

Declan crossed his ankles on their father's bed, whilst Molly tucked her knees up to her chest, sitting beside their mother. "Dad would fall asleep watching football in his relaxer chair, then get mad when you'd change the channel as if he was actually watching the game." He chuckled, remembering young Molly calling it the relaxer chair because every time Dad would say he's relaxing he'd be sitting in the reclining chair.

"Don't talk about them like they're dead," Molly snapped. "They're not. They are right here." She pointed to the machines. "The machines are beeping, that means they're alive. Their chests are moving up and down, that means they're breathing."

"I know, I'm sorry." He didn't have the heart to explain to her the reality of it. She said she knew, but he didn't think that she did. The machines were breathing for their parents.

"Sorry to bother." A doctor came into the room. "Declan, I need to have a word."

He looked at Molly, she'd surely want to be part of the conversation, she always needed to know everything. But this time, she nodded and stayed in her chair. When Declan rose, she pulled out her phone.

He followed the doctor into the hall and closed the door behind him.

"They were each other's next of kin. And as the eldest sibling—"

"Ainsley is the eldest," he corrected.

"I know, it's just information to be passed along." She flipped through the chart. "Your parents, Dorothy and Edward Holliday have signed an agreement. The agreement states that they do not want any extensive measures. They do not wish to live on life support."

"I'm sorry?" That couldn't be right.

"They must have felt like it would be their time soon because they came in to see me last year to make sure they did not extend thirty days on life support if that were the case."

He shook his head, not believing that his parents would do this. "This doesn't make sense. How would they have known they'd be on life support?"

"They couldn't, really. But I believe they were tying up all loose ends. Listen, Declan, it's very important that you hear this." She closed the chart and held it against her chest. "When the thirty days are done, we will be removing your parents from the life support."

"Why the bloody hell would you do that?" Molly yelled from the open door to the room. "Doesn't anyone believe they are going to make it?" As soon as the first tear fell down her cheek, she took off.

Declan sighed, closing his eyes. He hated playing tough and hoped that this didn't break him. "Do everything you can for the next thirty days." He glanced back into the room.

Their chests rose and fell in sync. "Are they in pain?" He closed his eyes waiting for the answer.

"No."

Chapter Three
Ainsley

A small part of Ainsley actually wanted to be angry. She had to get out of bed, pack a bag, hail a taxi, and be on the next flight out of New York. It was already half past midnight.

She ended up getting a flight at eight in the morning, so she packed her bag and set an alarm for 5:30 a.m. There wasn't anything she could do until she arrived in Holly Grove. It was going to be different being back home. It had been four years since she'd been there last...*I think.*

She tossed and turned all night; neither side of her bed was comfortable. She closed her eyes but opened them immediately. Sleep would not consume her. *Molly would be okay*, she told herself; she'd have Declan, she knew that. But she was still so young.

She had fallen asleep eventually because when her alarm went off, it scared her awake. Ainsley grabbed everything she'd prepared the night prior. She hailed her taxi, and he drove, weaving around the few cars that were on the road with them. She sent a text to

Declan to let him know where she was and her ETA. Before now, Ainsley hadn't talked to Declan or Molly in a long time, she was honestly surprised that Molly wanted her there. She felt like she was about to walk into her own interrogation. Were Mum and Dad really in the hospital, or was it some elaborate scheme to get her to go home?

Then she called her boss.

Katherine was a nice person, understanding...when things were done exactly her way.

"Ainsley," she said upon answering the phone.

"So...I'm about to get on a plane to England," she said, getting right to the point, clenching, waiting for the backlash.

"What? Why?" She couldn't tell if Katherine was angry or concerned, so she went with concern.

"Huge family emergency. Don't worry, I can still edit articles and blogs whilst I'm there." Ainsley wouldn't admit to being a people pleaser, but at that moment, she wanted to keep Katherine happy. "Actually, have you given any more thought to allowing me to have a column once a month?"

"I thought you didn't talk to your family."

"I didn't. It's all very complicated. About the articles?"

"Right." She sighed. "You know how much I valued you as a writer, but I think you're a much better editor."

THE HOLLIDAY INN

Ainsley nodded, even though Katherine couldn't see her. "Right." She tried so hard not to sound disappointed. She did love her job as an editor, and she knew how important she was, but she did miss her own stories.

"If you can get me something good by the twenty-third, I'll run it in the Christmas edition. But it has to be *good*."

Ainsley perked up. "Oh, thank you, Katherine."

"And take a few days to spend with your family."

They hung up and she waited impatiently for her flight, which had been delayed...twice.

Hours felt like days waiting for the flight to leave. She shifted on her seat, standing to walk, thinking that airports should invest in comfier chairs.

Declan called to check-in.

"What time is it there?" Ainsley asked.

"One in the morning. Molly just fell asleep. We're in the living room watching a romantic Christmas movie. I'm stroking her hair."

"Is she okay?" She couldn't help but feel some type of responsibility. Maybe if she'd been more present, if they had talked more, Molly wouldn't be so alone.

"I don't know." Declan sighed. "When do you get in?"

"Seven your time, in London. So, I'll be at the inn around eleven."

"Okay. We can go visit them when you get in."

She didn't know why it hadn't occurred to her that she'd have to visit them in the hospital. Would they be unconscious? Would they be their old selves, laughing and welcoming? Or would they be stand-offish because she hadn't come home in four years, and she'd left nearly seven years ago?

The siblings stayed on the line, both quiet.

"When's the last time we were all together like this?" Ainsley asked.

"We won't be all together." She didn't know what to feel at this statement. Relief? Anger? Disappointment? She knew their family was damaged, but it didn't seem right. "And never like this."

"I suppose you're right." The seatbelt light above her head lit up. "I have to go; the flight is taking off."

"See you soon."

She spent the entire flight thinking about seeing her younger siblings again. Would she be welcomed? The higher the plane went the harder it became to breathe. She hadn't talked to her siblings in what felt like years, there was an occasional text wishing happy birthday or happy holiday. Declan was right about one thing; they wouldn't really all be together.

❄ ❄ ❄

Ainsley wished she had taken a sleeping pill; the entire flight she was riddled with anxiety. Her head throbbed from being awake for so long, her eyes constantly felt like they were being weighed down by anchors. Surely, she shouldn't drive whilst tired, but she needed to get to the inn. Once she got the rental car, she stopped for coffee. *Mum would be so disappointed that the Americans got me to switch over to coffee so easily,* she thought. Tea was sacred in the family, though the Brits were widely known for their love of tea, Dorothy took it seriously. Coffee was less than. The only reason it was ever stocked at the inn was that their guests were typically from North America. Then she began the four-hour drive to The Holliday Inn.

The trip was a blur, and she stopped at a local cafe for another cup of coffee. "Ainsley Holliday?" She looked down from the wall menu at the person who spoke. "Ainsley!"

"Olive?" She'd changed so much. "Wow, you look incredible." Olive came around the counter and hugged Ainsley.

"How are you?" Ainsley was surprised how easily they got on; there was no bad blood between them. Olive looked almost happy to see her. Then again, she wasn't the one who broke up with Olive.

"I'm alright. Have you seen Declan?"

Olive's entire body shifted, and she tucked a piece of loose brown hair behind her ear. Ainsley gushed over how soft Olive's tan skin looked; Ainsley dealt with chronic dry skin in the winter.

"Sorry, I shouldn't have said anything." Ainsley waved her hand as if to wave away the comment.

"No, it's okay. I was sorry to hear about what happened to your parents."

"They'll be okay. Can I get a coffee please?"

"Of course."

Ainsley took the lid off to cool it down, immediately bumping into someone.

"Are you fu—" She looked up at who had the audacity to spill scorching hot coffee on her? "This is extremely hot," she said between clenched teeth. Tall, light brown hair, great beard, black glasses. If she wasn't in such a pissy mood, she *might* think he was attractive, she might have even flirted. *Not today, sir.* "Watch where you're going," she fumed. All she wanted was a comfy bed to lay down in and *this* was the price she had to pay. She'd been awake for over a day, not to mention extremely jet-lagged.

"Oh my...I am so sorry. Let me help," he stuttered, grabbing a napkin, and starting to pat her chest.

"What the bloody hell are you doing?" She stared at him, her jaw falling open and eyes wide in shock.

"I'm..." He looked at his hands that were touching her breasts. "I am so sorry." His face turned red, and he fumbled with the napkin, pulling away.

She pushed his hands away from her. "Then stop touching me," she snapped.

THE HOLLIDAY INN

He cleared his throat, regaining his composure. "I'm Gavin."

Ainsley narrowed her eyes at him. "I'm bothered. Goodbye."

She walked around him, trying not to think of her coffee-stained clothes or how her skin burned. Did *Gavin* really think introducing himself would charm her out of this mood? Though he was quite attractive. *Don't. Don't even go there.* The inn was thirty minutes away from the heart of town. Finally, she pulled into the driveway. The inn parking was practically full, so she parked in front of the one-level home her parents had built when they bought the inn. No one appeared to be inside and when she tried the door, it was locked.

"I'm already so over this trip," she grumbled as she trudged through the path that was recently covered by a soft layer of snow. She shoved her bare hands in her pockets and went to the inn.

"Whoever decided snow was essential to the environment clearly never had to live in it." She shut the front door behind her, and then grinned at her siblings who sat at the front desk.

"Ainsley!" Molly ran to her and hugged her tightly. "I'm so glad you're here." She was growing up into a fine young woman. Ainsley had expected to see the same ten-year-old kid who was shorter than her, but Molly was eye level now, her natural blonde hair tied in a ponytail at the nape of her neck. Molly's freckles weren't apparent in the winter as they were in the summer, at least Ainsley hoped Molly still had her freckles. Ainsley inspected Molly one more time, noticing she seemed to be at the end of the awkward teenage phase; she was becoming a beautiful girl.

"Of course, I'm here. You needed me."

She pulled back, looking Ainsley over. "That didn't stop you from not coming home in, what, four years."

Ainsley sighed. Her reasoning was complicated, she didn't want to taint Molly's perception of their parents if it wasn't tainted already. "Molly, travelling from New York to here in the winter is extremely difficult. My flight was delayed twice. I've been awake since five-thirty yesterday and the time difference is seriously confusing me." She took off her jacket. "I got burning coffee spilt on me, and I'm pretty sure Olive thinks I'm a charity case. Despite being a highly successful editor for a popular weekly journal in New York."

"You saw Olive?" Declan rose from his seat. "How is she?"

Ainsley shrugged. "She looked great, and I'm pretty sure she owns the cafe."

"How do you figure that?"

"It's called Oli's Cart. Have you two even talked?" she asked Declan.

"I kind of hoped I could get through this trip

without thinking about her." Though she knew the breakup was sudden between them, he didn't look as bothered as she thought he might be. *I guess time does heal wounds.*

"And how's that working?" Ainsley smirked.

"Terribly." He rolled his eyes. "Even though a great girl is waiting for me back in London, I thought of Olive the moment I came into town." Declan hated himself for it, five years had passed, and he was still the same pathetic boy pining over Olive.

"You've got a girlfriend?" Molly asked, finally joining the conversation. She loved Olive, maybe more than Declan did. Olive always offered for Molly to hang out. Olive was the big sister she deserved. Guilt pulled at Ainsley's heart; she wasn't good enough to be their big sister. At the first opportunity to get out, she did. Leaving everyone behind. She was surprised Molly greeted her with a hug.

"No, not a girlfriend. We went out for drinks and then I got your call." Declan barely made eye contact. He was never one to talk much about his personal life.

"Can someone please get me the keys to the house so I can wash my clothes and shower? I've been sitting in these coffee-stained clothes for nearly an hour."

"Right, sorry." Molly ran around the corner where the office was and came back with a set of keys.

"Thank you."

Her childhood room looked exactly how she left it: pink walls, a green umbrella girl quilt that her grandmother had made for her fifteenth birthday before she passed the following year. Pictures of her and Narine stuck in the mirror on the dresser from high school. *My god, we have changed.*

She used to share a room with Molly, but the age difference, when Ainsley became a teenager, was too much and she was given her own space. Molly missed it, but Ainsley didn't. She wasn't a nice teenager, always thinking she was better, that Molly was only around to bother her. She had a lot of regret about how she treated her sister back then, but even still, she loved her family.

She dried her hair with the towel and sat on her bed. She knew she should've tried harder to come back, tried harder to *want* to come back, but everyone thought she was crazy for leaving, especially for New York.

"Why not London?" Mum had asked. "It's a big city, but so much closer to home."

At twenty it felt like she was trying to hold Ainsley back. Everyone was. No one wanted to see her spread her wings and fly. She wanted to be her own person, learn who she was outside of being a Holliday.

"Why don't you want me to succeed?" she had asked.

"I do, but why do you want to leave your family?"

Her relationship with her mother had been

rocky ever since; eventually, she stopped showing up because an argument always broke out. She stopped coming home on small holidays, then she stopped coming home at Christmas, and then stopped altogether. She regretted it now, not trying to figure things out, not at least having a conversation about it, but she couldn't change the past.

In the kitchen, Declan sipped tea from their mother's favourite cup; it was white and pink that said MUM with each of the siblings' names on it. Ainsley curled her toes and pursed her lips.

Narrowing her eyes, she asked, "What are you doing with that?"

"Drinking my tea," he said, oblivious to what Ainsley was actually talking about.

"That's not your cup." She didn't know why she cared, it was argued she didn't even like her mother; but now that the circumstances have changed, everything in the past with her was water under the bridge.

"I know. I don't live here, none of these cups are mine." He didn't even look up to meet her eyes. He scrolled on his phone, sipping his tea.

"That is Mum's favourite cup, why are you using it?" She scolded him like a child.

"Because I wanted tea, and this is the perfect teacup." He finally looked at her "Why are you so worked up over a cup?"

"Ainsley, it's okay," Molly said. "It's just a cup."

"She could die, Declan, and you think her

things are *just* things?"

Molly's face fell. Ainsley realised her mistake; she covered her mouth, her body filled with guilt.

"Oh. Oh no. I'm sorry," Ainsley stuttered and pulled Molly close, but she didn't return the hug. "I didn't mean it. I'm sure they'll be fine." *It is just a cup.* She didn't care about her mother's things, she cared about her mother. But the things were what made her who she was.

"I'm ready to go see them." Molly's voice was muffled from being pressed against Ainsley. She glanced at Declan who looked stiff.

Chapter Four
Molly

Molly sat in the waiting room whilst Declan and Ainsley talked to the nurses. She fiddled with her fingers in her lap. Guilt ate away at her; she'd been so rude toward her parents that night. All she could think about was what she was missing out on. She looked around; a couple leaning together, an elderly man sitting alone doing a crossword. She wondered what everyone else was here for.

"Ready?" Ainsley asked. Molly wondered how she was still functioning after all she'd been through just to get there. On the outside Ainsley seemed collected and in charge, but what about on the inside? She stared unblinking at Ainsley, trying to read her thoughts. If she tried hard enough, maybe she could do it; she'd know all of Ainsley's deepest thoughts. But there was nothing.

Ainsley furrowed her brows. "You all right?"

Molly nodded and followed her siblings and the doctor.

"Your parents have signed an agreement that if they're on the vents for over thirty days to remove the life support," the nurse who led them to the room said. "We will do all we can to make sure they come back, but we want you to be prepared. As you're aware, they had made these arrangements last year."

Molly stayed quiet, picking at her fingers, and bit on the corner of her mouth. Would they be able to hear the siblings?

Ainsley and Declan stopped in front of a closed door. "The nurse said they're bruised, but not mangled," Ainsley said, but she forgot that Molly and Declan had already been to visit.

"Talk to them like they're awake. The nurse says it's good for us and them," Declan added. "Ready?"

No one had a choice. Molly thought she was probably the owner of the inn now. All of the responsibility was going to fall on her. Ainsley would go back to New York, Declan to London, all as if nothing has happened, as if she didn't exist to them. Would she even be allowed to own the inn as a minor?

She stared at the door, losing focus on everything around her. She gnawed at the inside of her mouth while her brain went through a loop.

"Molly, there's no need to spiral. We're going to take this one day at a time." Ainsley put her hand on Molly's shoulder. She had that look in her eye, the one where her eyes shifted back and forth when she thought about all that could go wrong. "Let's go in and tell them what's going on."

Molly nodded. "Okay."

THE HOLLIDAY INN

Declan opened the door; their parents lay on separate beds as if they were having an afternoon nap. The only difference was all the beeping machines.

"Hey." Declan flopped on a chair. "I've come home from London, probably for a short while, Molly is going to need help at the inn now that you two are laying here."

"Dec," Ainsley scolded. "Show a little respect." Molly sighed with relief; Ainsley did care about them still. "I've come home from New York, my boss is giving me the chance to have a monthly column, but she expects something great from me first." She looked at her hands, probably thinking the same thing Molly was, there was one of two ways Mum would respond to that if she could. Either super supportive, saying, of course, she could do it. Ainsley was a talent. Or she'd be condescending and say something like: "Maybe New York isn't right for you after all."

"I wanted to go to Hilary's with Amelia. Maybe if I'd been allowed to go, we wouldn't be here, with you like this."

"Molly, that is not helpful for anyone," Ainsley said softly.

"I'm sorry, Ainsley, but it's how I feel. I don't like that I'm angry about it, but maybe they'd be at the inn, cooking breakfast and wondering if this is finally the year Ainsley comes home. Or Declan stays longer than two days. Or—" She stopped herself. There wasn't a point in bringing up more past events than was right in front of them. The hurt between the three siblings was enough; they didn't need it from people who weren't even there.

Neither of them spoke. What could they say that wouldn't cause another fight? Nothing. Molly didn't want to hear anything from them, but she hated them staring at her like she was broken. She wasn't. She was angry.

"Well, Mum, Dad, Ainsley is here. She and Declan are here for the whole month from what I gather. A shame *this* had to happen to get them here."

"I'm here until we meet the lawyer. We can't do the reading of the will if they're still on life support," Ainsley said.

"Wow," Molly said sarcastically. "You really think that they're not going to pull through?" She stormed out of the room, looking for a public restroom to hide in. Her fists clenched, and despite wanting to punch something, she took calming breaths; it didn't help.

On her way, she ran into Teagan, a girl Molly went to school with, a year above her, someone who was considered an outcast. Her curled black hair hung down to her waist, she wore dark, heavy makeup, and skater clothing. Molly was always friendly to those she knew from school, but Teagan scared her. Just the look of Teagan freaked her out.

"Hey," Molly unintentionally said in passing, still desperate to hide in the bathroom.

"Hey. Molly, right?" Teagan had stopped

walking.

Oh, so I guess we're doing this. "Yeah." Molly turned her attention to Teagan.

"Molly Holliday," she said as if finally piecing everything together. "I am so sorry about your parents. Are you here by yourself?"

Molly checked behind her as if her siblings were going to chase after her. "No, my brother and sister are in the room. It's gotten a bit tense."

Teagan nodded. "I know what it's like. Not the sibling part, but the parent part."

Her mum died last year in a car accident. *Oh god, are my parents going to face the same fate?*

"I didn't mean to scare you. I just meant if you need anyone to talk to, I'm here. I know you have your friends, and I'm...but I've been where you are." She stepped around Molly.

"Hey, Teagan?" Molly shouted after her. "Thank you."

She gave a half-smile and kept walking away. Every time Molly saw her, she got a flutter in her stomach. It was like she was ready for Halloween at all times of the year in case someone decided to change the dates. But was the flutter really fear? That was the first real conversation they've ever had; she was so different than Molly originally thought she'd be. Her edges were soft, and she spoke kindly.

Molly stood in the middle of the hallway while nurses and doctors ran around her, caring for their patients that might actually make it out of there. Watching Teagan walk away, she hoped she'd turn back. She didn't. Why would she? They weren't friends. She didn't know Molly, and Molly *really* didn't know her. So why was she compelled to watch Teagan leave? Why was Teagan even there in the first place?

The Holliday siblings needed to come together, they needed to put their differences aside and forget the past. They needed to want to be together and want to do whatever they could to make sure their parents came out of their comas. But Molly was so mad, Ainsley was mad. She didn't show it, but Molly knew. Molly knew Ainsley didn't want to be around their brother. Not after what he did. But they should, they *should* want to be together, every Holliday.

Everything was getting more complicated as they got older. Molly wanted to live in the fantasy that they were happy, that they liked each other. That fantasy was easier to live in when none of her siblings lived near her. She could pretend that it was life that kept them apart. Now, though, they had to live with the reminder that there are unresolved issues between them.

Chapter Five
Declan

"Is one of us going to talk to her?"

"I'm not sure if she's genuinely mad at me or at the situation as a whole." Ainsley sat in the empty chair. "It's all so frustrating."

"Maybe you should talk to her then? You're the one who hasn't come home in three years."

"Four." She turned away.

Declan sat up straighter. "Ainsley, are you serious?"

She shrugged. "You know how they felt about New York. No one was supportive, eventually, it got easier to stay away. Especially with what happened the last time we were *all* together." She stared at Declan, explaining the situation telepathically.

Of course, he remembered. How could he not? It was the event that turned the whole family upside down. Ainsley had been furious about the whole thing; obviously still was. Fingers were pointed, feelings hurt, and people accused. It was a mess. They had never fully recovered as a family. All they did was the best they could.

She looked down at her hands in her lap. "I'm not proud of how it was handled, but I am proud of my job and the life I've created for myself, despite everyone's lack of faith in me."

"What's that supposed to mean?" Declan snapped. He wanted her to do her thing. She couldn't have been blaming him, he supported her. The family only ever wanted her to succeed. She was their sister. Declan believed they wanted her to do whatever she felt was best for herself, but Ainsley didn't.

"I don't want to get into this. I need to do some work, call the lawyer, and find something worth writing about for the Christmas edition."

"Could you write about Holly Grove? We're literally known for Christmas." Declan didn't want to argue either, whatever happened in the past was meant to stay there. This was the first time they were almost all together in years, the last thing they should do was argue.

She nodded hesitantly like this place was the last thing she wanted to write about.

"Do what you need to, I'm going to find Molly." Declan left the room, hoping things would go back to how they were before they were all old enough to think for themselves.

He sent a text to Molly, asking her to meet him in the lobby. He waited a long time. He suspected Molly was trying to avoid him and Ainsley. Eventually, she sat on the chair beside him.

"That was a lot of emotions back there."

"Yeah," Molly said with a sigh.

"The only way we're going to get through this month together is by communicating. No blaming, no harsh things. We've all grown up a bit, so we just need a little time to adjust to each other."

"I know." She sighed. "I can't stop thinking about how they would feel if they knew they were missing out on you and Ainsley. She talks about you guys all the time." She rolled her eyes. "It's a bit annoying, actually. You don't even live here, and I'm still being compared."

"Neither of us wants that. We aren't the enemy; no matter what, we're here for you."

Molly sighed, pressing her back deeper into the back of the chair. "I can't believe I still have to go to school."

"We can probably get you out for a day or two with a note if you want, but not the rest of the month; plus, you'll be on Christmas break soon."

"I know. Let's get Ainsley and get out of here."

Declan opened his phone to message Ainsley, and there was an unread message from Jamie, checking in on how he was doing. He was still unsure if he wanted to go for it. She was in London, she was attractive, and they were obviously compatible in more ways than one. But being back in Holly Grove, his thoughts lingered on Olive; he still hadn't seen her, but she consumed his thoughts. It was for the best that he stayed away from her, it would only hurt more having to leave again.

"Who is Jamie?" Molly asked.

"No one." He quickly locked his phone and

shoved it in his pocket.

"You're awfully secretive for a no one." Molly smirked.

"We've been on one date. Call Ainsley," he ordered.

"Let's stop for something to eat," Ainsley said once they were all in the car. "There's a great cafe that has really good sandwiches."

Molly and Ainsley exchanged smirks. Ainsley wiggled her eyebrows.

"It's not going to work. And even if I did see Olive again, we want different things. She's made it clear that she would not move to London. Ever." He didn't want to have this conversation, but he also knew his sisters, and they would press him until he blew up; he wasn't going to blow up.

"Fine. But you two are going to run into each other soon enough and realize you both made a stupid mistake." Ainsley folded her arms and pressed her back against the seat.

"It was five years ago. I've moved on. I've been dating. I told you about Jamie."

She smiled like she didn't believe him, which she didn't. "You should have seen her when I mentioned you. It was like the wounds were still fresh. I reckon she still fancies you."

"I'm driving; can we not do this whilst I'm trapped?"

"It's the only time we can talk about it. You won't talk about it otherwise."

"Maybe because I want to keep my love life private for me. I don't need to talk about who

I fancy with my sisters."

"Declan, come on—"

"Ainsley, I said enough." His tolerance grew thin, his patience wearing out. Did he want to see her? Yes. He wanted to see if the life she chose over him was worth it; because he wasn't sure his was. He wanted to see if maybe she regretted ending it as much as he denied he did. Whatever the truth was, especially if it was worth it, would hurt too much. There was no reason to pretend their situation was different this time. She was never going to go with him, and he was never going to stay. Seeing Olive on purpose would only hurt him more. He couldn't forget about their relationship, she meant too much to him, but he could move on. He could find someone just as nice, just as fun, just as sexy...

He wasn't here to rekindle a romance; he wasn't interested in that. He was only there to help Molly get adjusted. Plus, there was a perfectly nice girl back in London, where he lived, where he wanted to be, and where he wanted to continue living.

No, he wasn't here to rekindle an old romance with Olive, but he'd be lying to himself if he said he wasn't curious if things could change.

Chapter Six
Ainsley

Ainsley packed up her laptop bag for work. She didn't hold out much hope for getting any work done in the quiet house where her mum should be baking shortbread, checking over her shoulder to see if she was getting the work done, her dad watching the telly on a volume that was a bit too loud. Molly should've been painting on her easel and Declan on his phone watching random videos about film theories.

Declan had gone to the inn to help Molly prep dinner for the guests. He seemed to have taken on the role of the new innkeeper. Ainsley never thought of him as the innkeeper type, or the type to take the initiative to do that role; she was impressed.

"The cafe isn't going to be open when you get there," Molly called from the front steps of the inn. "They close at six."

Ainsley checked her watch. 5:45.

"Where can I go?"

"Denny's Pub is open until midnight." Molly rubbed her arms.

"Thanks." Ainsley waved. But Molly didn't go inside until she put the car in reverse.

Denny's Pub. Seemed a lot of new places had opened since she left town. Ainsley found

THE HOLLIDAY INN

parking, grabbed her bag, and went in.

It was a large open room, filled with booths around the edges of the room. In the centre was an oval bar with seating all around it. Christmas decorations hung from every inch of the room. Tinsel draped on the back of each booth, wreath on the door, and even mistletoe hung in the door frame. Even the bar looked like Santa Claus threw up on it.

"Ainsley Holliday, as I live and breathe." The man behind the bar held his arms in the air.

"Denny Ryder. How are you?" Ainsley sat at the bar, setting her bag on the chair beside her. The two graduated high school together and had a short lived relationship. She admired those who stayed in town; they were contributing to it, unlike her. She was selfish, she knew, it was written in between the lines every time her mother spoke. Would her mother's words ever stop ringing in her ear?

Denny leaned on the bar; a towel draped over his shoulder. "Fantastic, love. Have a seat anywhere and we'll get you a menu." He looked the same as he did in high school, maybe a few more smile lines and a full beard, but his soft green eyes were the same.

"I'll need a table with an outlet. You don't mind if I work, do you?"

"'Course not. Right now, the only table with an outlet is back there. You may need to share; someone is already there."

"No worries." She went off to the table. In

New York, no one would dare share their table with someone else, stranger or otherwise, unless they were there together. But in Holly Grove, everyone knew each other one way or another. Everyone was kind and willing to help out a neighbour.

"Oh, you've got to be joking." She sighed and sat opposite Gavin.

"Well, it's nice to see you too." He glanced up from his laptop. "Did the coffee come out of your clothes?"

"It did. Though it shouldn't have been there in the first place." She opened her laptop and found the email with the article she was to edit for next week's issue.

"Menu. Can I get you something to drink?" Denny asked, sliding a menu in front of her.

"I'll have an ice water and Greek salad please," she said to Denny without even looking at the menu.

"Sure." He took the menu away with him.

"The big city has changed you, or maybe the Americans have," Gavin said without even looking up from his work.

"Excuse me?" Ainsley shot a glare at Gavin. What gave him the right to talk to her that way? They weren't ever friends; he didn't know her to begin with.

"The salad. I don't ever remember you eating a salad."

"Remember me?" She was taken aback; her heart skipped a beat. She wasn't sure of the meaning of the skipping, but it couldn't have been a good thing...could it? He had to have remembered her from high school. He was a year older than her. A flutter filled her chest at the thought of being remembered. He didn't seem to remember her for being a Holliday; if he did, he didn't make it obvious. The family of the most successful inn in Holly Grove, they'd done so much for the town, they were like celebrities, which made it easier for the trauma of the family to get around town that much faster, despite never telling anyone what happened. Rumours about them spread like wildfire, but no one dared say anything to Dorothy or Edward, in fear they'd stop contributing to the town. Eventually, everything returned to normal.

But Gavin liked her, even after she yelled at him and blamed him. She couldn't figure out why. She hadn't been nice, but that didn't stop him. She'd be lying if she said it didn't intrigue her.

Denny placed her water and salad beside her laptop and topped off Gavin's drink with a smirk. She suppressed an eye roll.

"I have work to do." Gavin and Ainsley both turned to their computers. She finished the edits on Mallory's piece and emailed it back to her. She still had Tony and Natasha's pieces to edit, but she opened a blank document to brainstorm ideas for her piece for the Christmas edition.

"If you sigh any louder, I'm going to feel obligated to ask you what's wrong," Gavin said calmly. He was watching her over the top of his laptop.

"My boss is giving me a chance to write monthly, but this article has to be good. I'm drawing blanks on ideas."

Declan did mention writing about this town...that idea felt too easy, like a cop-out. She wanted a challenge, something that would inspire and feel authentically her. The problem was, she didn't know how she was.

Gavin did some clicking with a grin. "Come over here." He patted the empty space beside him.

She narrowed her eyes. "Why?"

"Just...could you just..." His sandy brown hair bounced while he shook his head and gestured for her to move from her seat to the one beside him.

"Fine." She moved. "What do you want to show me?"

He pushed his black-rimmed glasses up his nose. "Hopefully something that inspires you." He clicked on a picture in a folder, and it brought up Holly Grove at Christmas a few years ago, as per the time stamp in the bottom right corner. The mountains hovering in the background were barely lit by the town's Christmas lights. As he clicked through the pictures of the area, and the small businesses, the people, she remembered how much her parents loved this place, especially at Christmas time.

"Wait, go back." He did, after a moment of

hesitation. She pointed to the screen. "That's me."

It was a photo of seventeen-or-eighteen-year-old Ainsley, holding a cup of hot chocolate from Rebecca's Cafe before it became Oli's Cart. She wore a knitted black hat with a white pom-pom. Her hair was longer, to the middle of her back, and curled. Now it sat just above her shoulders. She was laughing at something Narine had said, she looked genuinely happy. She wondered if that was the last time her happiness didn't rely on an exterior factor.

Then she looked at the whole picture. "Narine," she whispered. Narine, her best friend at the time, touched her boyfriend's, Patrick's, arm. The three of them were mid-laugh. They'd lost contact, even though they promised each other they wouldn't. "Why haven't I seen this picture before?" Ainsley turned to Gavin, but he was already watching her. "Earlier you mentioned remembering me."

He nodded. "I graduated a year before you, but I took photos for the yearbook."

"Gavin." She tried to remember him. He was older now, seven years older. With facial hair and bigger biceps. "Gavin Taylor?"

"Tyler, actually." He smiled.

"Well, Gavin Tyler," she said, turning back to his computer. "Have you always taken such beautiful photos?"

"I have another I think you'll like." He

moved his mouse around and opened a new picture. It was one of the inn. The yellow glow of the lights shone under the roof, lighting up the front entry. Snow glistened on the roof, all the guest rooms were lit, most by the bed side table. The inn was made of mostly windows, and each room had a set of blackout curtains, of which none were closed in the picture. A Christmas tree, all decorated and lit up, stood in the large window in the sitting room. Her parents were putting the star on top.

"Oh, Gavin." Tears stung her eyes. "Have my parents seen this?"

"No. I took it last year when I was on my way to photograph a client. No one has seen this." She couldn't tell if he was disappointed that only clients would see his work. She could get his work out there. His photography deserved to be out there. Her feelings toward him changed then. She saw the kind of man he was through his pictures. She fought the urge to rest her head on his shoulder and look at the photo of her parents until her eyes hurt.

"Send it to me. And the other one." She took his notebook and pencil and wrote down her email. "I can make sure that people see this." She moved back to her side of the table.

"The town is happy to have you back."

"The town?" She raised an eyebrow, the corners of her mouth turning up slightly. "I'm not here for long. Only until we meet with the lawyer and slash or something happens with my parents."

He reached across the table and put his hand on mine. She snapped her head to look at him. "I was really sorry to hear about your parents."

She pulled her hand back. She'd told herself she wouldn't get close. She wasn't here for anything other than her sister. But the way Gavin looked at her made her breath hitch in her throat. "Me too."

He cleared his throat, busying his hands on his laptop. "Would you do it differently? If you knew this was how it would end, would you still leave?"

"I don't regret going to New York. I love my job, but..." This wasn't something she thought she would admit, and she would have denied it otherwise, surely. "But I would come home more. I'd apologize and work things out." She wiped her nose and dabbed under her eyes, even though there were no tears. "I don't know why I'm pouring my heart out to you," she said with a slight chuckle and shut her laptop and packed the rest of her things. "I'll be going now. I'm expecting an email from you with images."

He grinned. "Of course. I'll be in touch."

"Goodbye, Gavin."

"See you later, Ainsley."

Chapter Seven
Molly

Molly had been dreading going back to school. She hadn't seen her friends since before the accident, she knew she was going to be the talk of the school. Ainsley was already the talk of the town; everyone loved her when she was around, Molly didn't know that was why she held onto her resentment. The Holliday children were known, Molly didn't like that people knew her business, or thought they did. That's what happened in a small town when your parents ran the most successful inn. Everyone loved Ainsley until she left for New York and didn't look back. It was hard not to gossip about her. Molly knew everyone would be dying to know how she was handling everyone's return.

"Do I really have to go?" she begged Declan. Ainsley would be immune to her, but Declan has always been soft for his little sister. She rested her head on his shoulder while he poured steaming tea into a mug.

"Yes. Ainsley will kill me. Besides, both of us need to work, we'll go to the hospital for dinner. Okay?" He set his mug down and held her shoulders. He smiled softly and tucked her hair behind her ear, a gesture she would've expected from Ainsley, not him.

She rolled her eyes and untucked it. "Can you drive me then?" Molly pulled out of his grasp. She went down the hall to her room to get her school bag and brought it to the front door.

"Get Ainsley to; I've got to get to the inn." He transferred his tea from the mug to a to-go cup that hadn't been used in at least two years. Their parents preferred to have fresh tea at the inn. He patted Molly's back on his way past her to get ready to bear the cold.

Snow fell from the sky almost constantly in the mountains. Today it was light, like dust floating around. It was always colder up there than it was down in the town, where the schools and businesses were. Ainsley would likely spend the day at Olive's cafe. Molly wanted to spend the day at a cafe, painting, or at home curled in her bed watching anime.

"Ainsley, I need a ride to school," Molly called from her room where she readjusted her hair in the mirror hanging on her door. Ainsley had to be out of the shower by now.

"Ten minutes," she yelled back from behind her closed door.

Molly waited in the living room, texting with Hilary and Amelia. No one mentioned the accident or asked what happened, or even how her siblings were. If roles were reversed, she wouldn't know how to ask that either. Instead, they talked about upcoming exams and what they had planned for the winter break.

Finally, Ainsley emerged from her room with her phone between her teeth, digging through her purse. "Ready?"

Molly followed her to the car.

"You're going to be okay. If there's any major developments, I will come get you."

"I know, I just don't want to be the kid with dying parents."

"But you are. Set and stick to your boundaries. When you get there, you don't want to talk about it. Don't sulk. If you truly don't want it to affect your days at school, don't sulk."

Molly sighed, watching out the window like she was the main character in a sad music video. Snow covered the trees that flashed by. Her mother would be babbling on about something she'd have to do at the inn or trying to get Molly to cover the desk when she got home. She'd take that over Ainsley yelling at her co-worker asking if they can hear her yet. She hadn't realized how much she missed the constant talking. At the moment she couldn't decide which was worse, the guilt tripping or Ainsley yelling at her co-worker asking if they could hear her.

"Bloody service. Hello!" she yelled into the steering wheel. Neither of them were sure where the microphone was, but Molly wasn't about to say anything. "Mallory, are you there?" The line went dead. "Bloody hell. I'll call her back when I get settled at the cafe." Then they rode in silence for fifteen minutes.

THE HOLLIDAY INN

The awkward tension in the air draped over Molly like a weighted blanket. She didn't know how to talk to her sister anymore, or what to say to her at this point. She wanted things to go back to normal but didn't know what to do to get them there.

Ainsley pulled around to the drop-off lane at the school. "I'll be here to pick you up. Three-thirty, right?"

"I'll text you. I might get a ride with Hilary." Molly hopped out of the rental car that was at least six years newer than their dad's truck. Shutting the door, and adjusting the bag on her shoulders, she went inside.

She didn't want to answer any questions about what it was like or what she felt. She didn't even know what she felt. There were too many different emotions building up inside. None of them felt like they were what others wanted her to say. Winter break was so close, she just needed to get through two weeks of pity stares. Maybe her parents would wake up and then she wouldn't have to deal with people looking at her like she lost everything.

"Molly." She stopped to wait for Hilary and Amelia to catch up. "I just saw your sister leave. I can't believe she's back. How long are they staying?" Amelia asked.

They took their jackets off once inside the heated school. "Until the thirty days are up."

"You really don't think your parents will wake up?" Amelia asked.

55

"No." She hated that that was the truth. But they were older, and it was the reality of having older parents. She didn't know anything about death, or what to expect from this experience, but she knew that she didn't see them coming out of it.

"Molly, hey." Teagan stopped in front of her, ignoring Hilary and Amelia altogether.

"Hello," she answered, her eyes growing wide like they do in an anime show when the main character meets a cute person. "Can I help you?" They'd barely exchanged pleasantries. Except for that time at the hospital, this was the most they'd talked. The corners of her mouth tugged upward.

"I'm sorry about your parents." Molly wanted to sigh with an eye roll, but Teagan touched Molly's arm, and it was like she stopped breathing altogether. She could practically feel Hilary and Amelia vibrating beside her; if it weren't for the shock the touch sent up her arm, she would've glared at them. "They're great people."

All Molly could manage was a nod.

"If you need anything, like just to get away, message me." Her hand slid down Molly's arm to her hand, leaving a piece of paper behind. Molly watched Teagan walk away.

"Is that—" Hilary started.

Molly opened the piece of paper to find Teagan's number written on it. Her heart rate quickened as she sucked in a breath.

"Girl!" Hilary hit Molly's arm with a stupid

grin on her face.

"You want it?" Molly offered. "You can have it." Molly didn't know what intentions came with Teagan giving her number. Molly never thought she'd want to find out, but here she was thinking about what else she and Teagan had in common.

Molly wasn't typically into girls who looked like Teagan, but the way her hand felt sliding down Molly's arm made her reconsider pretty much everything. Molly's liking of women wasn't something that was widely known like Teagan's was, but the way Teagan acted was like she knew. They shared something, and Molly could feel it physically in her body.

"She gave it to you. She knows what you're feeling. She might be the only one who knows, besides your siblings," Amelia said.

Teagan's mum was in a similar accident just the year before. Though she died on impact. Teagan wouldn't know the feeling of waiting to see if her parents were going to die. She knew right away. *Is it wrong to envy that?* Molly didn't want them to suffer, or her siblings. This was all so emotionally draining.

"I don't want her pity."

"It's not pity, she's empathizing," Hilary said.

"No. It's not a good idea. We promised each other no dating this year," Molly said as a defence, but even though the thought of actually dating a person scared her, she was intrigued by Teagan's interest.

Molly's friends rolled their eyes. "That's because none of us could get a date. Maybe she'll ask you to the winter dance." Amelia smiled.

Molly liked Amelia, she was kind and gentle, but a little too naive. Her parents never fought, they were disgustingly in love, she had a younger sister, and they were devoted to God. Half this town thought God and Jesus were the greatest gifts to this earth. If he was so great, why was he taking Molly's parents away from her when she still needed them?

"You two would be so cute together." Hilary touched Molly's hair, draping it behind her back. It was shorter than Teagan's but longer than Ainsley's. It sat at about mid-chest; so did Amelia's ginger hair, and Hilary's straight blonde hair. Teagan and Molly were two opposites. Teagan wore dark makeup and Molly's was very natural. Teagan wore a lot of dark colours while Molly wore neutrals. Teagan listened to some type of grunge music and Molly loved pop. Nothing about them said compatible.

It was rumoured that her dad was trying to poach the inn from Molly's parents. Claiming they were too old to run a business as demanding as an inn in the mountains. And it was clear that she blamed her father for her mother's death since he was the one driving in terrible road conditions. Molly worried that with her parents gone, Declan wouldn't be able to handle the job and he would sell. Molly hoped the rumours weren't true.

"Just think about it, at least." Amelia nudged Molly with her shoulder. Molly smiled at her as if to say okay, just so she'd let it go.

Molly planned to toss the paper in the first bin she saw, there was no reason for her to want to spend time with Teagan. Nothing about the two of them as friends, or otherwise, made sense. But when she came up to the bin, she put her hands in her pockets, shoving the little piece of paper with Teagan's phone number a little deeper.

Chapter Eight
Declan

"Where is the coffee?" a bitter voice demanded.

"Sorry?" Declan looked up from the computer. On top of trying to get his mum's work into the computer and not on sticky notes spread across the desk, he also had work to do for Heather. He still had a job in London that he needed to at least pretend still mattered to him. Even though he didn't really want to do either one at this point. His main goal was to make sure Molly was taken care of.

"There's no coffee on the table." A very obviously American family stood in front of him. They looked like they needed coffee in an IV in order to survive. What was it with them and coffee?

"I'm sure I could find some tea."

The lady, with her ridiculously large top knot, scoffed. "Coffee. Are you dense or something? There was coffee the last time we were here. Where is Dorothy?" She all but cracked her neck to look around. "I haven't seen you before." She looked Declan squarely in the eyes with her hands on her hips. "She obviously hadn't trained you." Declan swore

THE HOLLIDAY INN

her head moved around in an effort to give him sass. This woman, in her forties, him in his twenties. After everything going on, he didn't have in it him to deal with the attitude.

He sighed. She was about to get a wake-up call. "I'm her son. She and my father are unconscious in the hospital. This is my first time trying to run the inn, and I have a job in London that I still need to do. So, if you could so kindly be a little more polite, maybe, just maybe, I'll help you get that coffee your body is so obviously addicted to," he said while maintaining his most professional customer service voice, adding a smile at the end, knowing his point got across.

Her mouth fell open, her cheeks turning red, and her son clapped his hand over his mouth. "I'm sorry to hear about your parents. Could you please make sure there is coffee tomorrow?"

"How about I go check the kitchen?"

She sighed. "That'd be great, thanks." She took her son to the sitting room, where normally there would be a ton of decorations, but it was empty, except for the furniture.

"Bloody guests," Declan grumbled opening every door and looking around everything. "Of course." He banged his head on the counter when he couldn't find any coffee. "Who sells coffee?"

"Knock, knock."

He turned to the back door. "Olive." He stood stunned. He was so positive that he could've gotten away with not seeing her his entire trip. But, of course, she was his parents' coffee and tea supplier.

"Declan." She stopped short. "I didn't expect to see you here. Where's Molly?"

"School. Someone's got to be here." There was bubbling in his stomach. Nerves? He watched her. He began to obsess over what she was thinking. His heart beat a little faster, his chest grew a little tighter.

Olive was as beautiful as the day he'd left. Her blonde hair was tied in a ponytail at the base of her neck and cascading over her shoulder, while she wore her toque.

She cleared her throat. "Weekly delivery. Give me a hand?"

"Sure." He followed her out the door to her company van. "How are you?" He tried not to feel weird, to not feel like there were some unresolved issues between them. Everything was black and white, they wanted different things and he would've done anything to not be in the position he was in right then, not to have the feeling bubbling up inside of him right now. He wanted to reach out and touch her back, to feel her skin on his again. It was too much too fast.

"Good. Got my own business." She smacked the side of the van with her company name and logo.

"I see that. Ainsley said too, congratulations."

At one point in his life, he was so sure she

THE HOLLIDAY INN

was the person he would marry. The person he'd have kids with, who he'd grow old with. Now she was someone he didn't know. They used to do everything together. She wasn't just a girlfriend, she was his best friend. He recognized her face, but she was a stranger to him. Nothing was more heart-wrenching. Everything from their past, the laughs, the kisses, the butterflies, the dates, came flooding back. He wondered if she thought about it too.

He suddenly remembered lying under the stars. It was summer, but it was still breezy there in the mountains. They were lying on a picnic blanket, she talked about wanting to own her own cafe, and here she was, doing it.

He felt overwhelming pride for her. She was achieving what she wanted, and him? He couldn't even stay in a relationship because he compared everyone to her, and it wasn't fair.

"How about you? How's the city?" They talked in passing, she'd go in the kitchen as he was going out to the truck, and vice versa.

"Good. I love London. I think you'd like it too." He stopped in his tracks and turned around to her. She was watching him amused, waiting for him to fumble over his words. "I didn't mean—"

A soft smile came across her face. "I know. I reckon I should mention that I'm seeing someone."

He followed behind her into the kitchen with the last box. He shut the door, keeping the heat inside. "Oh." He tried to ignore the sinking feeling in his chest. It had been five years, why would he think she'd wait for him, he certainly didn't wait for her.

"Me too, actually." It wasn't a total lie. He had just been on a date before arriving. "Her name is Jamie." He wasn't sure why he felt the need to give details, maybe to prove that he wasn't just saying it because she was. Maybe to prove he wasn't a pining loser who couldn't move on from his high school sweetheart.

"Peter."

"As in Peter Davies?" Declan chuckled. "Good for you." Peter was the jock that every girl fancied, it seemed. But Olive was Declan's, he had her heart in high school, and now...Peter still got her. Jealousy worked its way through Declan, but he ignored it; it was pointless to feel that way. It'd been so long since they'd been together, since they'd seen each other. She deserved someone who made her happy, even if it wasn't him.

"He's not like he was in high school. He's sweet enough." She leaned against the counter, folding her arms. She was comfortable here, even with Declan. He wished he felt the same, but he wasn't sure if he could be around her and not be with her. "It's still new, but we're having fun."

He nodded. She didn't have to explain herself to him, and he wasn't sure if he wanted the details. They stood on the opposite side of the metal table in the centre of the kitchen.

She looked good. Too good. He hated himself for thinking it. He hated that he thought they could pick up where they left off. She was with someone, and he—and he what? Jamie wasn't his girlfriend, she could've been. But not after seeing Olive and knowing that the feelings from years ago still lingered.

He missed Olive, that's what he feared most about seeing her, that he would miss her. Declan missed her touch, her laugh, her friendship. They were best friends before they dated, and now it was like they were complete strangers trying to make small talk. He loathed the person he was in that moment. He never walked on eggshells around her, but he was now.

Declan looked around the kitchen, maybe something would stick out that they could talk about. He wasn't ready for this moment to end.

"Excuse me. Did you find the coffee?" The same lady from earlier popped her head into the kitchen.

"Yeah, sorry. Delivery day, Olive needed help."

"Can I have it?" she asked when he didn't move.

"Oh right, yeah." Declan opened the box clearly labelled coffee and gave her a bag. "I assume you know how to work the coffee maker?"

"Thanks," she snapped, grabbing the bag out of his hand and closing the kitchen door.

"I don't think I'm cut out for the hospitality life."

She chuckled a little, tucking some loose hair back under her hat. "Just be yourself. Then they will have no choice but to love you."

"Olive, I'm really—" Was he really sorry for leaving? No. "I never wanted to hurt you."

She looked down at her feet. "I should go."

"Olive, please." He went to her, touched her shoulder, and she snapped around to face him. "I mean it. I *never* wanted to hurt you."

"Then why did you? You had every opportunity to stay, to choose me, to choose *us*." She stepped out of his grasp. "But you chose you."

Declan stood taller, narrowing his eyes. "You chose you too. What happened was not solely my fault."

She sighed, running her fingers over her eyebrow. "I know. It's easier to blame you since you're the one who left. It's easy because I didn't have to see you."

"I get it. But we're both doing good, dating. Moving on." He hated saying it and hated even more that it was true, or at least it was on her end.

"Right. Moving on. Good." She nodded then just left. No goodbye, she didn't even look back.

Declan's heart sank.

❄ ❄ ❄

THE HOLLIDAY INN

He should not have been the one left to tend to the inn. He knew nothing about it. Was he supposed to cook for them? They weren't even capable of getting their own coffee. They probably weren't supposed to be in the kitchen, but still. Declan tapped his fingers obsessively on the desk as he researched how to run an inn. He wished his mum had a step-by-step manual on how to do literally everything.

All they did at kids was check people in, he didn't remember what happened at mealtime or anything that happened after he handed off a key. Now, he was just expected to do it, and with the nagging feeling of how things ended with Olive in the back of his mind, it was hard to get anything done.

"Eddie!" a man yelled, entering the front door.

Declan looked around the lobby to see who he'd be talking to. "Sorry, sir, no Eddie here." Could he be talking about his father? Declan couldn't think of anyone who called him Eddie.

"Declan." The older man smiled. "Good to see you, mate. I'm here for my shift. Let your parents know I'll be in the kitchen."

"Sorry, who are you?"

"Albert. I'm the chef." He looked confused. Then glanced around the lobby, peering into the sitting room. "Where are your parents?"

"You haven't heard?" This was rough. He

wasn't sure how many more people he could tell people, though it did get easier each time.

"I was visiting my sister this past weekend."

Declan sighed and broke the news about his parents. The more he talked, the more he started to believe it could be a temporary situation. It was a dangerous thought, he knew.

Albert sat at the dining table, hand in his thin white hair. "What terrible news. I am so sorry."

Declan sat across him, not ever remembering meeting Albert. He'd been home last Christmas, he thought he would remember him. "I'm good. We're all working together to help out around the inn and the house."

"All of you?" Albert's eyes wrinkled, not believing him. Declan didn't blame him.

"Ainsley came home too. We have until the end of the month for them to pull through, if not, then we..." Declan couldn't utter the words. *We'd kill our parents.*

"Do I still have a job?"

"Yes, sir. I could really use you. You probably know more about this place than I do. I jumped in over my head."

"Of course. Anything you need." Albert rose from his seat, patting Declan's back. "Family of Eddie and Dorothy is family of mine."

Declan's shoulders fell back, and he rested his head on the table. "Thank you." He almost cried. He hadn't realised how much he actually missed his dad. They weren't close, he didn't tell his father everything, but he'd always been supportive. Declan could only imagine what Molly was going through. His heart ached for her. He and Ainsley forced her to go to school like everything was normal. She should be there. Ainsley should be there.

They were pretending the accident was minor, that after the thirty days were over they would just get up and come home. The truth was, they didn't know what would happen. Their parents could wake up in a few days or not at all. But once those thirty days were done there was nothing that could be done. Declan wanted to be around everyone. Loneliness crept inside him, tightening his chest, and he didn't think there was anything that could get it out.

Albert spent the day teaching Declan the basics. Payroll, checking in and out, cleaning a room, and staying organised, even though that wasn't his mother's strong suit. A cleaning company came once a week to do a deep clean of everything.

Declan hadn't realized how late it was until Albert mentioned starting dinner.

Panic ensued. "Where are Molly and Ainsley?"

Chapter Nine
Ainsley

All day. Ainsley spent all day staring at a blank document. *How the hell am I supposed to start?* She didn't even know exactly what she was going to write about. So, instead, she edited other people's work. Since that was her actual job. Before she was an editor, she was given topics to write about. This time it was 'make sure it's good.' The unlimited topic possibilities intimidated her.

After her fourth cup of coffee, Olive cut her off and gave her decaf herbal tea and a muffin. Ainsley complained about it but took it anyway.

"Hello."

Ainsley glanced up from her blinking cursor. "Gavin." She wanted to greet him with a smile, but that blank page was taunting her, killing her mood.

"Work?" He tried not to smirk while gesturing to her laptop with the cup of coffee in his hand.

"Watch where you wave that thing." She closed the laptop and pulled it a little closer to her. They both chuckled, recalling their first meeting. She was pleased that the hot coffee didn't tarnish her thoughts of him anymore.

THE HOLLIDAY INN

"I'm still struggling with what to write about. And I've checked my emails, there's no photos."

"Right, sorry. Have a pen?" She passed him one and he wrote on his hand. "There. When I get home."

She nodded, expecting him to leave. "You're here late."

"Late?"

"It's nearly six. They're about to close."

"Oh, fu—dammit." She packed up everything as quickly as she could. "I was supposed to pick up Molly from school three hours ago." She checked her phone, which, conveniently, died. "Declan is going to murder me."

"Relax, I'm sure it's going to be fine. Maybe she got a ride with a friend."

A ride all the way to the inn? That's more than out of the way. "Right, yeah," she said anyway, despite not believing him. She ran her hands through her hair and stopped at the nape of her neck. "I can't believe I forgot my sister."

Gavin put a hand on her shoulder. "It's okay. People make mistakes."

She pulled back. "You don't know me. In my family, you're either perfect or you get kicked to the curb. That girl has been through enough without me legitimately forgetting her."

"I'm sorry, I didn't think—"

"No, you didn't." Ainsley grabbed her bag. "Send me those pictures, please. I will pay for them; email me your price." She left him standing alone, glancing over her shoulder slightly.

She plugged her phone in when she got in the car, feeling bad about lashing out at Gavin; he was only trying to help. The phone and the car both needed to warm up. Finally, the phone turned on. She called Declan.

"Is she there?" Ainsley cut off his greeting.

"You mean you don't have her?"

"I messed up, I'm sorry." Ainsley felt like the worst sister ever; her one job with Molly was to pick her up, and she couldn't even remember to do that.

"Call her, I can't leave the inn." The sound of disappointment was apparent in his voice. She knew that sound all too well; it took her back to her mother.

"So, family means nothing to you?" her mother had asked her. They were on the phone discussing Christmas plans the year before. Ainsley again said she wouldn't be able to make it home for Christmas.

She didn't know what to say, except to scoff. Of course, family meant something to her, the family that actually showed they cared. It was hard for her not to see her mother all the time, but when she said things like that all the time, it made it easier.

"Maybe if I wasn't constantly reminded that I'm the disappointment, it'd be easier to go back." As soon as the words left her mouth, she regretted them. But they were her true feelings that she'd bottled up for too long.

"Well, sorry I'm a bad mother. I just hope you'll come home before I'm dead." Her mother hung up, leaving Ainsley's heart sitting in her stomach. She never thought her mum was a bad mother. She was rude sometimes and claimed to be supportive, but Ainsley only ever felt supported when she did something that her mother wanted her to do.

Now was not the time to dwell on the past. She hung up and immediately called Molly.

"Well, well."

Time to start grovelling. "I am *so* sorry. I got lost in work. I'm not used to having someone depend on me."

"I'm fine, thanks for asking." Ainsley's heart rate settled. "I got a ride with...a friend."

Ainsley sighed and rubbed viciously at her face. "Molly, I'm so sorry."

"I'm on my way home, don't worry about it." Her words might have said don't worry, but her tone said otherwise. She was rightfully angry. Molly had said she'd text her, but there was no text. Ainsley didn't know what she was supposed to do with that information.

She stopped by the store to get Molly's favourite dessert. She hoped Molly still loved chocolate cake as much as she remembered.

Everyone was still at the inn when Ainsley put the car in park in front of the house around seven. No one sat at the front desk. She peeked around the corner; all the dishes were cleaned off the dining room table. Then she heard laughter.

The sitting room was her mum's favourite place to be, especially at Christmas when she had it all decorated. When the only light came from the tree and the fireplace, it was her own special type of heaven. She and Ainsley had that in common.

Declan and Molly sat next to the fire while an older gentleman sat in the big chair by the window that the tree normally sat in at this time of year. A few guests had joined them.

"There was one time Dorothy was looking for something, God bless her, the poor thing looked everywhere for it. 'Course I can't remember what it was. Anyhow, she opened the kitchen door the exact moment I was coming from the other side. The fresh baked, full sheet of macaroons fell out of my hands and all over the floor." The older man laughed, generating laughter from everyone. "Your parents were good people."

"Don't say it like that," Ainsley blurted.

"Ainsley," Molly said.

"No." She held up a finger. "He's sitting here talking about them as if they're already dead." She set the cake down. "Sir, they are going to wake up. They have to." She glanced at Molly. "If today is any indication, they have to."

"So, you can go back to your child-free life? I'm sorry I'm such a burden."

"That's not what I said. Molly, you are not a burden." Molly stormed passed Ainsley, daggers in her eyes. "That's not what I said." She defended herself to everyone watching her. Sure, it might have been a thought; her life in New York was simpler, but she wouldn't trade Molly for it.

"You couldn't have joined in quietly?" Declan sighed. "I'm closing the front desk early. If you need anything it'll have to wait until morning." He brushed passed Ainsley too.

The few guests followed out until it was just Ainsley and the older gentleman. "I'm sorry, I didn't mean to—" She cut herself off and gestured to the empty room instead, with tears in her eyes. "I guess I bring more drama than I care to admit."

"It's quite all right, dear." He grunted as he rose from the chair. "You look so much like your mother." He touched her shoulder. "She'd be so happy to know you're here."

She pressed her lips together and looked down. "I don't deserve your kindness."

"Ainsley, everyone deserves a second chance and kindness. Be kind to others and use this second chance for good."

She wondered if this really could be a second chance for herself. Her mum wasn't aware she was there, what second chance could this strange old man be talking about?

He left immediately after being ominous. So, she put the cake in the fridge and made her way to the house.

Inside, no one was around. The telly was

off, no glow came from any room in the house, except under Molly's door. She leaned against the wall, ready to knock.

"She's so selfish!" Molly yelled.

"It's hard to understand. You've never lived on your own, you're used to being the centre of attention."

"So, I'm the selfish one?" Ainsley didn't remember Molly ever having an attitude. Were all teenagers like this?

"No. No one is selfish. We're here because we're the opposite of selfish. What I'm trying to tell you is we all need time to adjust to this new life."

"I don't want to adjust. I want Mum." Her voice cracked, and Ainsley opened the door. Molly's eyes narrowed at her. "Go away. You've done enough."

"Come on. I said I was sorry. You're sulking like I'm the reason this all happened. As Declan said, we all just need to adjust. Just because I forgot you once doesn't mean I'm going to do it again. We're family, we stick together."

Molly scoffed with the most dramatic eye roll Ainsley had ever seen. "Where was that logic four years ago? Huh? We'll never really be all together anymore. There's too much bad blood. The sooner we stop pretending everything is fine here, the better." She turned away. "Nothing has been the same since you left. It's like everyone would rather do their own thing than stick together."

"What happened four years ago is *not* my fault. That happened *to* me. We couldn't have seen it coming; not even Mum saw it coming."

Molly shrugged. "We can start over tomorrow. Right now, I want to be left alone."

Ainsley tried not to sigh; Molly was right. It'd be better if they went to sleep and started over in the morning. "I can respect that. Would you like something to eat?"

"No. You may leave."

"I love you, Molly. Always have, and always will." Ainsley closed the door behind her and leaned her head against it.

"She'll get over it. Don't you remember what it was like at fifteen?"

"Honest? No." She followed Declan to the kitchen where he prepared two cups of tea.

Molly's room was different than Ainsley remembered it, a sign she was growing up and she was missing it. It used to be pink, rainbows, and woodland creatures. Now it was solid purple and had a wall dedicated to Polaroids of her and her friends at various outings and activities.

"I'd like to think I wasn't so dramatic." Ainsley sat at the small breakfast nook while Declan added milk to the tea.

"Well, I remember you wanting to go to a party once. It was the be all, end all of parties or something to that effect." He smirked, knowing that she knew where this was going. He passed her the cup. "You begged, but they wouldn't change your shift. You claimed they were ruining your life. You snuck out, got caught, and had to work every weekend for a month."

Ainsley chuckled, remembering it. "I was so insufferable, they rarely asked me to work another weekend."

"All teenagers are insufferable. We don't know teenage Molly yet."

"When did you get so wise?" She smirked, narrowing her eyes. He was four years younger; he was supposed to be dumb and partying, getting girls and not thinking about the future. But he's always had his values. Wanting a family, wife and kids. Their parents always wanted that for their kids. Ainsley was the black sheep of the family, never seeing herself with someone, let alone having children. There was still so much more she wanted to do. She knew they were disappointed that she didn't or wouldn't give them grandchildren.

She was pleased with how they handled Molly's interest in women, though surprised was probably the better term. All they cared about was that she was the same person she was before. She was, Ainsley knew that deep down, Molly was still the same sweet kid.

"I can't believe she's fifteen." Ainsley sighed. She mostly couldn't believe that Mum went along with the pregnancy at forty.

Molly wasn't a kid anymore; when Ainsley left, Molly was eleven. Still into dolls and Legos. She was just getting into painting canvas after always drawing on paper. Ainsley missed the biggest growth of Molly and knowing she'd never get it back was the only regret she let stay with her. She would never get to see her sister grow from a child to a teenager. She missed it because she was scared of getting her feelings hurt by their mother. She'd never forgive herself for it.

"Hey, do you remember what party that was? I remember Narine wanting me there so badly."

"I think it was some guy named Gavin."

Chapter Ten
Molly

Despite wanting to throw it out, Molly held onto Teagan's phone number. She'd yet to put it in her phone. She didn't want to seem desperate. Hilary would try to spin it, saying Molly had a thing for Teagan, when, in reality, she might be the only one who understood. It was clear that her siblings didn't. They were older and on their own, they didn't need their parents like Molly did. Teagan would understand that.

"You're acting weird." Hilary narrowed her eyes.

"I'm not. I just don't want to talk about every detail of my life. It's quite a bummer right now," she said bitterly. The only thing new happening right now, that didn't leave her feeling helpless, was Teagan.

Amelia held her hands up in defence. "All right."

They threw their trash in the bin and walked through the hall. Everyone's life seemed to be filled with joy as they talked to friends, mostly about the winter break. Around the corner stood Teagan with her friends. One had short black hair with a pink fringe, and the other had brown hair, but her nose was pierced three times. Molly had made it clear that she wanted their friendship to remain a secret. No one needed to know more about her business. Everyone already looked at her with pity, she didn't need their judgement too.

To say Teagan was never part of the 'in crowd' was an understatement. She was the type to mock the in crowd, to mock people like Molly. Teagan wasn't preppy, but Molly participated in dress-up days and went to sporting events. Teagan ditched any time an organised event took place.

"Want to say hi to Teagan?" Hilary teased. Ever since Teagan gave Molly her number Hilary had been relentless about her doing something about it, at least in a joking manner. Molly didn't think she was ever serious when it came to being with someone so different.

"I'm good, thanks." But underneath her fear of what others thought, she really wanted to say hi to Teagan.

"She's kinda cute. If you're into the skater, goth chick type."

Little did she know, Molly was starting to. She didn't want to be. She didn't want to go through this stage in life without her mum. Sure, Ainsley may know things, she might even have good advice, and maybe, if her mum wasn't fighting for her life in the hospital, Molly might have chosen Ainsley to talk about this with. Now, all she could think about was her mum and how she'd love to see her with someone...to see her daughter happy.

When Molly first thought she wasn't interested in boys, she thought she was wrong. She was always asked if she had a boyfriend, or when she would have a boyfriend. But the thought of a boy touching, or god forbid, kissing her grossed her out. She sat down with her mum, without her father at first, and told her she was worried.

Her mother smiled. "There's nothing to be worried about, babe. Sometimes women like men and some like other women. Some like both. The only thing I care about is if you are still the same person as before. I care that you're kind, I care that you're respectful, strong, brave, willing..."

"I am." Molly was then, she wasn't sure if she was brave now.

That was a year ago. She hadn't been interested in dating, per se, but she knew that when she was, it would not be with a boy.

Hilary never bothered Molly about Teagan the rest of the day. She did offer a ride home with her mum, but Molly told her she had messaged Ainsley, even though she hadn't. Before school this morning she had told Ainsley she'd be going to Hilary's after school to do homework. She lingered by her locker until the school was mostly empty. Then, she put on her coat and hat and went behind the school.

As she rounded the corner behind the

school, the wind picked up, stinging her eyes, causing tears. She worried Teagan would think she'd been crying. She put on her gloves and dabbed under her eyes anyway.

"You okay?"

"Yeah, the wind." Molly leaned against the building beside Teagan.

"I was starting to think you weren't going to come." They stood in silence for a moment. "About yesterday—"

"I had a good time, but I stand by what I said. I want this to be a secret. I don't need Hilary or Amelia, or god forbid, my siblings, reading into this."

"And what is 'this' exactly?" She stood a little closer, so the backs of their hands touched.

"We're..." Molly didn't know. Were they friends? Was there more here that she didn't want to unpack? Could there be?

Teagan looked at Molly. "Do you want to go for a drive?"

"Yes, get me out of this cold." Molly followed beside her to her car; being seventeen had its perks. It was old, probably as old as the girls. They waited for it to defrost. "How long was it before they declared your mum dead?" Molly removed her gloves and fixed the fly-away hairs, when she took her hat off, in the tiny mirror.

"They gave us a month, but it was only two weeks before she...on her own. They say she died on impact, but my father couldn't accept it and forced the doctors to put her on life support."

Molly wanted to touch Teagan's hand that sat on the gear shift, but instead, she rubbed her own arms to distract her hands. "I'm so sorry."

She had a sad smile. "The not knowing is worse. The waiting to see what's going to happen."

"Yeah." Molly looked out her window. "It really sucks."

"How're all your siblings taking it?"

She scoffed. "Well, Ainsley and Declan are just fine." She rolled her eyes. "This is nothing more like a minor inconvenience for them. *I'm* an inconvenience for them." Molly picked at her nails.

Teagan's hand hovered over Molly's, hesitant that she'd pull away. When she didn't, Teagan lowered her hand. Her fingertips chilled Molly's skin.

"I'm sure that's not true. Anyone should be so lucky to have you in their life."

Their eyes met. For a split second, Molly thought Teagan's eyes glanced at her lips, and for a split second hers drifted to Teagan's.

Molly cleared her throat, turning back to the front. "So, that drive."

"I can drive you home, through the mountains."

"Sounds good."

They sat another moment, Teagan's hand still on Molly's before she removed it and put

THE HOLLIDAY INN

the car in drive and started off.

If anyone could see her now, they'd probably ask what she was thinking. Molly barely knew anything about Teagan. She was certain Ainsley would yell at her for not thinking better of getting into a car with basically, a total stranger. But she wasn't. Molly trusted her, maybe against any better judgement. She knew the emotions, the feelings, the thoughts. The ones Molly didn't try too hard to hide, anyway.

It was a half hour to the mountains, where the inn resided. They were bound to get into small talk territory.

"Tell me more about you," Teagan said, breaking the silence.

"What do you want to know?" There were things she couldn't say, things that were too much for the getting to know you portion. Things that would make her reconsider...whatever this was.

"What's it like having siblings so much older than you?"

"I liked it at first; they'd been through almost all of it. Whatever I needed advice for, they had it. It was easier going to Ainsley than to Mum sometimes." Molly looked out the window, leaning her head on the glass. "Once she left, I don't think things were ever the same. Now, it's like we're all strangers to each other. I don't know how to talk to Ainsley anymore."

"You could start by telling her about me.

The weird kid at school who started talking to you because her mum died too."

Molly couldn't stop the laugh that slipped out. "I'm so sorry." Molly covered her mouth. "That's not funny."

Teagan smiled. "It's not, but I'm glad to hear you laugh."

A heavy sigh escaped Molly's mouth when she saw the house come into view. The inn, not too far off, looked naked for this time of year. "Mum would've had this place decorated by now."

Teagan put the car in park, letting it idle. Molly wondered if she didn't want her to go as much as she didn't want to. "Sounds like you and your siblings need a bonding experience. Maybe decorate it together?"

"That's not a bad idea." Molly picked up her bag. "You're not the weird kid at school, you know. You're very kind."

Teagan's hand sat on Molly's shoulder, gently holding her down. "Don't tell anyone." Teagan scrunched her nose up and smiled, then her hand slid down Molly's arm into her hand. A mischievous grin came across Teagan's mouth. "It could damage my whole 'I don't care' vibe."

Molly smiled. "Well, we can't have that." Molly liked that Teagan's gentle side was reserved for her.

"Certainly not."

"See you tomorrow, Teagan." Their finger intertwined was all the confirmation Molly

THE HOLLIDAY INN

needed that Teagan did feel the same. There was definitely something between them. Molly brought Teagan's hand to her mouth, pressing her lips gently against Teagan's skin before she could second guess herself, she left the car before either of us could say something.

As she watched Teagan drive away, her chest tightened. She wished she didn't know what it meant. She wished she wasn't developing feelings for someone at pretty much the worst time of her life. But here she was, watching Teagan leave and counting down until the time she saw her next.

Inside the inn, Ainsley and Declan sat behind the front desk, staring unblinkingly at the computer screen.

"Do you know if Mum had a social media account for the inn?" Declan asked without looking up. "I'm looking, but not seeing anything."

"They have a website that they update like twice a year," Molly said, hanging up her jacket and kicking off her boots.

"Albert made chicken soup. It's in a pot on the stove," Ainsley said. She turned to Molly. "We're good?"

"Yeah. Sorry I freaked yesterday." Molly passed through the lobby, though the dining area, and into the industrial kitchen that had just been remodelled two years ago.

Molly brought her soup out to the lobby. "What are you looking at?"

"Inspiration."

"For what?" She hoped it wasn't—

"Remodelling. If we want business to keep steady, we need more appeal. I have a decorator coming on the weekend to decorate for Christmas. I'm sure she'll have some helpful tips for what we can do," Declan rambled.

"Especially about the furniture," Ainsley added.

"Wait, wait, wait. Hold on." Both siblings turned to her, concerned that she didn't understand. But she understood. She understood all too well. "You want to come here, after years of not showing up or being part of the family and its business, and just 'remodel?' Like all of Mum's hard work means nothing?"

Their faces changed. Regret?

"No, the opposite," Declan said. "I want to enhance Mum's work. The base is well done. It's the decor."

"Mum liked it this way. Soon, this will be all I have left of her. You guys will be fine, you have lives to go back to, but this *is* my life. You're throwing it away. I matter, you know."

Declan closed the Internet browser and gave his full attention to Molly. Ainsley stood. "That wasn't my intention. Why don't you work with me to help the inn?"

He only wanted the best for the inn, Molly saw that, but what did she know about running a business?

"First, we can start by decorating for Christmas together." Molly set her bowl of soup down. If she truly wanted them to be a family again, she needed to take charge. "Decorating the inn has always been a family thing. I want it to stay that way. No professionals."

"Fair enough. What do you think?" Declan looked over at Ainsley, whose arms were folded across her chest.

"I'm in," she said with a smile. "Saturday will be dedicated to decorating. What else you got?"

"Furniture can be updated, but that's it." As much as she'd like to think her mother liked the furniture in the sitting room, she knew it was old and time for some upgrades. The floral-patterned couch and the peeling leather chair didn't match the modern rustic vibe of the outside. People had expectations when they looked at the white and grey brick, all the windows that made the inn look new and modern. The furniture was far from modern and rustic.

Maybe having everyone together again would be a good thing. Well, almost everyone.

Chapter Eleven
Declan

Trying to balance his job and the inn started taking a toll on him by the end of the week. Declan had stared at the computer screen more than he has in a long time, and he was a social media marketer. A throbbing ache resided in his shoulders from bad posture. He did manage to create a couple of social media accounts for the inn, trying to get buzz around, maybe they'd get more bookings during the off-season. The town was still nice during the summer. The town loved hosting themed events. He remembered being dragged to most of them.

As he was taking the before decoration pictures, to do before and after shots for social media, his phone rang.

"Heather. I thought we weren't scheduled to call until next week." He went back to the front desk, in case she needed him to write something down.

"Are you coming back to the office?"

"Next week? I doubt. Everything is at a standstill with my parents. My sister is a child. I told you all that. Right?"

"Your work is falling short. I'm not sure what you're doing, but if you want to keep your job, you'd better start doing it." She spoke in a monotone.

"I'm staying on top of all my tasks for you, plus all the extras I need to do around here."

"You have until Monday, if I don't see an improvement...well, I'd better see one." The line went dead.

"I can't believe she just threatened me." Declan tossed his phone on the desk going to look for Albert. "Do you know any local photographers?" He popped his head into the kitchen.

"Oh, yeah. Call Gavin. Extremely talented," Albert called over his shoulder whilst cooking at the stove.

"Perfect, thanks."

Back at the front desk, there were at least fifteen people. "Where'd you all come from?" Surely, he'd remember seeing a booking for fifteen people?

"Signing in, under Darling. We're the wedding party."

His face went pale as he began to panic. "Wedding? Like a wedding, wedding? With a groom and bride and cake and...stuff?" he stammered.

The girl in the front looked around, eyebrows furrowed. "Uh, yeah. *Why* are there no decorations? Dorothy told me everything would be decorated just like on the website. Where is she? I'd like to talk to her."

Declan could help but stare at her. How could they not know there was to be a wedding?

"Hello? Are you new?" She snapped her fingers in his face. "Get me Dorothy or someone more competent."

Declan shook his head, bringing himself back to reality. "Sorry, Dorothy is currently unconscious in the hospital. I'm her son, Declan." He dug through the papers on top of the desk, bringing the large desk-sized calendar to view. There, in his mother's light blue writing, DARLING WEDDING.

"Oh god. Of course, this is happening." She held her forehead between her finger and thumb, rubbing gently, as if to massage the problem away. "There has been so many signs."

A middle-aged lady took the young woman's shoulders. "Emmie, there are no signs. You and John are meant to be together. For better or worse. This just happens to be the worse."

"Okay." Emmie, the bride, turned her attention back to Declan. "Can you follow directions?"

"Tell me what you need, and I'll do it," he said, desperate to make sure it went well.

"I need this place decorated for Christmas by tonight. The barn in the back, where the ceremony will be, also must be decorated. I have stuff and people for that. Dorothy said it was okay. I need all my guests taken care of tomorrow, whilst we're all getting ready. I've hired someone to cater, and they'll be here for that."

THE HOLLIDAY INN

"I've got two sisters. Between the three of us, I'm sure we can pull something together. Now, let's get you checked in," he said with a smile, hoping it hid his fear.

Ainsley picked Molly up directly after school, so they could get to decorating.

"How could you not know there was a wedding this weekend?" Ainsley complained. "Aren't you the self-appointed owner now?"

They each carried totes up from the basement of the inn, where all the decorations for each holiday were neatly organised by season. At least *that* was made easy for them. Each tote was also labelled with which room they were for.

"No. I thought it'd be easier if I did. You're so focused on your job, with no room for anything or anyone else." He glanced at Molly, hoping Ainsley wouldn't notice. Not that he was referring to only Molly, he thinks Ainsley needed someone nice to calm her down a bit.

"Oh my god!" Ainsley threw her arms in the air. "I forget her at school *once*, am I really going to be hearing about it for the rest of my life? Move on."

Molly chuckled, going to the record player in the corner of the room, and pulled out a Christmas record, setting it up as background music.

"Excuse me," an older lady, the bride's mum, said, peeking her head into the sitting room. "Is everything okay?"

"Oh yes, quite well. We always discuss

family matters loudly whilst strangers roam in the inn." Ainsley's statement was coated in sarcasm.

"Ainsley, this is the bride's mother," Declan said through gritted teeth. He turned his attention back to the guest. "How can I help?"

"I was wondering if you needed any help. There's just a lot to be done. Emmie is stressing a little. I have her in the bath with a glass of wine right now."

"I think the people in the barn could use some help."

She nodded. "Sure."

"We have to work together," he said once she was gone. "Whatever issues we're working through needs to be put aside. The wedding is tomorrow. Can we do that?"

"Yeah, fine," Molly said with folded arms, her hip popped out for dramatic effect.

"Good. Ainsley, you're in the dining room; Molly you're in the lobby, and I'll do the sitting room. Does that work for everyone?"

"Yes," Ainsley and Molly agreed, but both sisters wondered if Declan was capable of decorating to their mother's standards.

Molly adjusted the record player then went to the lobby with the tote labelled 'lobby.'

Splitting themselves up was the best option. Declan could only see them arguing if they did each room together. Which decorations would go where, it would be a whole thing and nothing would get done. Ainsley got to do the Christmas village in the dining room; that's

THE HOLLIDAY INN

where their mother had the longest table. Declan envied her a little; all of the siblings would always do the village together when they were younger. He wondered if she thought about that while doing it. He did save the tree for the three of them to do together. Maybe that would be the bonding they needed, that Molly wanted; it wasn't a lot, but it was important. The tree is what brought everyone together.

"Ready to do the tree?" he called to the girls.

"Yes!" Molly came running in. Ainsley was close behind. "What colours? Mum has different totes for different themes."

Ainsley looked around the sitting room surveying Declan's work. "I think we should go with the classic white and red."

Molly had already pulled out some ornaments and inspected them.

Ainsley opened a tote, starting to dig through. Molly and Declan sat around it too, like they were children seeing new ornaments for the first time. "Look at this." Ainsley held up a silver onesie with her birth year on it. "My first tree ornament."

"Here's mine," Molly said, pulling hers out. "And yours, Declan." She passed Declan his, which was a sneaker with his birth year.

"It's Mum and Dad's wedding date." Molly pulled out an ornament shaped like a cake.

"What's this—oh." The three of them fell silent as they saw another one with a year printed on it. Declan didn't know about the girls, but an ugly feeling rose in his chest. Hatred? He knew his mum wouldn't have gotten rid of it; it meant as much to their parents as his did, or Molly's and Ainsley's.

"Would it be wrong to not use this one?" Ainsley asked. It was wrong to ask, they all knew that. Mum would scold them for being hateful during such a joyous time of year.

"No," Molly said. "Put it back." She went to the kitchen.

Ainsley hesitated but did as Molly said. "I hate that."

"Me too. I wish I'd done so much differently. I'm sorry."

"It's not your fault, Dec. Blood doesn't make you family, and neither does marriage." She stared at the ornaments in the tote. "Family is about those you love and want to be around. Not this. Family isn't supposed to be conditional."

Molly came back with a tray of hot cocoa. Each mug was one that they used all the time when they were younger. The mugs were filled to the brim with marshmallows. Michael Bublé played in the background as they took turns putting decorations on the tree. Declan watched Ainsley close her eyes and take a sip of her hot chocolate, the crackle of the fire in the background, this was Ainsley's favourite.

Once they finished reminiscing and putting the meaningful ornaments on the tree, they went in with the bulbs and flowers. Their mum loved fake, white poinsettias being placed throughout the tree. At first, Declan thought flowers on a Christmas tree was odd, they were a summer thing, but over time they grew on him. Now, he couldn't imagine their tree without flowers.

"Time for the topper." Ainsley pulled out the large red poinsettia with ribbon and white leaves. "Molly, would you like to do the honours?" She passed the extravagant topper to Molly, whose eyes lit up.

"Really? Dad always did it."

"And now, you do it."

Molly took the topper, while Declan moved the ladder beside the tree. Their parents stopped getting real trees a few years back, once the kid had all grown up, mostly. Tree hunting was a huge part of their childhood. They'd run through the rows, seeing who could find the best tree first. There were more of them then. Remembering childhood moments like that was painful. He wanted to look back with fondness, with joy, but there was a lot of ache now. He couldn't imagine what it felt like for Ainsley. She'd gotten the worst of the treatment. And she felt the strongest about her family.

The artificial tree was easier to carry and work with. As it slowly became just Molly, hunting for the perfect tree seemed less needed when they could purchase one and it would be perfect every year. Declan did miss the smell of the real tree. But Ainsley found pine scented bars that she put throughout the branches, hidden in the back.

Declan held the ladder whilst Molly climbed to the top. Ainsley took pictures. They'd go great on the website, but he knew that wasn't her first thought.

"How's it look?" Molly asked.

"Looks great. Do you need something to secure it?"

"Yeah. I think there's ribbon in the tote over there." Molly gestured with her head, as her hands were busy holding the topper in place.

Ainsley turned around, at the same time someone was about to tap her shoulder. They startled each other, getting tangled in the tree lights that didn't work. With a grunt, they tumbled to the floor.

His hand made sure that her head didn't hit the floor. Their eyes met, and Declan swore Ainsley smiled at him. He pushed the hair out of her face.

"I'm beginning to think us running into each other like this is becoming a habit." He grinned. Declan couldn't take his eyes off them, he tried to keep his disgust off his face. Was he going to try to kiss her? Would she let him? Who was he? Declan blinked and thought he saw her eyes drop to his mouth; he tried to hold back the grimace on his face. He wanted her to be happy, but this was getting weird.

Declan cleared his throat. "Ribbon?"

"Oh, right." Ainsley shimmied herself, and the man got up, offering his hand to help her stand; she took it. "Gavin, my brother Declan and my sister Molly. This is Gavin, he's a photographer who's been trying to help get some creative juices flowing." She passed Molly the ribbon.

"Looks like he got some type of juices flowing," Molly mumbled. Declan snorted out a laugh he tried to hold back.

Ainsley blushed and shot Molly a look filled with daggers. Poor Gavin was so clueless. He stood there with a friendly smile on his face.

"Shut up." Ainsley punched Declan's arm.

"I'm here to meet Emmie, the bride. So, I should probably do that." Gavin turned around and left the sitting room.

It was so new to see his sister into someone, if that's even what this could be called. He turned to Ainsley and wiggled his eyebrows.

Chapter Twelve
Ainsley

"No," Ainsley said firmly, pointing her finger in Declan's face. "My life is in New York. I won't get involved with someone here." Not that she had many options in New York either.

"Why?" Molly asked, coming down from the ladder. "Because then you'd have to stay here?"

Ainsley knew what they thought they saw between Gavin and her when they tumbled to the ground. It was almost directly out of a movie. And she'd be lying if she said she didn't feel something in the pit of her stomach. A tingle crept through her body just thinking about it. She thought he'd kiss her, or at least try. She wouldn't let him; it would only complicate things. She was adjusting well to Holly Grove, she had a routine now, and she couldn't have a man ruining it. No matter how handsome.

"This isn't about you, Molly." Ainsley sighed. "I've established myself there, I built myself and my life there. *If* I were to be interested in dating, he'd have to be in New York."

"What's wrong with staying? Is your job really more important than us?" She tried to be tough, to look intimidating; but she was still a child. Ainsley did want to stay for Molly, she was her kid sister, Ainsley loved her, but she didn't think she'd be able to let go of all the bad that happened here.

"No, but my happiness is." Ainsley didn't want to get into it, but maybe if Molly knew then she would finally let go of whatever she thought was going on. "I spent a long time trying to free myself of the guilt Mum had unintentionally placed on me. I hated leaving you behind. I know they have been good to you, but they, especially Mum, put these ideals on me. Used me to live her life and guilted me when I didn't do what she thought I should. I won't stand here and be guilted for the life that actually brings me joy, after a long time of feeling resented for it, by a child who doesn't understand." Ainsley took in a deep breath, letting it out slowly.

"I am not a child." Molly's tone implied she wanted to stomp her foot on the ground, but she restrained.

"You are. Because if you were an adult, you'd understand why I can't just leave my job." Ainsley held her stance. The more she stayed here, the more she missed it; it messed with her head. She missed the way things were long before she stopped coming home. She missed something that didn't exist anymore, and probably couldn't again.

"Then why are you even here?" Both of the girls were getting heated. Declan stood watching them like some type of soap opera, with no real clue how to defuse the situation. Granted, neither did Ainsley. "I thought that decorating the tree would bring some peace between us. Clearly, I was wrong." Molly stormed out of the room and, moments later, out of the inn.

"What?" Ainsley glared at Declan. "You think I'm in the wrong." It wasn't a question. Ainsley normally wouldn't care what he thought, she was the eldest. But the way he looked at her then, like she had broken something, like what she had just said to Molly was at all comparable to what truly broke this family. She wasn't the one who did that. They were all broken a long time before this.

"I think you were a bit harsh. You go out of your way to remind us that this is temporary. That we're just a temporary part of your big successful life. That kid looks up to you, you're her idol, but you've made it abundantly clear that she's not so much of a consideration to you."

Anger wrapped around her heart, clenching. "I'm not the one who tore us apart."

"No. But you're also not willing to help put us back together." Declan walked past her, leaving her to think about it. Her eyes began to sting.

He was right, which she hated. She didn't want to live in the past, she wanted to move on, to have a future with them, but she wasn't

THE HOLLIDAY INN

sure she could get over what wasn't there anymore. Family was something that she thought would make it through anything, would have each other's backs, no matter what; she couldn't even live up to her own expectations.

"Hey, sorry," Gavin said, announcing himself. He was propped against the large entry way into the sitting room. "Are you alright?"

Ainsley looked at the tree. Everything had been fine just ten minutes ago. They were laughing and smiling. If Declan hadn't made that stupid comment about—Gavin. If he hadn't shown his face, if they hadn't fallen...

"I'm fine, but I'm going to need you to leave." She couldn't look at him as she said the words. They hurt, because she'd started to think of him as a friend, and now, because no one was capable of thinking of them as friends, she needed to shut it down. "Whatever you thought was here, was wrong." She bowed her head, hoping he didn't hear her. She was here for one reason, and she couldn't lose sight of that. She was there for Molly and then she was gone. Tears filled her eyes, and she crossed her arms over her chest. She enjoyed his company, but that's all it could be. No one wanted to believe she could be friends with a man. Anger continued to fester inside her.

Gavin moved beside her. He didn't say anything, just stood there staring at the tree with her.

"They'd be so disappointed in me. My parents." A compulsion to speak took over. Emotions flooded her and she couldn't arrange them, not alone, not quietly, not in her own mind. She'd kept him at a distance for good reason, she had a specific way she wanted to live her life, and no one understood it.

"I don't think that's true. You're here, I think that's all they truly wanted. Be here with your siblings."

"How can I? There's so much that's unresolved. Molly and I can't be in the same room without an argument ensuing. She hates me for leaving. I can't blame her. I love my life in New York, and she sees that as loving life without her."

"Do you? Enjoy life without her?"

She turned her whole body to face him. "No. I missed her terribly. Every time I had to say goodbye was like ripping tiny pieces off my heart."

He met her gaze. "Maybe you should tell her that."

"She'll never get it."

"It's tricky."

"It is."

Ainsley turned back to the tree; the threat of tears spilling over was still present. The tree was the only other source of light in the room, excluding the other decorations with lights and the fire. The fire crackled in the background. Under different circumstances, this might've been romantic. Standing there in the Christmas glow with an attractive man. They'd be intertwined with each other in a blanket by the fire. He'd be working on his pictures, and she'd be editing someone's article. It wasn't something she longed for, like Declan, but it couldn't be so bad to want that. She never thought she'd picture some type of future with someone, everyone always wanted something different from her. And she certainly never expected to think about that with Gavin. But he was here, he cared.

"There's a..." He trailed off, thinking she didn't hear him.

"There's a what?"

He chuckled, looking down at his feet for a moment. "It's stupid. There's a play tomorrow night. Would you—would you like to go with me? My niece is in it, and I promised I'd go, but I have—"

"You have an extra ticket?" she guessed.

"Yeah." He chuckled awkwardly, rubbing the back of his neck. He looked at he through his eyelashes. The deep brown of his eyes calmed her. Her tense body relaxed.

"Okay." The word left her mouth before she could process what was happening.

What's the worst that could happen if I stayed?

❄ ❄ ❄

"Molly, you bring this tray to the groom's room, Ainsley, this tray to the bride's. Albert, wait in the kitchen for Olive, she'll be here soon to prep the desserts." Once everyone had their tasks, Declan sighed, leaning over the counter. "Thank god it's a small wedding."

He was right, there was no way they'd be able to pull off a big wedding with only a day's notice. Ten people were going to be in attendance; mostly immediate family. It made it easier for the siblings, and Ainsley could be out of here in time for the play.

"Oh yeah," Ainsley said aloud. "I need to leave at six-thirty."

"Why?" Declan picked up a tray of snacks; he would call them hor d'oeuvres, but they weren't fancy enough.

"Gavin is taking me to a play. It's an elementary school play his niece is in."

"Gavin, huh?" The way he said it, was like he'd known this was going to happen all along. He even smirked, not bothering to hide it.

"Don't do that." She followed him to the sitting room, where he offered finger foods to the family of the wedding. "Don't act like this is some big revelation. We're friends from high school, catching up." Lie. They were not friends in high school.

"Right." He nodded. "And you're going to do that in a dimly lit room whilst watching a romantic Christmas play. That makes total sense." His voice riddled in sarcasm.

"Sarcasm is my thing. Also, there is nothing romantic about children."

"No, you're thing is taking that tray up to the bride and her friend, so they don't starve on her wedding day."

"Fine." She huffed.

"And you're forbidden from talking," he called after her.

"What? Why?"

"Because you're a cynic. Romantically challenged. This is a wedding day. Full of love, got it?"

But when she entered the bride's room, she was in tears. How could she not say anything?

"I brought—are you all right?" She set the tray on top of the dresser.

The bride was staring at herself in the mirror, crying. Big tears, ugly crying. The maid of honour sat on the bed on her phone.

"She's getting it all out now, so she doesn't ruin her makeup for pictures."

"Smart." Ainsley hung around for a moment too long, but when she turned to leave, the bride stopped her.

"Are you married?"

Oh god, Declan would kill her. "No."

"Engaged? Dating?"

"No."

She groaned, rolling her head back then dropping it on the desk.

"Look, if you're scared, that's okay. It's a big commitment, but you wouldn't be here if this wasn't what you wanted. Right?"

She nodded, sniffling. "Yeah. That's right."

"You've got an inn full of people committed to helping you through today. Even people who only met you and learned of your wedding yesterday."

"I'm ready to marry John. I love him. Maybe I'm just nervous to stand in front of everyone." She wiped her eyes. "I'm going to get my makeup on, the photographer should be here soon."

As if on cue; "Knock, knock." A voice came from outside the door. "Photographer's here."

"Come in," the bride called, turning her attention back to her reflection in her travel mirror.

"Hi, Emmie. Ainsley." Gavin nodded.

"Gavin." Ainsley touched his shoulder on the way out. A tingle shooting through her hand and up her arm made her want to touch him again.

Nothing was happening and it still felt like it was going too fast. She leaned against the wall in the hall, pausing for a breath. No attachments. She had a life to go back to. Friends, a job, it was all waiting for her in New York. At this point it was more of a reminder to herself that it couldn't last. And yet, she got fluttery when she saw him.

"What are you doing?" Molly asked, appearing out of nowhere.

She felt like a teenager who nearly got caught with a boy in her room. Molly studied her, waiting for an answer.

THE HOLLIDAY INN

"Just giving the bride her snacks. I'm going to see if Declan needs more help."

"I've never seen him so engrossed in something. Do you think he's trying to stay distracted because Olive is here?" She followed Ainsley down the hall, to the stairs to the main level.

"Olive is here?"

"You didn't know she was catering? It's like a soap opera. Do you think they'll get back together?" There was hope in her eyes. They all loved Olive, she was so sweet and kind, and she treated Declan well. He was obviously in love with her. But they wanted different things. Neither would be happy if they had to give up their dreams.

Ainsley shrugged. "Declan's job is in London; Olive doesn't want to leave Holly Grove. One of them would have to give in, and I don't see either happening."

"So..." Molly started. "What's going to happen to me and the inn if Mum and Dad don't make it?"

Ainsley stopped, pulling Molly into the office, closing the door behind us. "Is that what's been bothering you?" She held Molly's shoulders in her hands.

"I guess. I don't really want to move to London, and I *really* don't want to move to New York. No offence." She smiled apologetically.

Everything finally clicked for Ainsley. "I get it now. How about tomorrow after breakfast

109

we visit Mum and Dad and come up with a plan for *if* something were to happen."

Molly relaxed. "That's a good idea. I think it'd put me at ease to have a plan."

"Good. For now, I'm going to find Declan."

"I'm off the clock, I'm going to Hilary's."

Ainsley hugged her, pressing Molly's head against her shoulder, trying to reassure her that nothing bad would ever happen to her. Ainsley wanted to protect her from anything evil that would hurt her. But she couldn't. Molly was growing up, and Ainsley needed to let it go.

Molly left the inn and Ainsley followed the sound of clattering dishes to the kitchen.

Olive was at the oven checking the desserts, Albert was cooking the meals, Declan sat on a stool in the back corner of the room.

"What's going on?"

"Albert prefers to cook alone. Olive messed up the first batch of cookies so now, she has to remake them. The cake is on a truck somewhere on the road and we're not sure if it's going to make it here on time." He looked like he needed a drink.

"What do you need?"

"A drink." *Maybe I do know him after all,* Ainsley thought, trying not to laugh.

"If it helps, the bride is happy, and all is going well."

He nodded, but his face didn't change, just adjusted himself on the stool.

"Did you put some kind of pressure on

yourself?" She hopped up on the stool beside him.

"It's so stupid. But if this doesn't go well, how can I run the inn?"

"Who said you had to run the inn? Do you want to?"

"No. But you're not going to do it."

"Let's slow down. We found out about this last night. It's going well, all things considered. Let's visit our parents tomorrow after breakfast and come up with a plan if things go south."

"When do we meet with the lawyer to go over their will?"

"A few days before Christmas."

Declan let out a sarcastic laugh. "Happy Christmas."

Chapter Thirteen
Molly

Molly had lied so effortlessly to Ainsley. She did feel guilty about it. She was Molly's older sister; she should be able to tell her that she was actually going to see Teagan. Ainsley wouldn't tease her about it, she didn't want to talk about whatever was, so obviously, going on between her and Gavin. She would only encourage Molly to talk about it on her own terms. But still, Molly couldn't bring herself to mention Teagan.

When they were together, it was like the rest of the world didn't exist. Molly didn't have to hide any part of herself with Teagan, she knew it all and still wanted to be around. She wondered if her friends did too, but they walked on eggshells when it came to her parents, and she didn't want to deal with that right now.

Molly got into Teagan's car, hoping no one was watching her from the window. But the wedding was consuming Declan, and Ainsley wanted to prove that she was a good person.

"What do you want to do today?" Teagan asked, pulling out of the driveway. Another reason she didn't want to tell anyone was because she was older. She could drive, and

Molly didn't even have a learner's permit.

"I don't know, all I know is I don't want to hang out at a wedding."

"Do you like books?"

Molly wasn't much of a reader; the only books she read were required reading for school, and even then, she didn't usually read the whole thing. She liked comic books, not a lot of people considered that literature, and she liked films. But if Teagan wanted to look at books, Molly would be happy to. "You want to go to the bookstore?"

"Why do you sound surprised?" Teagan grinned, looking at Molly for a moment before focusing her attention to the road. The plow always kept the road to the inn clear.

"You don't look like the reading type."

Teagan laughed, giving Molly the same feeling as seeing the inn decorated for Christmas did, only this was deeper. Less superficial; this was real. "Oh yeah, I actually own a limited edition of Shakespeare's *The Tempest* and *Taming of the Shrew*."

Molly tried not to make it obvious how surprised she was, but her eyes were bugging out of her head. "Really?"

"No!" Teagan laughed. "I read comic books."

"Oh! That makes more sense." Molly laughed along with her but stopped.

"Hey, it's okay to laugh." She glanced Molly's way when she didn't answer. "I know it feels wrong to laugh when your parents are barely hanging on." She reached over giving Molly's knee a gentle touch for only a second. Her heart sped up.

"I shouldn't ever want to laugh again, but it comes so easily when I'm with you." So did the honesty. Molly could play it cool by telling Teagan she was just fun to be around, but that wasn't the whole truth. The butterflies danced around in her stomach, and Teagan put her hand on Molly's. It was so natural for them to be together, they held each other so effortlessly, not a single thought went into their touch. It had never crossed Molly's mind to even look at Teagan until now. She had almost missed out on the best thing in her life.

"Why do you feel like you shouldn't want to laugh again? Do you think your parents would want you to live in a constant state of neutral emotions, or even sadness?"

Molly sighed heavily. "No, Mum would probably be angry at me if she knew laughing felt wrong. She was fun. Well, when she wasn't yelling and berating me for not doing something her way."

"Do you want to tell me about her? We've got the time; town is still twenty minutes away."

So, she did. Molly spent the rest of the drive telling Teagan about how at the beginning of her birthday month her parents would have a game for her. Every morning leading up to her birthday would be a cup that she got to punch out and get a little gift. Sometimes socks, sometimes candy or chocolate. Their Christmas Eve tradition started with Ainsley; they'd get pyjamas and treats, and they'd watch a Christmas movie that Mum planned beforehand, that way the kids wouldn't spend the whole time arguing which film to watch. They'd all end up falling asleep in the living room.

Molly secretly hoped Ainsley and Declan would carry on the tradition, even if they were to wake up with nothing under the tree. The oldest kids hadn't done it in so long, but Molly still did it with her parents. Declan only came home on Christmas Day, leaving London early, to make it for brunch. But Ainsley hadn't been home in years. Did she even remember the Christmas tradition?

"Sounds like you had a great relationship with them."

"Have. I *have* a great relationship with them. They're not gone." She refused to say 'yet.' She wasn't ready to be an orphan. That's what she'd be. If both her parents died, she would be an orphan. Declan and Ainsley would refuse to move back to Holly Grove to raise her and she'd end up in an orphanage.

"Where's your head at?" Teagan parked on the side of the road on the main street. It was impressive that there was parking on the main road on a Saturday afternoon this close to Christmas.

"It's stupid. You wanted to see the library?"

"Let's stop by Oli's first."

The girls walked side-by-side. Molly kept thinking Teagan's hand would brush against hers like you'd see in the movies, but it never did. Teagan did, however, pay for Molly's hot chocolate. Molly wrapped her hands around the cup, thankful for the heat it gave off in the cold air. The pavement was cleared of snow and the streets were too, light snow fell out of the sky like a film. It was going to be a nice day, despite everything.

"Molly?" She turned around to the sound of her name, even though she recognized the voice immediately, she still hoped she was wrong. She had been hoping to avoid this situation.

"Hilary, Amelia," Molly said, pretending to be excited to see them, she was nervous they'd say something.

"Molly and...Teagan?" Hilary started to smile. The four girls stepped out of the way of walkers trying to do their Christmas shopping.

"No." Molly cut her off. She kept her tone soft, non-threatening. "There will be none of that. I'm setting a boundary. You are not allowed to treat this," she waved her hand between her and Teagan, "like we're dating." Teagan had a smirk on her face as she sipped her drink. This was amusing to her. Molly was defending their friendship, and though Teagan liked her; she was happy that Molly wanted their friendship to remain. Molly tried not to get flustered, but she knew her friends would

THE HOLLIDAY INN

assume she was dating Teagan if they spent any time together. That was why she didn't tell them.

"What else am I supposed to think when you tell me you have a wedding to help with at the inn and I catch you sneaking around town with her?" Hilary asked.

She did have a point.

"Maybe." Teagan stepped forward. "I can't speak for her though, she thought you'd jump immediately to the dating conclusion, like you just did, and she was trying to avoid that," Teagan said. She had a point too. "Just because we both like girls doesn't mean we're going to date each other. Two lesbians can be just friends."

Relief washed over Molly that Teagan wasn't mad at her for her quick defence. Teagan really wasn't like anything Molly expected her to be. Her kindness and gentleness were heartwarming.

"Is that true?" Amelia asked. She was less aggressive with gossip than Hilary was, but not sharing something personal between the three of them seemed to hurt her.

"She did just see me standing beside her and assumed we were on a date. We are not dating, we are friends."

"I'm solely here to offer my counsel." Teagan looped her arm through Molly, pulling her a little closer, and not helping their case. There might be feelings between them, but that didn't mean they needed to act on it,

Molly was sure she wasn't ready to date anyone yet.

"We can offer her counsel too. *We're* her best friends." Hilary couldn't hide the jealousy in her voice.

"Did your mum die in a car accident? No? Then you can't possibly know what she's going through."

"Whoa." Molly pulled herself out of Teagan's grasp and stood in between them. "This isn't a competition on who is more deserving of my friendship. You're both acting like children." Molly faced Hilary and Amelia. "I can have more than two friends. It doesn't mean I love you guys less. No one is going to take your place as my best friends."

Hilary and Teagan continued to glare at each other.

Molly rolled her eyes. "Do you know how stupid this is? You're fighting like I have to pick one of you. I don't and I'm not going to. Hilary, Teagan is a friend, that's something you're going to have to accept. We have things in common that you and I don't. And Teagan," Molly turned to her next, "I'm not a broken possession of yours. My mum taught me to set boundaries, so here it is: I am my own person. If neither of you can accept that I have other friends than I'm going to remove myself. Clear?"

Molly hadn't been assertive towards either of them before this, so this must've looked like a tantrum. Setting boundaries and sticking to them always felt dramatic and overreactive, but Molly knew it was necessary. She wanted to keep them all in her life, she hoped they didn't get mad.

"I'm going to the library with Teagan now. If you guys want to come over tomorrow after lunch, I don't think Ainsley or Declan would mind."

"Works for me," Amelia said.

"I'll bring my paint." Hilary's demeanour changed. She smiled.

"Good, I still have some canvas left over from last time."

Teagan followed Molly in the opposite direction of Hilary and Amelia, towards the library.

"You handled that well," Teagan said.

"When you grow up around adults, you learn a lot. So, you read comic books. Do you like to watch anime?"

"Only like a lot!" Molly was happy to have the topic changed to something they both identified with but wasn't depressing. "It's the only thing I watch."

"Me too! Ainsley used to judge me when we were younger."

"You talk about memories with Ainsley and Declan, what about what's going on now? Are you making new memories?"

Molly couldn't contain the scoff. "Barely, and not fun ones. Yesterday we almost did, but she has to continue to remind us that her life is no longer here."

Teagan thought on it for a moment. "What if she's having a good time and has to remind herself that it's not going to last?"

"I guess I never thought of that." *Was Ainsley really having a good time?* That could change everything. There had to be something that could be done about Gavin. Molly tried to suppress her evil grin from spreading across her face.

If Ainsley wasn't having a good time, however, that would mean she'd go back to New York, she'd have to choose between moving to London or New York, the inn would probably be sold, and she'd never see her friends again. Molly looked at Teagan, her chest tightening. Molly couldn't lose her, whatever was going on with them, friendship or more, she couldn't leave it without seeing it through. She had to do whatever possible to keep Ainsley and Declan around. They'd be a family again; she'd have her people again.

Chapter Fourteen
Declan

Olive wouldn't even look at him, and he hated it. She was the caterer and he was the venue; they were supposed to communicate with each other. The cake was supposed to have been delivered and on the table in less than ten minutes, but there was still no cake. Albert had since left, after washing the dishes and leaving some in the dishwasher. Ainsley was god knows where, and Molly was still out. Declan was on his own, and the caterer wouldn't even glance in his general direction.

Where is the damn cake! He huffed, falling back into a stool at the back of the kitchen. He hated the feeling in his chest, being around her. He shouldn't want to be with her, they wanted different things, but the way he felt all those years ago bubbled back up.

"Calm down," Olive said. Her soft voice was loud in the silence of the kitchen. "It's coming." She knew him still, even after all this time had passed, they weren't all the different; older, yes, but different? No. The idea that she still knew him gave him hope that there was a chance between them. He didn't let the fire burn too bright in his chest, but there was a fighting chance still.

"It was supposed to be here an hour ago." Declan liked that she was talking to him now, but how could he calm down? All the pressure that he put on himself was riding on this wedding to go perfectly, despite only learning of it the day before. He unknowingly put his entire self-worth on the outcome of this wedding. Stupid? Perhaps.

"It's December in the mountains, the roads are probably icy. They're just taking their time. Just chill out." Her words were harsh, no sense of comfort, yet he was comforted. The way her eyes darted his way when she spoke to him, the slight turn up of the corner of her mouth. It was all the same. Everything he had loved about was still there.

"If the bride leaves a poor review, it's on you," he grumbled.

Olive sighed; she knew him well, despite years of not talking. She had to know that he was still the same Declan. "What's really going on?" She pushed herself off the counter and sat on the stool beside him. It was the closest they'd been since their breakup. He held his breath, only for a moment. She smelled of dough and cinnamon. A scent he had forgotten about. He longed to bury his face in the crook of her neck, kissing her skin gently, hoping to get a taste of it.

"You're not going to get any bad reviews. Now tell me. What's really troubling you?" She hesitated to put a hand on his arm but decided against it.

She wasn't his person anymore, he shouldn't bare his soul to her, and he knew that. But he also didn't care. This would be his one chance to show her his thoughts and feelings, he needed to take advantage of it.

"I'm failing everyone." He turned away from her slightly. "I don't know how I managed it, but everyone I care about is disappointed in me."

"Oh, I'm sure that's not true." Olive slid her hand, innocently, across his shoulder as she got up to get them leftover cookies. Declan took it with a halfhearted smile. She remained at the centre of the kitchen, at the island. He didn't show her, but he was disheartened when she didn't return to him.

"It is. I disappointed you when I left for London, Mum was disappointed I didn't come home more. Molly is angry because she thinks we don't love her enough to up-end our entire lives that we've spent years building. And Ainsley is upset because I keep teasing her about Gavin."

Olive stayed silent for a bit. She knew he was right, everything he said were facts. But perhaps that didn't mean he failed them. He was human, after all. He had always put so much pressure on himself to be the perfect Holliday son. His mother held expectations for him, and he couldn't live up to them.

"I'm not disappointed that you left. I was upset at first, obviously, but it taught me that I can really only rely on myself." She meant it as a compliment, but he didn't take it that way.

"That's worse. We should've talked more."

"We were barely eighteen; I'm pretty sure we didn't know what a mature conversation was." She chuckled a little, making the corner of his mouth turn up. The sound of her laugh was like magic, always able to cheer him up. It was nice that some things stayed the same.

"You're probably right." He finished his cookie.

"I have a confession." She poured two glasses of wine, passing one to Declan. He suspected he shouldn't drink on the job, but a few sips couldn't hurt. "I'm not actually dating Peter Davies. We did go on a date—two actually. But it wasn't right. He wasn't it."

"Oh." Declan tried to hide the growth of a smile with his glass. "Why'd you tell me otherwise?" The curiosity on if she told him for the same reasons he told her he was seeing someone was too strong to suppress.

"I don't know." She leaned back on the counter before jumping on it, like it was her kitchen, and she did it all the time. Olive was relaxed. She looked at Declan in his—parents'—kitchen, wine glass in hand, and cheeks a little flushed. "I didn't want you to think you were the reason I'm single."

"Am I?" He didn't want to sound too eager, but hope consumed him. After all, she was part of the reason he was still single. He compared every girl to Olive. Maybe it wasn't

THE HOLLIDAY INN

fair, but if he didn't feel half as good as he did when he was with Olive, he didn't want it.

"Maybe in the beginning, but I really enjoyed being single. I built a successful business, I have a rescue dog called Winston, I see friends whenever I want."

Declan nodded, his heart sinking only a little. "I lied too. I did go on a date with someone before I came here, but it wasn't anything. It wasn't going to go anywhere." How could any relationship go somewhere when he constantly compared them to what he had in high school? And what if he had been building it up in his mind all these years, and they weren't as good as he remembered? He was sabotaging himself, but he couldn't help it; he knew she was it. Olive was his person. *I just hope I can still be hers.*

She nodded slowly, taking a long sip from her glass. "I guess we're a bunch of liars."

"I guess so." He smirked back at her.

Their eyes locked as they both took another long sip from their glass. Something unspoken shifted around them, maybe it was all in his head, but could they be understanding the same feeling? Could she want him back?

"Hey, Dec—what kind of weird energy did I just walk into?" Ainsley looked between him and Olive, then thought better than to hear what excuse they were about to give. "Whatever." She waved her hand. "They're ready for the cake."

"Stall, it's delayed," Declan said; Olive

125

tucked a long curly piece of hair behind her ear.

Ainsley stood taller, hands on her hips. "What do you mean delayed?"

"I come with cake!" The back door flew open, letting in the early December chill. The three of them helped the delivery man carry the box. They helped unload the satin-looking cake, the bottom tier looked like it was made from lace.

"The cake is here," Ainsley announced to the crowd, as they wheeled it out into the dining area; they responded with cheers.

Some family members made toasts, everyone wishing the bride and groom well. Declan watched Olive. She stood back against a wall, watching the newlyweds. It was the life they had both seen with the other, and often talked about as young kids in love. He always wanted to do and say the right thing, always letting someone else take the lead. He wondered if she wished she had done things differently too.

"You're creating a life together now," Emmie's mum said. "The family you create is your priority now. You'll do wonderful things. You'll be wonderful. It's okay to prioritise yourself, but don't forget those who have loved you all your life." Everyone clinked glasses.

Ainsley's eyes were on Declan until he finally met her gaze. He didn't want her to feel guilty, Molly was the one accusing them of not loving her enough.

At that moment, he knew what he had to do; if it came to it—if their parents didn't make it out of their comas—he didn't necessarily want to, he liked his life in London. But, if it came down to it, he'd move back. He would run the inn. He'd take care of Molly, and maybe, just maybe, he'd get a second chance with Olive.

❄ ❄ ❄

At the hospital, after a quiet breakfast where no one talked about the night before, the Holliday kids piled into their parents' room. Three chairs, the one by Mum and Dad were the same, the third looked like it was brought up from the cafeteria. Declan took the extra chair that sat in between both parents.

"Hey Mum, Dad," Ainsley said, making an effort to touch their father's bed and not his body. "We had a successful wedding yesterday that your planner did not mention. So, thanks for that."

Declan knew that the sarcasm coming out of Ainsley was well-intended, but it didn't sit well with Molly; her eyes narrowed at Ainsley, and she adjusted herself in her chair. Their parents were on the edge of their life, and she was there accusing them of, what, setting them up? Declan tried to ease Molly's mind, giving her a look, and gently shaking his head, as if to say not here.

"I'm hanging out with a girl," Molly muttered. Declan turned his attention back to her.

"I'm sorry?" Ainsley said.

"Not romantically, we're just friends. She's been through similar." Molly gestured to their parents.

"Does she know about the friends thing?" Declan persisted. He remembered her first coming out, was a year ago, maybe? Time was funny, but he was happy she was comfortable enough with who she was to be her true self. Not that she went out and paraded herself, even before they knew. It was her own business, and it didn't matter to Declan. He only cared that if she did date, it was someone who made her as happy as Olive had once made him.

"Yes." Molly rolled her eyes, crossing her feet at the ankles on their mum's bed, pulling her phone from her jacket pocket. "This is why I wasn't going to say anything. I knew you guys would get weird about it."

"So, should we come up with a plan in the event that this," Ainsley waved her hand to our parents, "doesn't end well?"

"I am not moving to New York," Molly said.

"I know. I highly doubt I'll be able to transfer here. There would be a lot of logistics, and a huge contract. Not to mention lawyers and currency exchange—"

"I get it," Molly grumbled.

THE HOLLIDAY INN

"I thought about it a lot last night," Declan said. "I'll do it. I'm sure I can manage my job and the inn and take care of Molly. She's practically taking care of herself already."

Molly peeked up from her phone. "So, I don't have to live in an orphanage?"

"Did you honestly think that we'd let that happen?" Ainsley asked.

Molly shrugged. "Until a moment ago, I didn't think either of you wanted the burden of living with me."

"It's sorted, let's move on to the next matter at hand. The lawyer. I called him and he's booked, unless they were to die before our meeting." Ainsley adjusted herself in her seat, to appear taller.

"What if the inn goes to you?" Molly asked

"I'm sure the lawyer has dealt with something like this before."

"Even if Mum and Dad left you their greatest accomplishment, you'd still turn it down?" Molly asked. It wasn't her typical snarky remark, it was a genuine question.

Ainsley was quiet, Declan didn't know how to process anything that was happening. Were they finally coming together, understanding each other?

"I don't know, but I know that it would take a lot of consideration." Ainsley sat up taller. "I know that you think that I'm selfish and probably a horrible sister, and I have been. I'm sorry for hurting you, for making you think that I don't want to move here because of you.

That couldn't be farther from the truth."

Molly put her phone in her pocket. Declan sat in between his two sisters, not knowing if he should move or leave to give them privacy.

"I know that I'm angry, that I seem angry all the time. But I'm not. I'm scared." Tears welled up in her eyes to which she averted them away from her older siblings. "I'm losing my parents, my sister doesn't want to come home, my brother is—" Molly sighed. "Declan, you've been kind. But you're a people pleaser."

"We've all got issues, but we're better together, the three of us. Aren't we?" Ainsley asked.

"I think so. Look at that wedding we did," Declan spoke up, relieved to see his sisters coming together.

The three of them sat in the silence of the room, except for the steady beeping of machines.

"You know, I always felt like the disappointment of the family. I didn't want the same things for my life that they wanted for me. I took off to ease that feeling. Being here is a constant reminder that I'm not the daughter they wanted. And they may never wake up for me to change." Ainsley pulled her knees to her chest and hugged them close.

"You don't have to change. It's your life. They're here to guide us, but it is ultimately our choice what we do with our own life."

As the words left his mouth, he knew what he wanted for his life. If you had asked him

THE HOLLIDAY INN

two days ago it would have been a completely different answer, but he was so sure of this, he was willing to risk it all. Besides, what did he really have to lose?

Chapter Fifteen
Ainsley

Everything was right again. Molly moved her chair next to Ainsley to show her pictures she'd taken recently. Ainsley was mostly interested in what the girl Molly was hanging around with looked like, and more importantly, if she was good to her. The girls actually giggled, talking about crushes they had in the past, and Declan sat on the other side of the room, trying to do the work he was falling behind on for Heather.

Though the location was less than ideal, they made it work. They were together with their parents, despite it all. They were even laughing together. Everything seemed okay at that moment. That was until our mother's machine started frantically beeping.

"What's that mean?" Molly sat up, worried, dropping her phone on the floor.

Ainsley ran to the door, her heart racing. "Help! My mum. Someone, please!" Several nurses came into the room. They ignored the siblings, working out whatever was going on with their mother. Ainsley stood back against the wall, holding Molly. She clutched Ainsley's shirt, keeping her eyes on commotion. Declan sat up, watching the nurses click buttons and push meds.

"Page general," one nurse said.

"What does that mean?" Molly asked. Her arms were wrapped tighter around Ainsley. She held onto Molly as if she were her own daughter suffering a heartbreak.

"We think your mother may need another surgery."

A doctor in a white lab coat entered the room. "Oh, Dorothy Holliday," he said. "Who is her next of kin?"

The three of siblings looked between each other, all assuming it was their father. "I am," Ainsley spoke up. "What do you need?"

The doctor flipped through the chart. "They are on a thirty-day time frame, but if you feel the surgery is unnecessary..."

"Of course, it's necessary!" Molly yelled, tears welling up in her eyes. "How could you say it isn't?"

A pang filled Ainsley's chest seeing her sister in such distress, even if she knew the surgery wouldn't save their mother, she agreed for Molly's sake. Ainsley was sure there was no way their parents were coming out of this, they were just here to humour the thirty days, to abide by their parents' wishes. But she knew. Whatever was happening, was only going to delay the inevitable.

The doctor wheeled Dorothy out of the room, making it appear much larger than it once was. Molly rested her head on Ainsley's shoulder, and she rubbed Molly's back, shushing her like an infant. "It'll be okay," she said. "The doctors will take care of her."

"I'll go get some lunch. It'll do us good to eat something," Declan said.

"Can you go to Oli's?" Molly muttered with a sniff.

The uncertainty was written all over his face. Did he really want to run the risk of seeing Olive? Ainsley thought the night of the wedding they were getting along. It was clear he still had feelings for her, she hoped Olive did too. What would he tell her? "Yeah. What do you want?" After getting the order, Declan left, leaving the girls alone with their unconscious father.

Finally, Molly pulled away, sitting back in her chair. "I don't understand. They were both doing fine."

"Some complications take longer to appear." Ainsley didn't know if that was true or not, but it seemed to give Molly some comfort. "Molly, we have to—"

"I don't want to."

Ainsley sighed, bowing her head. "I know, but now it is a very real possibility that after these thirty days..." But the words wouldn't come out. Not when it could very well be happening in the operating room beneath them. *Our mother may never wake up, and once the thirty days hit, the plug must legally be pulled. Why couldn't they have signed a full DNR? End it, why make everyone suffer.*

It was an hour after Declan came back with

THE HOLLIDAY INN

their order from Oli's Cart when the doctors wheeled their mother back into the room. She didn't look any different; tubes still coming out of her mouth, hooked up to IVs. The three siblings watched the doctor as the doctor checked her over.

"Her appendix ruptured," he said with a chuckle. Molly narrowed her eyes at him. "Sorry. It's just with all the injuries she sustained, we never thought to check for an enlarged appendix."

"So, she's okay?" Ainsley asked.

"Well, given her circumstances before and where she is now, yeah. She's back to the same." Which wasn't the news anyone wanted to hear or give. "Right, well I have some other patients to check on. You three have a good rest of your day."

They thanked him, with a nod of their heads, on his way out.

"Good rest of our day," Molly spat. "Yeah, we'll do just that with our parents—"

"Molly, let's take a breath," Ainsley said. She put her arm around Molly, who, in turn, put her head on Ainsley's shoulder. Ainsley didn't want to get her hopes up, but maybe this meant things were going to be better. Declan sat in the chair closest to the window, looking out at who knew what. They were all in our own little world, wishing they could tell their parents about it all.

❄ ❄ ❄

Ainsley sat at her usual table at Olive's Cafe. It was hard for her to believe that she'd been here so much that she had a usual table, and a usual order at that. It was Monday, the second week in December, which meant that the Christmas festivities were going to begin. She didn't know which events fell when, but knew she needed to participate if she wanted an authentic article for the Holiday Edition. She liked Christmas, the lights, the decorations, the magical feel in the air where people believed in magic, even the adults. What she didn't like was coming home for Christmas and being badgered on letting go of her crazy New York dream, or when she was going to settle down with a man and have kids.

She loved her job and her friends, but everything else in New York was so…but if she were to tell anyone she didn't like the rest of it, she'd no doubt get told 'I told you so' and practically be forced to move back. She was too proud to admit they may have had a point with moving away young and fast. So, she sucked it up for the love of her job. If she were to come back, it would be on her terms. But she didn't know what those terms looked like.

She sighed heavily, burying her face in her hands, and someone cleared their throat.

"Gavin," she said without lifting her head.

"You mind?" He gestured to the chair in front of her, even though she wasn't looking at him.

THE HOLLIDAY INN

"Go ahead." She closed her laptop so she could have a proper conversation. It wasn't like she was in the middle of anything, she wasn't even at the beginning. "Are you stalking me?" she asked with a grin.

"No, though it does feel that way." He chuckled. "Want to talk about it?" He gestured to her laptop.

"Nope. Is there a schedule of the Christmas activities?" She took a sip of cold coffee.

"On the bulletin at the community hall. Is that what you're going to write about?"

She shrugged. It felt like a cop out. "It's something. It's a start. The article is due in ten days and I don't even have an opening line yet. I'll take anything at this point." She packed her bag, stood, and slung it over her shoulder. "You want to come?"

Gavin perked up, though trying not to make it obvious. It was clear he liked her, whether it was friendly or more, she didn't mind. He was good company and she'd be lying if she didn't feel some type of spark light up inside of her when she saw him.

"Sure." He shrugged with a half grin.

Ainsley dropped her bag off in her rental car that she parked on a side street.

The air was chilly, but not cold enough to chill one's bones. She could walk with her winter coat open, exposing her favourite burgundy turtleneck knit sweater. She placed a matching knit headband around her head, covering her ears, and shoved her hands in her pockets.

Few people walked on the pavement, and those that did were not in a hurry. It was vastly different then walking the streets in New York. Everything was calm. Enjoying the weather, some kids twirled and giggled while their parents offered kind smiles on their way past Gavin and Ainsley. Some kids jumped in the small snow pile on the edge of the buildings. One, walking backwards, walked right into Ainsley's legs.

"Oops," she said with a smile.

"Oh, sorry," he said.

"Timothee," his mum, she assumed, called. "Oh. Ainsley."

She stopped in her tracks. "Narine."

The two stood in front of each other, taking each other in; not really registering anyone around them, at least on Ainsley's end. It had been years since they talked.

"It's so good to see you!" they both exclaimed, wrapping their arms around each other. "I was so sorry to hear what happened to your parents. I wanted to reach out, but didn't want to overwhelm you," Narine said. "Didn't want to cause a distraction, but I see you've found one anyway." Narine smirked.

"Oh, he's—"

"Hey, Gavin." Narine gave him a hug.

Ainsley stood there confused. "You two know each other?"

"He did my maternity shoot for Timothee, and we have a booking for this one." Narine rubbed her belly.

"Oh, congratulations." Ainsley laughed, finally seeing Narine's husband. "Patrick, how are you, mate?"

"Good, thanks, love." They half hugged; he kissed her cheek. "Been a long time."

"So long. Married?" Ainsley asked, noticing the ring on his finger, but not on Narine's. Her fingers must be swollen. She heard that could happen. Nothing about bringing a child into this world sounded fun to her.

"Three years," Narine answered, cautiously. "We would've invited you but—"

"Girl, don't even worry about it. I get it." Ainsley smiled. It was mostly true; she did understand why she didn't get an invite. She probably wouldn't have invited herself either. They fell out of touch, like so many high school friends do. It was natural, sucked, but natural. But she did get to see pictures on social media, and it was small. Just their immediate families. "I'm so happy for you both. You look really happy."

"We are." Patrick pulled Narine into his side. "I've loved her since our first date." He planted a kiss to her temple.

In high school, Ainsley would've rolled her eyes and laughed, but she didn't think they were those type of friends anymore. So, instead, she smiled and said, "That's sweet." It felt fake. Like she was an imposter trying to convince the people before her that she was the true Ainsley.

"So, tell me, what's going on here?" Narine pulled Ainsley aside, while the men played with Timothee in the snowbank. Gavin was a natural with kids, or at least with Timothee. Surely, he'd want some of his own one day. Yet another reason why staying here would be a mistake.

"Nothing. We were going to the community hall to see the Christmas bulletin. I'm working on an article."

"Christmas bulletin, huh." Narine had a devilish look in her eyes. "You two should come over for dinner on Friday."

Us two? she thought. There was surely no *us two*. "I don't know..." How did you turn down someone you once were so close with? Narine and Ainsley were practically joined at the hip, inseparable, they loved each other like sisters, still did on Ainsley's part, but it felt strange to be invited with Gavin. Like they were a package deal.

"Patrick, shouldn't Ainsley and Gavin join us for dinner on Friday?" Narine glared at Patrick as if to mentally threaten him to join her side.

"Of course, they should." Patrick, he never could stand against Narine. "I'll cook steak."

Ainsley wanted to scold him for encouraging her, but how could she turn down steak? She was mostly obligated to agree. Gavin looked at her with a smile. He knew it too. At least it was with people she knew and grew up with.

"I think they've tricked us."

"I'm afraid so." She grinned back.

"Oh, good. I'll message you the details. Come on, Timothee, we need to go."

"Bye, Narine." Ainsley wrapped her arms around her friend. It was like the goodbye they never officially got. They hugged each other a little tighter, a little longer than usual.

"Bye, Ainsley."

Ainsley watched her walk away before continuing to the hall with Gavin. They moved to the side so as not to bump into those walking toward them, his hand brushed against hers, and Ainsley released a small gasp at the shock that shot up her arm. They both turned to look at each other and she wondered if he felt the same thing.

She didn't want to give in, she couldn't. The way he was with children, he'd want his own and she couldn't lead him on. But it felt so good to be with him. She felt like herself, he was fun, he was like her. She only hoped neither of them grew too attached before her time there ended.

Chapter Sixteen
Molly

"Good news is I won't be sent to an orphanage," Molly said.

Hilary tucked her hair behind her ear. "Was it ever a question that you would?"

Molly shrugged. She didn't want to get into that now. It'd been hashed out with Declan and Ainsley, there wasn't any reason to talk about it anymore. "All I'm saying is we're good now."

"That's great," Amelia said. "I know things were rocky there the first week."

"Rocky is an understatement." Molly closed her locker and followed the girls down the hall. "But we seem to be really good again. The wedding on the weekend pulled us together, I think." It was good to feel like her siblings were back, that they were all back to normal.

Molly loved that they decorated the inn together, that they got to decorate the tree. Even with their parents in the hospital, it was them, together. Teenagers get a bad rep for not wanting to spend time with their families, and any sign of emotions is a sign of weakness or some bullshit, but this was what Christmas—the holiday season—was all about.

"Molly!" someone called behind the girls.

THE HOLLIDAY INN

They turned around to see Teagan lightly jogging toward them.

"Oh no," Molly whispered. Teagan looked different today. Pretty. Not that she wasn't pretty before, but different. A good different.

"Hey," she said, catching up. "Glad I caught you. You left this in my car." She held out Molly's pink hat.

"Oh." Molly took it, looking around. "Thanks, I—" She didn't know what to say. She had made her feelings clear on wanting their friendship to remain private, but here they were, very public. Molly's fingers touched Teagan's when grabbing the hat. Her heart pounded. This wasn't about not wanting the public to see them; it was about not wanting to admit any type of feelings that might be there. Molly was secure in her attraction towards other women, but she wasn't secure in the teasing that came with having a crush. "See you around, I guess."

"Molly, come on. Really?" Teagan's brows pulled upward together, her eyes growing wider; her tone riddled with disappointment. She wasn't one for showing feelings, but she did with Molly. They were each other's vulnerability partners. They cared for each other, deeply, quickly. Maybe too quickly. Molly didn't know what she had gotten herself into. She liked Teagan, sure, but this felt very public, like everyone was watching their every move. She was a self-acclaimed outcast, Molly didn't care, or she told herself she didn't care, but she knew what came with talking to Teagan. Teasing, ridicule, torment. But when she looked around, no one was even looking at them, only Hilary and Amelia. Maybe no one truly cared. Maybe there wouldn't be any teasing that came with it.

All three of them waited for Molly to say more. What could she say? She had no experience with talking about her feelings. "We'll talk later," she said. Teagan nodded and turned around, walking away.

"What was that?" Hilary asked, obviously offended on Teagan's behalf.

"I don't know." She didn't. She chickened out. She cared too much about people caring what she did or who she talked to. She cared too much about being teased. Teagan was standing in front of her looking different. Her long hair was in a ponytail, slung over her shoulder, her makeup wasn't heavy. She wore browns instead of blacks around her eyes, which were such a nice colour brown, almost gold. Even her lipstick wasn't black, but a nice shade of neutral pinkish brown.

"You completely disregarded her," Amelia added. "After the fit you pitched on Saturday, I thought you'd want to hang out with her more."

Molly sighed, glancing over her shoulder. Teagan was leaning against the lockers, scrolling on her phone, like nothing was amiss. She looked up, eyes locking on Molly. She gave a small wave; Teagan raised her chin

THE HOLLIDAY INN

slightly and turned back to her phone. Molly's heart sank, she did to Molly what Molly had just done to her. She deserved it. She was being a terrible person to Teagan.

Molly didn't mean to disregard her. She wanted the opposite. She wanted to pull her close, to bury her face in Teagan's hair that she was sure smelled like smoke, like a blown out candle. Molly shivered.

"What's going on?" Amelia asked.

"I just have a lot going on." Which was true, she shouldn't even be worrying about if Teagan liked her, the thing between Teagan and her should be the last thing from her mind, with Declan and Ainsley home, with her parents in the hospital. Her attention should be there, not on Teagan and her flowing black locks. But it was, and she cared what Teagan thought of her.

The urge to stomp her foot and let out a muffled scream was overwhelming, but she remained composed. Molly wanted to run away from everything. She didn't want to have feelings for someone. She didn't want to deal with whatever was going to inevitably happen with her parents. She felt suffocated by Hilary and Amelia for hovering, constantly asking how she was doing. Their jealousy over Teagan was misplaced, she wasn't looking to replace them. She didn't know. She couldn't explain what she wanted.

Molly did want to rip her hair and scream to release all the tension from her body.

"I forgot something in my locker, I'll meet you guys later." She didn't even wait for them to reply before she turned around and went back towards her locker...towards Teagan. She hoped she was still there. She needed to act before she lost all her nerve. Molly shoved all her school things back in her locker and then stood in front of Teagan who barely glanced up from her phone. Molly fiddled with her hands, her feet rolling back and forth from the outside and back in.

"What? I thought we weren't supposed to talk in public?"

"Let's leave." Molly's palms began to sweat. *Gross.* Her mouth went dry, she tried to swallow, but it was like sandpaper. *Why is this happening to me?*

Teagan locked her phone and paid Molly her full attention. "Leave?" She smirked. "Aren't you the epitome of a scholar?"

"Maybe I don't want to be that girl anymore."

"What do you want, Holliday?" She looked Molly in the eye. Her lips curled in a half smirk now. Teagan watched Molly and it felt like sweat was pouring down her back, but she was dry.

Teagan was testing her, pushing her buttons. Molly looked around the hall, people were standing around but weren't really looking at them.

Teagan scoffed. "Always caring what people think of you." She pulled her phone back out.

"Talk to me when you're ready to let it go."

Molly's fingers tingled; she thought her eye twitched. She pushed Teagan's phone down from her face, pushing her so she was standing straight against the wall then kissed her. Teagan was stiff at first, then melted into Molly, cupping the nape of her neck. Her lips were soft, her kiss heated. Molly pulled away.

"I..." What could she possibly say after that? What was she thinking? *Oh my god. I kissed her.* "Oh god."

Teagan grinned. "Still want to leave?"

"I don't think that's a good idea." Was Molly the one to say that? Her brain was malfunctioning after what she'd done. She was out to those that mattered, her parents, siblings, and best friends. Teagan knew, and if she didn't, she did now. They didn't care, they loved her regardless of who she was attracted to. So, why did it bother her so much?

"Meet me behind the school at the end of the day," Teagan said, then walked away.

Oh my god...what the hell did I just do? Molly ran into the bathroom and slammed the stall door shut. She paced around the tiny box, chewing on her lip, ripping dry skin off. This wasn't the way things were supposed to go. Teagan was just a friend; she was just helping her through something that she'd been through before. Teagan wasn't supposed to be someone Molly wanted to kiss, let alone actually kiss. Molly wasn't the type to just kiss people. She'd never kissed a person before.

She shuddered. She didn't think she'd ever wanted to kiss someone, but Teagan was looking at her, almost daring her to do something. Molly was in over her head. It never occurred to her that this—her first kiss—would happen.

"Molly?"

"Yeah?" She tried to keep her voice as even as she could, biting down on her thumbnail. She didn't want to bite the nail off, but needed to do something with her hands. Her body was taking up space and she didn't know what to do with it. Her whole body felt in the way. *In the way of what?* She was hyper aware of everything. After shaking herself to get a grip, she opened the door.

Amelia leaned her backpack against the wall, waiting. "Do you want to talk about it?"

Her eyes popped out. "Don't tell me you saw that." She ran cold water over her hands and gently dabbed it on her face, avoiding her eyes.

"Hilary went to class. Since I don't have class with her, I thought I'd back track and see how you were. Then I saw you talking to Teagan and then you..."

"I can't believe I kissed her." Molly rested her head in her hands. "And now I have to go the entire school day waiting to know what she wants to say to me. She's probably going to tell me to leave her alone now. I was probably just a charity case to begin with."

Amelia followed her back to her locker,

where she shamefully grabbed her school things again. *I really asked her to cut school...* She could hear her mother's voice ringing in her ears. *Foolish girl.*

"Why do you say that?"

"I'm nothing like her. You've seen her friends. They all probably listen to grunge music and host blood sacrifices on the weekends."

"You like her, obviously. So, you have to decide if they are people worth getting to know. We've all practically grown up together anyway."

Amelia had a point, they've all known each other since elementary school, it was just a matter of getting to know who they are now. All Molly needed to do was get past the raccoon eyes, baggy clothes, and black...everything.

She looked at her own outfit, orange leggings and an off-white knitted sweater. They were opposites, there wasn't any chance that something serious would happen with them, and it scared Molly to think that it could. At fifteen, the last thing she needed to think about was a serious relationship. Or any relationship. She thought that was her problem, she might have been attracted to girls, but knowing she wasn't ready for a relationship was what got her through. But Teagan came along and swept the ground from under her feet and messed the whole thing up.

"Promise me you won't tell Hilary. We did

promise no relationships this year."

"I promise. But for your sake, I hope you don't go down a spiral alone. Promise you'll talk to Ainsley or someone."

"I promise." She said it, but she wasn't sure she meant it. Ainsley wouldn't want to deal with this. She was so far out of high school; Molly was sure any sense of it would make her run. Or romance. Molly cringed. Romance. She didn't want it. She felt too young for it. Wasn't she? She had way more important things going on than the need for a relationship. *This is so stupid.*

The day dragged on; Molly didn't think the final bell would ever ring. She both anticipated and dreaded going out to meet Teagan behind the school. It was their spot when they were friends, hiding behind our other friends' backs. Would she want to end the friendship? Molly had crossed a line. She was so far over the line she couldn't find it.

Lunch was a tough hour to get through, she hated lying to Hilary, but until she knew what was going to happen with Teagan, it needed to stay that way. Hilary was easily jealous when people she cared about seemed to stray. Molly didn't want to give her something to get worked up about. She blamed it on her parents. Her mother had to have emergency surgery and she was still shaken up about it. It wasn't a lie, there was just more piled on top of it.

THE HOLLIDAY INN

When the final bell dismissed her out of History, Molly nearly bolted out of the room. She wanted to keep her cool, she wanted to be the girl who was easy going, but she wasn't. She cared way too much what people thought, what people were going to say.

"Do you need a ride home?" Hilary asked, coming up to meet Molly at her locker. "Maybe we could hang out at the inn. You know how much I adore the aesthetic of that place. It's so rustic meets chic." She smiled. "Plus, that fire place in the sitting room, to die for."

"I'm meeting Ainsley at Oli's, but maybe later." Molly checked the time on her phone. "I'll message you later."

"Oh, all right." Her voice rang with disappointment, and her face fell a little, and Molly wondered if she suspected if she was really meeting Teagan. They split up, going in opposite directions.

Molly messaged Ainsley on her way to the back of the school, asking her if she was going to be at Oli's, and if she was okay with Molly meeting her. Ainsley agreed and as Molly rounded the corner to the back of the school, she put her phone in her pocket. She needed to be present for this. Whatever was going to happen, heartbreak or otherwise, she wanted to feel it. Her mother's voice echoed in her ear again, *you made your bed, now lie in it.* Whatever the outcome was, Molly was ready. But she really hoped Teagan wasn't angry. Molly took in a breath, the air nearly freezing the inside of her nose, burning her lungs.

"Hey," Molly said as casually as she could.

"I'm a little surprised you came," Teagan said. She leaned so effortlessly against the school. She didn't care what anyone thought of her. She was comfortable in herself, in what she liked and who she was. Molly could never, but she wanted to.

"Well, I did start it." Molly leaned beside her, shoving her hands deeper in her pockets. "I'm sorry." What else could she say? "I'm sorry I kissed you." That was better, though it came out more as a question.

"You're sorry?" Teagan sounded surprised.

"Yeah. I shouldn't have done it, but the way you were looking at me..." Molly kept her head and eyes froward. "I felt like I needed to prove to you that I didn't care what people thought."

"And?"

Molly turned her whole body to face Teagan. "I care so much. I'm freaking out. The people who matter know I like girls, and they don't care, but..." Molly genuinely wanted to cry, but the cold probably would've turned her tears to ice the moment they escaped her eyes. "I'm not like you or your friends. I want to disappear in a crowd, I don't want to stand out. I don't want people to see me or talk about me."

"Hey, hey...let's settle down." Teagan stepped closer, her hand placed gently on Molly's cheek, rubbing her thumb softly. "I like you, Molly. But if you don't like me or don't want to be with me because of whatever reason, I will respect that. We can stay friends if that's what you're more comfortable with."

"R-really?" She was crying soft, slow tears. How pathetic was that? Molly was the one who kissed Teagan and now she was standing in front of her crying because, why? Why? Because maybe someone would know she had feelings? Maybe she was human and liked how Teagan made her feel? What did it matter what anyone thought? Molly didn't know why she cared so much about what people thought of her, but she did know how good she felt standing this close to Teagan.

"Of course. You're going through a lot. I'm here for you in whatever way you want me. If we're the kissing type of friends, I can't say that's not what I want, but if we're just the type to drive around and talk about stupid stuff, then I'm happy with that too. *Whatever you need from me.*"

"Can you...hug me?"

As soon as Teagan's arms wrapped around Molly, she broke. Everything from the past seven years flooded her and she cried. She cried for Ainsley leaving, she was Molly's icon, the person she looked up to. She was Molly's best friend and she just left. Molly cried for Declan who didn't see a life here with Olive, she cried for *that* night. That night that everyone refuses to acknowledge. She was supposed to be fine after that? It lived rent free in her mind, it kept her up, and it broke her heart. They'd never truly all be present after that; they'd never be whole.

Teagan didn't say anything, nothing about being cold, nothing about how it'll be okay, nothing about how Molly was going to be fine. She just held Molly close, as close as their parkas would allow, and rubbed her back. She rocked them gently, side to side. Molly realized was wrong to judge Teagan based on looks, and she was wrong to judge Teagan's friends. She was probably the nicest person Molly had ever met. There didn't seem to be any agenda with her.

After what felt like an hour, Molly pulled back, wiping her face and her nose. "God, I probably look like an idiot," she said with a slight laugh.

"No, more like Rudolph." Teagan tapped Molly on the nose with a grin.

"Shut up." Molly pushed her, laughing.

Teagan laughed too. "You don't need to make a decision now. We can continue to hang out as the non-kissing type of friends until you do decide."

"That'd be really great." Molly sniffed. Teagan pressed her lips to Molly's forehead. "Could I get a ride to Oli's? I told Ainsley I'd meet her there."

"Sure."

As they walked, their hands brushed against each other, Molly couldn't stop the smile. Never did she think she'd like someone while in high school, or at all really, but

Teagan made her stomach flutter.

Molly rubbed her hands together while Teagan started the car and waited for all the windows to defrost. She passed Molly the AUX cord to play whatever music she wanted on the short drive. She could worry about Teagan judging her taste in music, thinking that it was weird or too poppy. But Teagan passed it to her, she knew what she was getting into. Molly decided to put on some Queen and a wide smile spread across Teagan's face.

"You like this?" she asked. "Like genuinely?"

"Yeah, why?"

"You watch anime, you listen to Queen, you're basically my ideal girl."

"But?" Molly asked, knowing it was there.

"You're fearful," she said casually with a shrug. "And I meant what I said before. I am here for you in whichever way you need."

Molly was fearful, more so than she might have ever been, but she knew in which way she wanted Teagan around.

Chapter Seventeen
Declan

After the surprise wedding, Declan was grateful that the inn wasn't hosting any events for Christmas. He didn't think he could survive another event, let alone one for the entire town. His parents were beloved in this place, and he knew he could never do them justice. He did hope he could make them proud though. They used to host a Christmas Eve party, the inn was the place to be at Christmas, but with them in the hospital it made sense to cancel it. Declan could never throw a party like that. Maybe next year, it didn't feel right to party with them in their condition.

He was falling behind in his actual job, so that was going to be his main focus. Molly was gone to school, Ainsley went to Olive's cafe as usual to work. He wasn't used to working on his own, there was always people around, people coming to him to ask questions. He was the information guy. He started working on ads that could be run over the course of the next few months. Heather was keen on promoting the health benefits of her pills. When he first started there, it was required that staff take the vitamins, so they knew

THE HOLLIDAY INN

what they were dealing with, and they had to stop any previous vitamins.

He, personally, didn't really notice a difference from taking it as opposed to not taking any, which he didn't take any vitamins prior to working with Heather. Maybe his hair was thicker? But he used a lot of staff's testimonials in the ads, claiming them as user reviews, which wasn't technically a lie. He needed them done quickly, so he didn't bother to look for new reviews on the website. In hindsight, he should've, it might have made all the difference when Heather called him later that day.

He was getting ready to lock up the front desk. All the guests would be gone to town to watch the battle of the bands—the first event to kick off Christmas—which Molly insisted on going to.

"I don't want to be late," she grumbled at him, all dressed at the door. "If you're not in the car in five minutes I'm driving myself." She left the inn to start the car.

He sighed and answered his ringing phone. "Hi, Heather," he said as cheerfully as he could. "What can I do for you?"

"What did you just send me? Surely you don't think I can use these."

"What's wrong with them?" He sat in the chair to look through the images he had set her. They looked fine.

"They look like they've been thrown together in a pinch. Are you in a pinch,

Declan? Have I not been more than accommodating to you and your situation?"

He sighed again. "No, you've been great." *Great pain in my ass.* "Tell me what you want fixed and I'll make the adjustments tomorrow."

"No. Declan, I have been more than generous with giving you time. I warned you if your work was not up to par then I would have no choice."

He sat up straighter. "Wait, you're *actually* going to fire me?"

"What choice do I have? I have people here, in London, who actually want the job. Who are *doing* the job."

He gave her five years of his life. For five years he had taken her stupid vitamin, he'd done her ads, her social media, her everything. And *this* is the repayment he got? Fired? Because his parents were in the hospital, and he had to be there for his family? He scoffed as anger fuelled him. That job was his only reason for staying in London, now that he didn't have it...he could do anything. "Fine. Fire me. It's the last tie I have in London anyway." He hung up the phone.

He decided to sell everything he had in London and move into his parents' house. That was the plan all along, right? So, why did he, all of a sudden, resent the idea? A pit formed in the bottom of his stomach, now that he didn't have a choice, that he was really going to have to live there and work at the inn, the possibility that things could go wrong all over again with Olive settled in his brain. What if their problem wasn't that he left, but that they just didn't work? He loved her, he still did, it was painfully obvious in the way his heart raced and he got awkward when he saw her. He wanted to do things right this time.

Declan wanted to be able to leave London on his own terms. In no way was this on his terms. He sank deeper into the chair at the front desk. Everything was falling apart. He wanted to be there for Molly, he really did. He missed his family whilst he was away, but it wasn't going to be the same without his parents.

The more he thought about all he had done for Heather and how easily she had let him go, the more anger filled him. His fists clenched at his sides as he fought the urge to swipe the desk clean.

"You know I was joking about driving myself, right?" Molly plowed through the front door to the inn. "Uh, you okay?"

He didn't know what he looked like. Confused? Heartbroken? Betrayed? All those things felt true. "Heather just fired me."

"Oh. That sucks." Molly trolled on the balls of her feet, still eager to leave, no doubt.

Whilst Declan sat, staring at the table, in disbelief that this could've happened, Molly's eyes darted around the lobby. There was no one there, everyone was in town waiting for battle of the bands to start. Molly stood on the balls of her feet and rocked back on her heels. She clapped her hands in front of her, pursing her lips.

"Oh my god, okay! Get in the car." Declan slammed his hands on the table and stood. "Why are you so eager to get there? It doesn't start for another hour and a half." Hilary and Amelia weren't even in a band; at least he didn't think they were. Wouldn't Molly be in it if they were?

In the car, she tapped her hands on her knees, then rubbed her hands on her pants, like she was wiping away sweat.

"Are you nervous?"

She scoffed. "No. I have nothing to be nervous about," she said. But Declan wasn't convinced, and he didn't think she was convinced either. He bet it had something to do with the girl she was talking to, the one she claimed was 'just a friend.' If she made Molly this nervous, she must be pretty special.

The whole ride to town, Molly drummed her hands on her knees. Declan tried not to sigh every five minutes, but it was starting to get to him. She was obviously keeping something from him, but he wasn't sure if he cared enough to ask.

"Will you stop that!" he said louder than he intended. She stopped, snapping her head toward him. "Sorry." He sighed. "I didn't mean to yell. It's just...the tapping." He was irritated, this thing with Heather, his job, and the still lingering feelings for Olive was adding up. He didn't want to be angry about any of it, but it consumed him.

"Sorry," she muttered. "I guess I am a little nervous."

"Why?"

"Teagan, the girl I told you I made friends with, wants to introduce me to her group of friends. They're playing tonight."

He nodded, wanting her to go on. Maybe her silly high school feelings would distract him from his very real problem of having to get all his stuff from London to Holly Grove. "And?"

She groaned and pressed her the back of her head into the headrest. "And sure, we've grown up together, and while technically we know each other, we don't *know* each other. What if they don't like me?"

"Then they are incredibly stupid. You're fun."

"But they're into dark makeup, weird hair colours, and heavy metal. I'm into a natural look, boring hair, and pop." It wasn't entirely true, she liked to listen to classic rock, but Declan didn't say anything. "I'm not the usual type that they hang out with, or like."

He found parking in the community hall parking lot, which surprised him. Usually the tourists got there early, otherwise they'd probably get lost parking on the side roads.

"Does Teagan like you?" He felt like Ainsley should be having this talk with Molly. Declan tried to channel his inner Ainsley, thinking what she would do and say.

Molly turned her head to the side, keeping her eyes down. He took it as a yes.

"Then why does it matter if her friends don't?"

"Because friends have a huge influence on us teenagers. That's why I didn't tell Hilary and Amelia. I knew Hilary would get all weird about me having a thing for her. She gets jealous."

"You would stop being friends with Teagan if Hilary told you to?" It didn't make sense to Declan. Molly didn't seem like the type to be influenced so easily.

"No. I don't know. They were my friends first."

"So, you're nervous to see Teagan? Do you *like* her?" Declan teased, an amused grin spreading across his face.

"Okay, we're done here." She opened the door and headed toward the hall.

Declan turned off the car with a smirk and followed her. The room was bright, people were gathered in one big crowd; there were no obvious cliques, though the tourists were easy to spot leaning against the wall with whoever they came with.

Christmas music played through the speakers, just from a phone, while they waited for the event to beginning. He couldn't see Molly anywhere, so he went over to the bar and ordered a Coke.

"Hey." He turned to the small voice. "Here alone?" Olive asked. He relaxed in her

THE HOLLIDAY INN

presence, the edges of his mouth turning up slightly. Everything that happened a half hour ago didn't matter anymore. She came to see him with a smile on her face. His shoulders fell as the tension left his body.

"I brought Molly, but she ran off to see her friends. Are you? Here alone, I mean." He couldn't stop the rush of his heart, hoping she'd say yes.

"Yeah. I just love supporting the local kids. I heard it's going to be a really good show." Olive also ordered a Coke.

"Would you like to watch the show with me?" Declan asked. It would be an unofficial date. If things went well tonight, he might have the courage to ask her on a real date. What else did he have to lose? Though, if she rejected him, he wouldn't be able to run home to London. He lived in Holly Grove now. But he also knew that he would kick himself if he didn't give it another try. She was his one that got away, and he had the chance to reel her in again. He needed to try one more time.

She hesitated for a minute, then smiled. "Yeah, I'd like that."

Relief filled him. She grabbed his hand and pulled him through the crowd. Her hand felt natural in his, like all those years apart never happened. He knew why she was holding his hand, so to not lose him, or rather he lose her. But he liked it. He gave her hand a squeeze and she looked back at him, sending his heart aflutter.

They sat at a table with a semi-blocked view of the stage.

"I heard about your plan to take over the inn."

"How'd you hear that?" He hadn't told anyone besides his sisters.

"Please," she said with an eye roll and a grin. "So, it's true?" He swore there was hope in her eyes, like she wanted him to stay, wanted him again.

"It is. Actually, I just...left my job in London. So, it's official." He couldn't risk her thinking less of him for getting fired. He still wasn't exactly sure why he was fired, since he was keeping up with the work. Besides, he really didn't want to get into it. "I'm staying."

She tried to stop a smile from spreading across her face, she took a drink to hide it. "That's great. I bet Molly is really excited to have you."

"I think she's most excited that she doesn't have to pack up her entire life and move somewhere new." He didn't want to talk about Molly. He wanted to talk about new chances, a fresh start, them trying again.

"And are you happy with your decision?"

"I am. It was the right thing to do."

She nodded but looked away from him.

"Hey." He placed his hand on her arm. "What just happened?"

She took in a big breath, tipping her head back. "I'm not sure what to think, Declan."

"What do you mean? We have a second

THE HOLLIDAY INN

chance. These opportunities don't always happen."

"A second chance? We're just figuring out that we're still friends; it's so fast, Dec. You choosing to stay now, means you always had the ability to stay, you just didn't have anything worth staying for." Her eyes fell to his hand on her arm. He dropped it.

Declan narrowed his eyes. What was she saying?

"I wasn't worth staying for. Now, that you choose to, or you're forced to, stay, you were always capable of staying."

"Of course, you're worth it. I was eighteen, I was stupid, I wanted more of what we had here."

"We could've had more, but you left." She folded her arms.

He bowed his head. "I know. I'm sorry. I wish I knew then what I know now. I would've made so many different choices."

"I don't know what to think. I like having you here; we've fallen back so naturally, but I just need to think about this for a little bit." She turned toward the stage, where a man stood in front of a microphone. The screeching sound of the feedback pierced their ears.

"Welcome, everyone! Our bands are eager to play for you. So, let's give a warm welcome to our first band of the night, Toxic Rebels!"

The crowd erupted in applause and 'woohoos.' Olive clapped, leaning back in her chair. Their view was semi-blocked, but the band came out and the crowd settled; most people took a seat, and it was easier to see the stage.

Molly sat in the right corner, watching. Could that be Teagan's band? Molly didn't look engrossed in them but was paying attention. So, Declan did too.

"We're the Toxic Rebels! Who is ready to get the night started!" The crowd cheered again. Then the band started playing. If it was the group Molly was talking about, them liking heavy metal wasn't apparent. They were more rock than metal. But they were loud.

The girl started singing. Declan tried to really listen to the words. The singer looked Molly's way on occasion and Molly would give a little wave. The song was about falling for someone completely unexpected. He looked at Olive.

She wasn't unexpected, he'd always had feelings for her. Even after five years apart and at least a hundred dates later, she was still the one he compared everyone to. She was the standard. If no one made him feel the way she did, it wasn't worth pursuing.

He needed her to feel the same about him.

Chapter Eighteen
Ainsley

Ainsley had spent the day at Olive's cafe, Oli's Cart. She couldn't remember anyone calling it Oli's Cart, despite it being branded on everything in the cafe. She got some semblance of what she wanted her article to look like. She was going to talk about the town at Christmas. It made the most sense. What other thing do you write about when in Holly Grove at Christmas?

She had finished editing a piece and was closing her laptop when Gavin came in the door and came right to her table. "Are you going to battle of the bands?" he asked without any form a greeting.

She checked the time on her watch. "I was planning on it. I need it for my article."

"Good. Do you want to go to dinner with me?" He got right to the point; she had to give him credit for being upfront.

She rubbed her lips together, stalling. "Are you asking me out?"

He removed his hands from the chair, putting them behind his back. "I..." He second-guessed himself. She didn't mean for him to doubt himself.

Ainsley raised her eyebrows. "Are you?"

She thought she wanted him to. Dating. It was exhausting. Man after man continuously disappointed her. Eventually, she gave up. It was easier that way, and soon dating didn't even cross her mind. But Gavin stood in front of her, asking her to dinner. Was it a date or was it not?

"Battle of the bands doesn't start for a couple hours. You have to be hungry."

As if on cue, her stomach rumbled. "I am, let's go."

They left the cafe and went to Denny's Pub. The two sat at the bar, it was casual, with no pressure to talk or get to know each other as if it were a real date. Ainsley relaxed.

"Did those pictures help your writing?" he asked, while they waited for our order of food. Denny served them their alcohol. The community centre was within walking distance, so Ainsley didn't mind having a drink or two.

"They did, thank you."

He nodded, with the corners of his mouth turning upward slightly.

"What?"

He shrugged with a grin as he brought the beer bottle up to his lips. "The whole premise seems a bit basic."

"Basic?" She wasn't offended, she knew it was basic, but her deadline was fast approaching, and ideas were far and few between.

"I feel like you could go deeper with it."

"How?"

"What was it like as a kid versus an adult being away for so long?"

"Huh." She hated to admit it, but it was intriguing. Being in the Christmas Capital of Europe, where she'd grown up and been accustomed to the season, did feel different to her now.

"I think it could take your article from good to great."

"I'll think about it."

Their food was placed in front of them, and they began to eat. "So, Gavin. Tell me about you."

He let out a sarcastic laugh. "Well, my parents divorced when I was young. I thought I'd be doomed to repeat their mistakes, so I swore off dating."

So, it wasn't a date. They were just getting food. *Then why did he burst through the doors with such purpose? The only purpose being to ask me to dinner?*

"I know it's a bit of a red flag. Women don't like when you don't plan a future."

Ainsley rolled her eyes. "Plan. There's so many uncertain variables that it's so hard to plan."

"That's what I say. I just know that once they start asking 'where is this going' I'm doomed. Why does it always have to go somewhere?"

"Exactly!" Ainsley said. "Like we can just have fun without worrying about a ring or marriage or children."

"Do you want any of that?" She could sense his reservations about asking.

"I'm not sure about the marriage, maybe if I meet the right person, but I do not want children. You?"

"No. No kids. And my mother keeps asking when I'm going to meet a girl and give her grandbabies as if my sister doesn't have three." Gavin huffed.

"It's the worst! No, I won't change my mind. I like kids fine, but I like being able to eat ice cream for dinner, or skipping meals to work, and you get in trouble if you don't feed your kids. It's not a life for me." Ainsley shook her head.

"I don't think I've met a girl in this town who isn't obsessed with wanting a wedding and babies. It's like it's required to be a woman in this town."

"Please. I travel. You can't get on a plane on a whim with a kid."

"I don't think I've ever been more attracted to anyone," he said, then immediately froze. "I am so sorry. I shouldn't have said that."

The bluntness shocked her, at first, but she didn't mind that he said it. If she was being honest with herself, she was attracted to him too. They shared the same values and hopes for their lives; it was one of the reasons she had reservations to begin with. The men she used to date in New York always said they wanted to be a dad; which really translated to they wanted a woman to do all the work and they get credit as being a dad. She wanted no part of that life.

"I think the battle of the bands is going to start soon. Do you want to head over?"

"Yeah, let's go." They each paid Denny for their meal and drinks. "It's so cold," Ainsley complained when they stepped outside. Gavin slid his hand into hers. It was warm and sent a tingle up her arm. She shoved her other hand in her pocket.

It was weird to hold his hand. Nice, but weird, like it wasn't supposed to be there. She couldn't decide if she wanted it there or not. Before she could figure it out, he let go and opened the door to the community centre. She thanked him whilst he held the door open for her. A large group filled the main floor, a stage was built in the back with guitars, drums, and other equipment that the bands would need to perform.

"Do you want something to drink?"

She thought maybe she had enough to drink, her insides were warm, and she was thinking about Gavin in a different way. He leaned against the bar on his elbow, his fingers laced together. His plaid shirt sleeves were rolled past his forearms. She sucked in a breath, taking her bottom lip slightly between her teeth. Her body heated up, she rubbed her hands together, trying to rid her body of its newly developed feelings.

"Glass of red," she said. He nodded once

and turned his attention to the bartender.

Oh my god. He ran a hand through his hair and offered her a little grin. *Oh my god. I am attracted to him.* She needed to calm herself down. He paid the bartender and gave her the glass.

"Let's go sit."

"That's probably for the best," she muttered mostly to herself. He looked confused but didn't say anything. Instead, he went to a free table. "I'm surprised there's a table."

"Everyone seems to be at the bar."

"Mm, will probably sit when the show starts." Ainsley looked around, maybe she could see Declan or Molly and they could all sit together and there wouldn't be a heavy feeling around her. She kept her drink to her lips, maybe then she wouldn't think about his.

"Did they do battle of the bands when we were younger?" Ainsley asked.

"I don't think so. I think they did more craft shows."

A man came out of the corner of the stage and stood in front of the microphone. The feedback pierced through the room. "Welcome, everyone! Our bands are eager to play for you. So, let's give a warm welcome to our first band of the night, Toxic Rebels!"

The crowd erupted in applause and 'woohoos.' Gavin clapped, leaning back in his chair; he was so relaxed, he definitely didn't look like he was battling some inner feelings like Ainsley was. They sat close to the stage,

THE HOLLIDAY INN

then she noticed Molly on the opposite end of the stage when the singer looked her way and winked.

"We're the Toxic Rebels! Who is ready to get the night started!" The crowd cheered again. Then the band started playing. They were loud. Or Ainsley had too much to drink. What was Gavin drinking? It didn't look like alcohol. Was he staying sober to be able to drive? If he offered to take her back to his house, she would force herself to refuse.

The girl started singing. Ainsley focused on that, on the band in front of her. Maybe it could distract her enough from these quick feelings. The singer looked Molly's way on occasion and Molly would give a little wave. The song was about falling for someone completely unexpected.

Of course, it is. Ainsley glanced at Gavin, who looked her way at the same time. He smiled softly, then turned back to the band. He was completely unexpected. She didn't want to fall for anyone. It was easier that way. Especially with the life she wanted. He claimed to want it too, no kids, no attachments.

What was more no attachment than a girl who lives in a different country?

"What?" he asked.

Ainsley was still staring. They were too close. Her cheeks got hot, but all she could think about was kissing him. So, she did the only rational thing any logical person would think of. She took his face in her hands and pressed her lips against his.

When she pulled back, she couldn't tell who was more shocked, him or her. "I am so sorry."

He grinned. "It's alright. Do you want to go outside?"

Yes, but I shouldn't. "Yes." They left the building before the first band finished. She felt like a teenager again, sneaking out to talk to a boy. It was thrilling.

"What was that?" He shoved his hands in his pockets, leaning against the building.

Ainsley kicked at the snow. She wasn't a teenager, and that meant she had to communicate like the adult woman she was. "I don't know." *Nice communicating.* "You were looking at me, and you at the bar...and at Denny's. It's all very confusing."

"You think *you're* confused?" He laughed. "I swore I would never find someone I wanted to be with, someone worth risking it all. And then you show up with your perfect hair, and your grumpy look over spilled coffee, and I needed to know you."

"Please!" She rolled her eyes. "There's no one out there who doesn't want a wife to care for them and someone to bare them children. And you come along and prove the opposite, that you don't want kids and you like to travel, and you don't want strings attached."

"What could be more no strings attached than a girl who lives in a different country?"

he asked innocently. They were the same, knowing that he was exactly what she was looking for tightened her chest. She wasn't ready to open herself up to love, to romance, but there he was. Her perfect man. Her heart quickened and she feared what could happen in a month's time.

She pressed her body against his, grabbing his jacket collar, and kissed him again. This time it wasn't an impulse. His hands came around her waist, despite her puffy jacket, and held her closer. When the door opened, she pulled herself away, turning away so no one could see her face. She wasn't embarrassed or ashamed to be kissing him. He was hot, she should be flaunting that she was the one kissing him. But she still felt like a teenager who sneaked out and didn't want to be caught.

"Do you need a ride home? I need to get home, still have a lot of pictures to edit, that are due tomorrow."

"I'm not going home with you."

"No." He laughed. "To your home."

"Oh. I should find Declan. If you're leaving."

"Do you want me to stay?"

Of course, she did! Were her lips on his not obvious enough for him? Did she have to spell it out that she actually liked being around him? It was overwhelming how fast the feeling came, like it was all at once. But she wanted to see him again, not casually like before, but this like. Where they would hold hands and laugh.

"What are you doing tomorrow night?"

"You tell me," she asked, her inside sparking.

"The Christmas light walk."

"They still do that?" she asked, a grin spreading across her face. Since when did she care about romantic walks in the snow?

"Yeah. I can meet you at Oli's at sunset?"

"Yeah, that'll be great. See you tomorrow, Gavin."

"Yes, you will." He gave her a kiss on the cheek and left for his car.

Ainsley watched him walk away, giddy that she had a date with him; he turned back once and gave a friendly wave. Once he was out of sight, she fell back against the wall, her foot slipped on the ice on the ground, and she fell into the snowbank.

"This feels right." Sighing, she rested the back of her head on the wall.

"Ainsley, what are you doing in the snow?" Narine asked, offering her hand.

"Oh, I just slipped." Ainsley wiped the snow off. "Did you see the first band?"

"No, our sitter for Timothee was running late. Did you?"

"Yeah, I'm not sure how many have performed now." It felt like she was out there with Gavin for hours, just the two of them, kissing in the snow with muffled music playing in the background. "Let's go."

She and Patrick followed Ainsley into the centre. Immediately, she saw Declan and Olive sitting at a table. "Come on." Ainsley pulled Narine to the table. "Hey, guys!"

Olive greeted the women with a grin, but Declan glared. They were sitting close, like Gavin and Ainsley had been. Maybe that's just how the chairs were set up. Narine did feel a little close. If the chairs had not been that close, she might never have kissed Gavin.

"How many have performed?"

"This is number three. They just started," Olive answered.

Ainsley nodded, but all she could think about was what had happened with Gavin. This wasn't supposed to happen. But it wasn't like it was love, god no. No strings attached. It was just fun, they were going to have fun, and nothing deeper was going to come from this. It couldn't.

Chapter Nineteen
Molly

Declan drove Ainsley and Molly home, apparently Ainsley had been drinking. Molly didn't even know Ainsley liked alcohol; they still had a lot to learn about each other, but Molly was willing. She missed her siblings and wanted to know who they were now.

The ride was quiet all the way to the inn, all of them in their own little world. Molly didn't know what Ainsley or Declan was thinking about, (she bet Ainsley didn't know she saw her kiss Gavin) but Molly couldn't stop thinking about Teagan. Until Teagan invited her to Battle of the Bands, she didn't know Teagan and her friends had a band, let alone a good one. Teagan sang, and she was really good at it. Teagan was so confident on the stage with everyone watching her, but she only looked at Molly. Like Teagan was singing to her—about her. It was a feeling she'd never felt before; one that made her eyes light up, and her heart sing. She was embarrassed and smitten at the same time. But she couldn't take her eyes off Teagan; Molly knew that her feelings ran deeper than the non-kissing type of friends they agreed to be.

When the band was done, Molly went

THE HOLLIDAY INN

backstage. She was going to meet Teagan's friends, officially. They were all kind, wishing Molly well and offering condolences about her parents. Teagan pulled Molly into a hug, wrapping her arms around Molly's neck, and thanked her for coming. Molly hugged back, not sure where to look, Molly didn't want to look at the band members, so she closed her eyes and nuzzled in the crook of Teagan's neck.

Teagan was sweaty from being on stage, but Molly didn't care, it was still a comfort.

"What did you think?" Aria asked. She had a different punk look than Teagan, with short black hair and a hot pink streak. Here eyebrow was pierced too.

"You guys were great," Molly said.

"You sound surprised." Teagan laughed.

Molly shrugged. "I guess I am. When you think of high school bands, they don't typically sound good. What's the prize?"

"First place is five hundred pounds," Imogen answered. She had natural brown hair, nothing added, no piercings in her face either.

"Wow, that would be awesome. I should get back out there, Hilary and Amelia said they were going to come too."

"We'll catch up later?" Teagan asked, her hand slipping down Molly's arm into her hand. Molly nodded, her heart pounding.

Molly rounded the corner and pressed herself against the wall. Her little crush on

Teagan was getting harder to deny.

In the car on the way home, she kept thinking of the butterflies in her belly. Never did she think she would be this person. The person who got feelings for someone. That was for older people, not her.

Declan parked in front of the house. None of them moved. Molly's phone chimed, Teagan's name appearing on the screen, pulling everyone out of a trance. Declan was the first to leave the car and go into the house. Ainsley sighed, following Declan. Molly opened the message and followed Ainsley.

`Thanks for coming tonight. I liked seeing you outside of school, sorry we didn't get any alone time x`

It was obvious Teagan liked Molly, but she couldn't figure out why. Molly wasn't anything like Teagan. She had no cares about what people thought of her, Molly cared so much. Molly didn't want to stand out, she liked blending in, but being with Teagan meant being noticed because she was easy to see.

Declan shut himself in his room. Ainsley in hers but left the door open. Molly changed into her pyjamas, taking off her mascara. She sucked up whatever pride she had and went to Ainsley's room, knocking on the door.

"What's up?" Ainsley asked, not looking up from her laptop.

"Can I talk to you about something?"

This caught her attention. She closed the laptop, and tossed it aside. "Of course."

"It's about Teagan." Molly sat at the edge of Ainsley's bed, crossing her legs. She didn't know what she was going to say, how much she would say, but she got comfortable.

"That's the girl you mentioned at the hospital?"

"Yeah. I think she likes me in more than a friend way."

"Do you like her?"

Molly sighed. "I don't know. I kissed her. I didn't mean to, and now I think that she thinks that means I want to be together."

"Whoa, wait. Back up. *You* kissed *her*?" She looked impressed, but Molly scowled. "Which is obviously a bad thing." Ainsley corrected herself.

"I'm just very confused. Do I think she's attractive? Sure. Yes. Do I want to kiss her again? Maybe. Probably. Do I want to be her girlfriend? I don't know. It feels…"

"Foreign? Uncomfortable? Unusual?"

"Yes." Molly bowed her head, looking at her hands in her lap. Surely none of those feelings were to be ashamed of. Did Ainsley feel them when it came to Gavin; was that how she knew?

Ainsley tapped Molly's knee a few times. "Kid, there's nothing wrong with that. You're fifteen, you're not supposed to know what you want."

"Really?"

"I'm twenty-seven, you think I know what I want?" She leaned back against the headboard. "I did something tonight that really could mess everything up."

"You kissed Gavin."

Ainsley's eyes widened. "What? How'd you know that?"

"I saw you when Teagan's band was playing. Can we get back to me?"

"Right, sorry. Listen, there's no reason for you to have all the answers. Try one thing and if you don't like it, then that's fine."

"What about her feelings? She sent me this text." Molly pulled the text up on her phone and showed Ainsley. "It's clear what she wants, and if I try a relationship and don't like it, then I'm just hurting her for no reason."

"That is tricky."

"What do I do?"

"I can't tell you what do to, mainly because I don't know. If I had all the answers I wouldn't be in the same situation."

"So, you like Gavin?"

"It's more complicated than that. It's not like you and Teagan, you both live here, you both have access to each other. Gavin and I...we want the same things and it's that we don't want anything serious."

"Wait, so that was nothing serious?" Molly saw Ainsley's face after the kiss. At least she thought she did. Maybe she guessed wrong. But they left together...and she came back alone. If she couldn't figure out how to make it work at twenty-seven, how was Molly supposed to know how to make a relationship work at fifteen?

"It shouldn't have happened. We're just having fun together. You're young, you don't need to be worrying yourself with the needs of a relationship."

"It's not that I don't want to, it's that I really don't know. We're good friends, I like being her friend, but I also like when her hand slips into mine, or when she leans a little closer."

"All solid relationships start with a friendship."

"Are you and Gavin friends?"

She thought for a moment. "Yeah, we are."

This talk wasn't at all helpful, Molly still didn't know what she wanted to do. She didn't think Ainsley knew what she wanted to do about Gavin either. But at least she wasn't alone in the confusion about wanting a relationship.

Molly had missed her sister. She liked talking like this, like they were the same, like there wasn't twelve years standing between them. "Do you want to watch a movie?"

"Yes! Grinch?" Ainsley asked hopefully.

Molly rolled her eyes but smiled. "Sure, but you can't say the words. I'll get some snacks."

Ainsley groaned; she could recite the movie word for word, everyone found it annoying. "I'll get the movie on my laptop."

Molly went to the kitchen, digging through the cupboards; they really needed to get some groceries. She found a bag of unopened crisps in the back of the snack cupboard, dumped them all in a bowl, and went back to Ainsley's room.

"What would Mum say?" Molly asked.

"About what? Us watching a movie?"

"About what I talked to you about."

"Oh. Well, I think she would tell you that you're a smart girl, and you shouldn't have to do anything just because someone else wants you to."

"Yeah, that makes sense." Molly pulled the blanket over her legs.

Molly didn't want to do anything just because someone wanted her to, that didn't feel right. She also didn't know what was expected of her. Did Teagan think she would want to be in a relationship with her just because she wanted one from Molly?

Molly was glad her mum wasn't here to worry about her, she knew how much her mum wanted her to feel comfortable being herself. She didn't want her mum to see her struggling with this. But she also really missed her. She missed the hugs she would give when she thought Molly wanted one, even though she groaned about it, she still hugged back. She always hugged back.

Oh, Mum...

Molly snuggled closer into Ainsley, not intentionally, but it was the closest she could get to her mother without her being there. Molly never realized how much her mother did for her until she was no longer around. *I hope she comes out of it...*

THE HOLLIDAY INN

❄ ❄ ❄

Molly woke up the next morning in Ainsley's bed. She wasn't anywhere to be seen, but the bedroom door was open. Molly grabbed the scrunchie off her wrist and tied her hair into a low ponytail, leaving the room.

She followed the smell of freshly made tea to the kitchen, where Ainsley and Declan were talking about movies. *Did they watch the same type of movies?* They laughed. Molly wasn't sure what changed, but she was glad to hear the sound of laughter.

"Hey."

"Morning," they said simultaneously.

"Am I late for school?" She looked at the time on the stove. She still had time to get ready before Ainsley would take her to school. "I'll have a cup of tea," she said, sitting beside Declan at the island. Ainsley poured a cup, added some sugar, and set it in front of Molly. "What are we talking about?"

"Do you remember being obsessed with this one movie?" Ainsley asked. "I can't for the life of me remember what it was, but I know you wanted to watch it all day every day. You'd watch it back-to-back from morning to night."

"Really?" Molly scrunched her nose. "I don't recall." Molly pulled out her phone to look through her Instagram.

"There was like four movies you've ever done that with," Declan said. "Mum gave in all the time. I reckon it was easier to put you in front of the telly while she worked."

"Maybe that's why you're so addicted to your phone." Ainsley pointed to her. Molly set her phone aside, face down.

"I'm not addicted to my phone."

"Please." Ainsley rolled her eyes, and Declan laughed. "Can't be any worse than Declan, he'd run around the entire house naked as the day he was born."

"Hey!" he shouted, and they all laughed. It felt good to be like this again. "It's not fair that you have all the embarrassing stories of us."

"I'm the eldest, it's my job," Ainsley said proudly. "Finish your tea so we can leave." She finished her cup and rinsed it in the sink; leaving Declan and Molly alone, Ainsley went to her room to change for the day.

"I don't think I like that she knows embarrassing things about me," Molly said.

"She's only going to use it for evil," Declan agreed. "Not sure when, but I know she'll tell Olive or Teagan."

"What do you know about Teagan?"

He shrugged. "Just what you told me last night." He drummed his hands on the counter. "I need to get ready for the inn. I reckon I'm late but can't tell."

"You're the boss now."

He stopped mid-stride. "That's right." Then he kept walking.

Molly didn't know exactly how it worked; they hadn't met with the lawyer yet. There was a lot to this she didn't understand. She mostly just agreed with what Declan and Ainsley said. It was easier than asking questions.

When she finished her tea, she went to her room to get dressed. She settled on a typical outfit, black leggings and an oversized sweater. She took out the scrunchie and brushed through her hair. "Ready!" she shouted to Ainsley.

"Coming!"

Molly knew she had at least a few more minutes, so she put on some mascara.

"Hey," Ainsley said, meeting her in the hall. "The mascara looks good on you; makes your eyes pop."

"Thanks."

Molly followed behind her. Ainsley looked relaxed; way different than when she first got here. She wore white jeans and a baggy blue sweater. She had her hair up in a half-up bun. Her makeup was more minimal now than it was when she first arrived. Molly took it as a sign she was comfortable there. The thought made her smile, she let herself hope that Ainsley would reconsider staying here.

Chapter Twenty
Declan

Declan sat at the front desk, but today was different. He was in charge of the inn. At first it was just a theory, something that could potentially happen, but now it was reality, there was no job in London to go back to. No safety net in case things didn't work out. *Who let me be the one in charge of running this business?* He was sure he was the least qualified person to do the job. Albert probably knew more than he did.

"I hate to be that guy, but do you know when you'll get payroll out?" Albert leisurely walked up to the front desk.

"Payroll?" Declan snapped his head toward Albert. "I have to do that too?" Albert furrowed his eyebrows at Declan, who tipped his head back and groaned. "This wasn't what I signed up for." Except that it was. He had made the executive decision to oversee the inn, and that meant he was the boss. He had to do everything that his parents did. They never gave anything a second thought, and he can't stop thinking about all the little things that needed to be done.

"Are you going to be okay?"

"Yeah, I just need some time to get used to

this. I didn't do any accounting at my other job."

"There's a great accountant in town."

"I know who to call, thanks." Declan pulled out his phone. He hadn't responded much to Jamie's texts. Mainly she wanted to know how things were going with his parents. He kept the replies short. But he needed her. He felt bad contacting her only when he needed her, but she was the best accountant...*I think*.

"Declan, how are you?" Jamie answered. She didn't sound angry that he had been dodging her. "I heard about the incident."

"That Heather fired me? Yeah. I'm doing okay. Listen, I need your help."

"Sure, what's up?"

"I'm running the inn. I'm one hundred percent in, but I know nothing about payroll or business expenses."

"Do they have accounting software?"

He clicked through every app he could find on the desktop, then he went through the bookmarked tabs on the internet, finally finding one. "Yes, but I don't know the login. Hold on." He went into the office to check the safe. Sure enough, there was a piece of paper with all the usernames and passwords. *Thank you.* He silently said to his mum.

He got logged into the system. "It's a lot."

"I know it's intimidating, but you won't need every function. Alright, so here's what you're going to do..." She walked him through the entire program, step-by-step. He silently thanked whatever god there was that she had the same program. He followed along, writing down the important bits, though it all felt important.

There was a lot riding on him getting it right. He couldn't remember a time when he felt such pressure.

"Declan?"

"Yeah?" He was distracted, he was too busy focusing on the task at hand. He needed to figure out what to pay Albert, what he owed Olive for her weekly deliveries. Did his parents have a cleaning service, or did they clean every room themselves? "Yeah, sure that sounds great. I gotta go. I'll call you later." He responded without hearing what she said. He ended the call not knowing it would come back to bite him. Flipping through the papers on the desk, he had no real intentions of talking to her again. It was nice at first, but his life was going to be here now; he wanted it here, with Olive. He just needed to figure out how to ask her out properly.

Maybe there was a schedule around that would help Declan run the inn to the best of his abilities. "Albert," Declan called heading toward the kitchen.

"Yes, sir?"

The term sir took Declan by surprise. But he was Albert's boss now, sir was appropriate, but it felt so strange to be called sir by someone so much older.

"Is there a schedule around for cleaning and

THE HOLLIDAY INN

other tasks?"

"Check the calendar in the office. I think there's a cleaning crew who comes once a month to do a deep clean of everything."

"Do you know how to clean the rooms?"

He smiled, wiping his hands on his apron. "There's a clipboard that your mum has when she does the walkthrough."

Declan nodded. He was sure he had all the information, but where did he start? The entire process was overwhelming.

In the office, he sat at the desk. It was strange. It was his father's seat. He was the guy who knew how to run the payroll, the one who did the accounting part of the inn. Declan had no clue if he was capable of filling his father's role.

He grabbed the clipboard that had a checklist of what his mother did to clean a room in preparation for a new guest.

He sighed heavily. "I have to do this to every room?" The first thing he would do was check the budget to hire a housekeeper. He didn't want to be the maid service too. Until then, he needed to get started.

Declan went up the stairs and grabbed a laundry bin out of the closet. "Okay," he said pulling out the clipboard. "I need cleaner." He went through the different brands on the shelf; there was a cleaner for everything. However, many different rooms, there was something for it. He sighed heavily.

"Hey." He jumped at the sound of her voice.

"Albert said you were up here." Olive picked up a bottle from his cart, checked it out, and put it back. Was she judging him? He didn't know how to properly clean or sterilize a room.

"Yeah, just deciding which cleaner to pick. I think I've said that word so many times it doesn't feel like a word anymore."

"Do you want some help?"

She offered all on her own. He tried not to seem too eager to spend more time with her. "Some guidance would be great. What are you doing here anyway?"

She slipped into the closet, which was already a tight fit for him. "Your mum ordered extra supplies for December, so I'm bringing them in."

Declan nodded. Her shoulder pressed into his arm whilst she stood looking at the shelves of cleaners.

"You'll need the sanitary wipes, bathroom scrub, and some air scent." She grabbed each of those things putting them on his cart. "Do you need help cleaning?"

"You want to help me?"

She shrugged. They weren't in the confines of the closet anymore. He missed her touch, whether it was on purpose or simply because the closet was too small. "I didn't plan on being in at the cafe today, so I'm all yours."

All mine. He liked the sound of that. "I'd love your help."

They went to the first room; it had been

THE HOLLIDAY INN

vacant for two days. The wedding party had left, and no one was booked in until the weekend. She started on the bed, while he wiped every flat surface down. She piled all the blankets in a big ball in the middle of the bed, and before he could bring her the laundry bin, she threw them at him with a mischievous grin. He stumbled back with a grunt, and she let out a laugh.

Declan laughed too, seeing how easy they fell back together was something he didn't expect. He wanted it but didn't think it would happen. Here she was, standing on the far end of the room, giggling, looking at him.

The impulse came and he jumped on it, scared if he didn't now, he'd never get the chance again. "Do you want to go to dinner with me?"

She stopped giggling, but her face was still soft. "I was wondering when you were going to ask."

Declan grinned and tossed the ball of blankets in the laundry bin. "Want to meet at Denny's at six?"

"That sounds perfect." She came around the bed to him. Her hand on his arm sent a shock through his body. "I've really missed you, Declan." She reached up and kissed his cheek. "I'll see you tonight."

He stood there, even after she left the room, probably even left the inn. *She agreed?* He still couldn't believe it after he finished the room and all the other rooms. He tossed the laundry down the shoot that went right into the laundry room in the basement. He really needed to hire another person. Who would want to do laundry and clean rooms for a living?

What else did he need to do before he left?

"Declan." Albert peeked his head into the office.

"Yes, Albert?" He checked off the last thing on the list and put the clipboard down on the desk.

"Can we talk?"

"Sure, have a seat."

Albert did. "Listen, I saw you going around today, and honestly you looked a bit stressed. Is there anything you need me to do?"

Would it be smart to hire Albert on as more than the chef? Could he handle it? Declan wanted to jump at the request. He wanted to immediately hire him on to do more, but this wasn't just an inn, it was his home. Declan needed to be sure that whoever joined the team would be here for a long time. He didn't know how much longer Albert would be around; his age did concern Declan, whether he wanted to admit it or not.

❉ ❉ ❉

Declan made sure that Ainsley and Molly knew they were going to be alone for dinner. He didn't tell them why, just in case his date with

THE HOLLIDAY INN

Olive went badly. They were going to Denny's, it was a pub, mostly casual. He didn't want to look like he was putting in too much effort, but he wanted her to notice that there was an effort. He rolled his eyes. "When did I become such a girl about this?" he muttered to himself.

Ainsley would slap him if she heard that thought. *Boys are allowed to care what they look like,* she'd say. He styled his hair into a coif in the bathroom mirror, put on a bit more deodorant, and met Ainsley and Molly in the kitchen.

"Well, don't you look dapper," Ainsley said with a smirk as she leaned against the counter, folding her arms across her chest.

"Hot date?" Molly grinned, licking a spoon.

"Ice cream for dinner? Really?" Declan judged.

"No. I have a frozen pizza in the oven."

"I'll see you guys later." He grabbed his coat and left the house, starting the half hour drive to Denny's.

Inside the bar was all decorated for Christmas. Garland draped across the bar in the middle of the room. Large bulbs hung from the ceiling, and a Christmas tree sat in the corner all decorated with bulbs, snowflakes, ribbon, and a giant bow for the top.

Olive waved from the booth beside the tree. He took in a breath and went over after getting a beer from Denny.

"Hey," he said. "Thanks for agreeing to

meet me."

"You sound like this is a business meeting. It is a date, right?" Olive looked hopeful.

"Yes. It's a date." He was nervous, making this whole thing uncomfortable. He needed to shake it off. "Tell me about your life now."

"You would love my rescue pup, Winston; he's a German Shepherd. He's the light of my life, you know?"

"I do. I remember you always wanting to adopt a dog." Warmth filled him, whether it was the alcohol in his beer, or the feeling of her talking about the things she passionate about, he didn't know. But he didn't care where the feeling came from. She was here, her long dark hair fell straight over her shoulders, her curves...

Her light blue eyes focused on him whilst she took a sip of her wine.

"How are you since the other day?"

"Better. Everything happens for a reason; I'm starting to think I know what the reason is." He reached across the table and took her hand in his.

The corners of her mouth turned up slightly. "You know, I spent a long time getting over you. I thought that if we were to ever see each other again, I wouldn't feel anything but neutral towards you. But that's not what happened."

"What did happen?" He knew what happened for him, he was still in love. Maybe it was because he knew her or thought he did.

THE HOLLIDAY INN

She was familiar. She wasn't not the same girl as she was in high school. She was so much better, stronger, fierce, talented, the list went on. She was sure of herself and that was insanely hot.

"I saw you and you looked the same, but with facial hair. I was taken back to being eighteen and the butterflies filled my stomach. I thought that going on a date with Peter would help, but all I could think of was you."

They talked over eating, paying more attention to each other than their food. They laughed together. Declan knew that she was his endgame.

"Do you want to go for a walk?" he asked when they were obviously done eating.

"The Tree Light Drive walk is about to happen; do you want to do that?"

"Yeah, that sounds fun."

The Tree Light Drive walk was a walk up Tree Light Drive, where the group would admire the decorated houses. The street was the best-lit road in all of Holly Grove.

Declan paid the bill, and Olive smiled at the ground, thanking him. They stepped out into the winter air, and he took her hand in his.

"Are you ever going to talk about what happened between you and your siblings?"

The question took him by surprise. How could he answer that? He wanted to be truthful, he wanted to tell her everything that happened, but it wasn't his story to tell. He was a bystander.

"We tried to get along, we were young, I don't think we understood that just because you're related through marriage doesn't make you a family."

"You don't consider them family?"

"It's complicated and happened a while ago. I think Ainsley is the most affected by it. She had this idea of what family was, of what our family was, and it got destroyed. I think that's ultimately why she stopped coming back. Family wasn't the same and she didn't know how to handle that."

She gave his hand a squeeze. "I'm talking about you, Declan. You're part of that family too."

"I know, but I didn't get into the fight. I purposefully stayed out of it, and I think because no one sided with Ainsley, she took it as us being against her."

Olive nodded, listening.

He wished he'd done something, wished he had cared more. Maybe then it wouldn't have taken so long to connect with his sisters. They'd always been close when they were kids, no matter what, and then the night of the fight changed everything.

"Do you still want marriage and kids?" he asked, changing the subject.

"Wow, jumping right in." She laughed.

He could see the group up ahead, soon they wouldn't be able to talk privately. He needed to know if they still wanted the same things, if not, there was no point in continuing to pursue a relationship.

"I do. I've always wanted marriage and kids."

He sighed with relief. "Me too."

"You're not going to propose, are you?" she teased.

"Not tonight. But I can't make any promises about tomorrow." They laughed together, meeting up with the group.

"Well, hello," Ainsley said. Gavin stood next to her.

"You didn't tell me you were coming here."

She rolled her eyes. "Neither did you. Actually, you didn't tell us anything." Ainsley looked between him and Olive. He knew he was in for a teasing later.

"Is Molly here too?" Declan looked around. He didn't want her to get her hopes up. She loved Olive when she was a kid, the last thing he wanted was for her to get attached again and something bad happen. This was only their first date. Their second first date, but he was determined to do it right this time.

Chapter Twenty-One
Ainsley

Ainsley didn't know what Declan was planning for the night, but she didn't expect him to do the Tree Light Drive Christmas light walk. Hell, she didn't expect her to do it. The cold was never something she found particularly enjoyable. Whilst mostly everyone was wearing jackets and mittens, she had a long sleeve shirt, sweater, jacket, hat, and mittens. She didn't mess around when it came to winter activities; mostly she never did them.

"Don't worry, we won't walk with you, wouldn't want to do something to embarrass you," Ainsley teased Declan.

"You can walk with us, I don't mind." He put his arm around Olive, who looked at him and smiled.

"Oh." She looked at Gavin who shrugged. She was hoping to walk alone with Gavin. Olive didn't seem to mind either. "When do we start?"

"Any minute," Gavin answered.

Ainsley saw Molly at the other end of the group, standing with Teagan, Hilary, Amelia, and some other girls she recognized from the band the night before. It pleased her that Molly wasn't one of those girls who ditched her friends to hang out with her crush. They seemed to be getting along well, laughing.

"You two look cosy," Ainsley said.

Declan played it off, but she knew that he was excited to be back with Olive. That girl was the love of his life. He pulled her a little close and she nuzzled into him.

"When you know you know," he said.

"Alright, everyone, we are going to begin! If you haven't gotten a cup of hot chocolate, you can do so on your way past the booth, courtesy of Oli's Cart."

"You do a lot for the town, don't you?" Declan asked.

Olive played it off as nothing. "It's what we do for each other. Come on!" She pulled Declan to catch up with the group, though they stayed trailed behind. Gavin and Ainsley followed them at a distance.

"Do you want to catch up with the group?" Gavin asked.

"No." Ainsley took his hand in hers, though she didn't feel any warmth due to her mittens. "I like trailing behind."

"Never in my life did I think I'd meet someone who wanted things like I did," he said. "And to think, Ainsley Holliday. It's really messing with my whole life plan."

"You say it like I'm someone famous."

"You might as well be in this town. Your parents are so well known and so beloved by everyone. We feel like we know you." He hesitated. "But we don't."

She hoped he wouldn't ask. Everyone knew that something happened to the family, that there was a reason they left home, a reason one of them never returned. Their parents didn't like to talk negatively about their kids, so surely, they came up with a flourished version of the truth. *They left to chase their dreams and follow their hearts.* Not to get away from everything and each other.

"What happened between you guys? You and Declan seem okay."

"We're good." It was true, she was mad at him for not being on her side, but now it felt foolish. There didn't need to be sides anymore.

"That's all I get?"

"It happened a long time ago, and though I'm still incredibly angry about it, it's in the past, and it's just the three of us now."

Ainsley thought she knew what family was. You chose each other no matter what, whether you were born into it or marrying into it. You're a family, you choose each other. You're supposed to be there for each other. And to be left behind, without even a second thought, was devastating.

"Are you okay?"

She hadn't realized she'd stopped. Her eyes were staring at a house, but her brain hadn't registered it. "Yeah." She shook her head. "I just don't like talking about it, it gets me into a weird mood."

"Of course, let's just look at the Christmas lights."

THE HOLLIDAY INN

She wanted to be present with him, she wanted to admire the hard work that went into making the displays, but her heart wasn't in it anymore. She kept thinking of them being kids and doing the Christmas light walk with their parents. They lived for the traditions of the town.

But now the kids were grown, moved on with their lives, except for Molly. She was stuck here, forced to grow up and have her firsts without her mother around.

The Holliday family used to do every Christmas activity together, now they were separated and doing them with other people. They couldn't even come together enough to do the things they used to with their parents, who were most likely never going to experience this again.

"We can leave if it'll help." Gavin rubbed Ainsley's arms, stepping a little closer.

"No, I want to be here." But she wanted to be there with her family, the family that she thought they were, the family she wanted them to be. Clearly, no one else felt the same, they were happy to go off with their new loves and she was standing there, freezing, with Gavin, someone who didn't want anything serious, someone who never saw a future with anyone.

"Ainsley, we might not have been friends long, but I can see that you'd rather be anywhere but here."

She sighed. "I'm sorry I'm not better

company. I should just leave."

"Come back to my place, we'll put on a stupid movie and drink something hot and when you're feeling better, then you can go home."

"That sounds really good." She relaxed, giving him a soft smile.

He took her hand and led her back toward the main street. How could he not want anything serious? He would make someone the perfect boyfriend or husband. He knew exactly what she needed, and he didn't hesitate to offer, even when she said otherwise. Her chest filled with gratitude and admiration for him.

There were supposed to be no strings attached between them, but how could there be no strings when he did all the right things?

Gavin didn't pry the entire drive back to his one-storey home. There was a kitchen, living room, bathroom, and two bedrooms, one of which he made into his office/studio. It was a cute and cosy home. He grabbed a bottle of wine out of the pantry and two glasses. Ainsley sat on his couch whilst he put on a Christmas movie but made it quiet, so it was background noise.

"I didn't mean to ruin your night," Gavin said, holding out a glass to her.

"You didn't. It's me, I get all in my head and I feel all these big feelings which I never learned to deal with properly."

Ainsley swirled the wine in her glass

around. It had never been her drink of choice, she found the taste bitter, but she took it, not wanting to be rude. "Do you ever feel like you're constantly wrong about people? Like you think that they'll be one way but turns out it's the complete opposite?"

"Hmm, I'm not sure."

"You don't see their true colours until it's too late, and you're the one who gets hurt because you had these expectations of them."

"Is that what happened with your brother?"

"Yeah." *My brother.* It felt strange, but that's what he was, despite everything. She always thought family was supposed to have your back no matter how small or big the circumstance was, but that was not the case in the Holliday family.

The next morning, Ainsley woke up disoriented, she didn't remember going home. She sat up on the bed. She was not home. *Oh no.* She wasn't home, and she was in his clothes. *This is not good,* she thought. Ainsley left the bedroom, which Gavin was not in, and followed the smell of bacon and eggs to the kitchen.

"Good morning."

"Gavin," she said, worried.

"You changed yourself, I slept on the couch," he said without looking at her.

Oh, thank god. She poured a cup of tea from the kettle and sat at the table. "I have to go all the way back to the inn to get my work just to come back to town to work. Molly." She shot up from the table getting her phone.

Several missed calls and texts from Declan and Molly. But there was a sent message to Declan that told him she was fine and staying over at Gavin's house. *Oh great, that's just what I needed.*

"Declan is going to take her to school. It's all sorted."

"Did you call him?"

"He called you this morning, I answered. I didn't want him to worry about you."

"Thanks." The panic subsided and she sat back at the table. "You're cooking breakfast," she observed.

"I always make breakfast. I have a full day of editing and photo shoots, so I'm going to ask that you eat and leave." He peeked at her over his shoulder.

"I can do that," she said as he put a plate of food in front of her. Though, if she were being honest with herself, she was disappointed. "Thank you." He sat in the only other chair at the table, across from her. "Thanks for letting me crash here. I don't usually spend the night."

"We had fun. We watched movies and ate a lot of popcorn."

"Yes, I do recall." It was nice having a friend. A friend...*Narine*! Ainsley was supposed to go to dinner at her house on Friday with Gavin. He was her plus one. Was it a double date? It was too soon after waking up to freak out like this. "Can you drive me to my car?"

"Of course."

After breakfast, she helped him clean the dishes, and she put on yesterday's outfit. He drove her to her car. The drive was silent, but his hand found its way into hers. Comforting, yet. She knew how this was going to end, but why wasn't she more concerned about the stirring feeling in the pit of her stomach?

He parked behind her car on the side street. "Will I see you again?"

"There's a bake sale tonight for the youth centre and then I do believe I owe you a walk through Tree Light Drive?" Ainsley said, hoping it didn't come off as desperate.

"Yes, I do believe you do," he said with a grin. "I'll meet you at the community centre at five-thirty?"

"That's perfect." Ainsley gave his hand a squeeze and then kissed his cheek. "See you tonight."

She got to the inn in what felt like a record time. Declan was sitting at the front desk, clicking aimlessly at the computer. He looked dazed, barely blinking, head resting in his hand, mouth hanging open slighting.

"Are you okay?" Ainsley asked him.

"Huh? Oh, yeah." He shook his head and focused on her. "So, you spent the night at Gavin's house?" he asked with a smirk.

"Don't go there." She held a finger up to him. "I'm going to the hospital to check on

Mum and Dad. You want to come?"

"Yeah, that'd be good. Let me just tell Albert."

"Alright, I gotta run to the house to change. Meet at the car." She practically ran to the house to change, knowing it shouldn't take long for Declan to talk to Albert.

Ainsley settled on leggings and a sweater. She was going to the hospital, comfort was ideal, plus she wasn't trying to impress anyone at a hospital. Was she even trying to impress anyone here? What about Gavin? He didn't need to be impressed by her, he seemed to like her despite everything. *Ugh, now is not the time.*

She met Declan at the car, where he was sitting in the driver's seat of his; so, she slid into the passenger seat.

"Why do you want to go to the hospital?" he asked, pulling out of the driveway.

"I want to make sure they're doing everything they can within the thirty days." In reality, she missed them. She used to get bothered by her mother constantly asking when she was getting married and having children or constantly degrading what she wanted to do with her life. But she cared. Mothers have a strange way of showing they care.

The car ride was silent, neither of them really knowing what to say. Just a morning ago they were laughing over movies, now, on their way to the hospital, nothing. It was like

THE HOLLIDAY INN

they were giving a moment of silence.

When he parked, they found the elevators and went up to their parents' room. Someone was standing over their bed. Two people. Who was here? Did the hospital allow visitors other than her, Molly, and Declan?

Ainsley stepped into the room and her entire body caught fire. Anger pulsed in her veins. "What the hell are you two doing here?"

"How could you not tell us?" Jude asked.

"Get out." Ainsley kept her voice firm and steady, despite wanting to scream.

"He has a right to be here," Angela said, stepping around Jude. Her orange hair fell straight over her shoulders. "They're his parents too."

Chapter Twenty-Two
Molly

"I saw you talking to Teagan after her band performed," Hilary said whilst they walked through the halls on their lunch break.

Molly wasn't ready to talk about that with her friends; she hadn't figured out her feelings yet. She did have a nice conversation with Ainsley about it, though it wasn't too helpful. "Yeah. Are you guys going to the bake sale tonight?"

"My mum wants to. She loves anything that involves sweets and supporting the children," Amelia said. "Are you?"

"Probably. Ainsley has been insistent on going to all the events." Molly rolled her eyes, but she couldn't refuse any sweets.

"Do you want to come to my house this weekend to paint some more?" Hilary asked. It was the one thing the three of them had in common. They all loved to paint. "I can ask Mum if she'll get some snacks and soda."

Molly wanted to, but she was sure Ainsley and Declan would want her to go to the hospital, there were only two weeks until they were required to pull the plug on their parents. Her heart sank, fast. She didn't expect the feeling. *Pull the plug.* What a grim thought.

"I'll have to ask and let you know."

"I got some new paints with my birthday money. Mum said if I wanted some from her, I'd have to wait until Christmas," Amelia said. "I think I'm getting new paint brushes too."

"I need some new brushes; mine are getting hard from me neglecting to wash them immediately," Molly said, pulling out her phone which had chimed. She stopped dead in her tracks.

"What's going on?" Hilary asked.

"Declan wants me to go to the hospital," Molly answered slowly.

"How come?" Amelia asked.

Molly locked eyes with her. "Jude is back."

"Whoa," Hilary and Amelia said simultaneously.

"He's coming to get me, should be here in a few minutes." Why was Jude back? What could Angela possibly gain from coming here now? "I guess I'll see you guys later." She left them to go to her locker and gather her things. Then she waited out front for Declan to arrive.

At the hospital, Molly followed Declan up to the waiting area where Ainsley sat frantically bouncing her knee, chewing her thumbnail.

"What's going on?" Molly asked, sitting beside her sister.

"They've been in that room for an hour, at least."

Molly looked to Declan, not sure what to say, and not really sure why she was here. She was a kid, what could she say or do to help in this situation? She still thought of Jude as part of the family, but maybe Ainsley didn't.

"What are you going to do?" Molly asked.

"I'm going to demand them tell me why they're here."

Molly hadn't seen Jude or Angela in over three years, but as they walked toward the other three siblings, a shiver went through her body.

"Are there any rooms vacant at the inn?" Angela asked as if everything was completely normal between all of them. Her hand clenched Jude's and she held him close to her.

Jude had gained a substantial amount of weight since they last saw him. He was bigger than their father now, tall like him too. He had weird blond facial hair and looked like he just got off a night shift if they had night shifts wherever he worked.

"Yeah, I can get you one when I get back."

"Declan!" Ainsley yelled in a hushed tone.

"What?"

Ainsley groaned. Her face was the worst at hiding how she felt, but Molly thought that when it came to Angela and Jude, she didn't bother to try. It was far too obvious how she felt about them.

"Is there a problem, Ainsley?" Angela asked with a smile. It wasn't a real smile, even Molly could tell it was a challenge.

Ainsley rolled her eyes and gave a sarcastic smile. *Can smiles even be sarcastic?* "No, not at all," she said through clenched teeth. "See you at the inn."

"Let's get some lunch, Angel," Jude said causing Ainsley to scoff with the most dramatic eye roll.

"Angel," Ainsley said when Jude and Angela were gone. "That name couldn't be any more ironic if it tried. How hard is it to add the last A?"

"I don't understand what's going on. Why was I pulled out of school for this?" Molly sat in the empty chair beside Ainsley.

Ainsley buried her face her in hands. "God, I could punch her in her smug little face."

"Again, I ask, what am I doing here?" Molly looked between Declan and Ainsley. This wasn't her battle to fight. She was Switzerland in this situation. She shifted in her seat watching Declan watch Ainsley.

"How could you tell them you had vacancies?"

"Was I supposed to lie and turn away revenue for the inn because our family doesn't get along anymore?"

"*Yes.*" She glared at him. "Do you remember when they expected us to all go to them for their first Christmas? It was the last Christmas that I came home because I couldn't do this anymore. I couldn't pretend that we were something we weren't."

"Can we talk in private?" Molly asked. They all went to the room their parents lay in. This visit was different. The air in the room had changed; it was colder, but the temperature was the same as the last time they were there. Did Angela really have that kind of presence?

"What do you mean by pretend to be something we aren't?" Declan asked. He checked over the machines hooked up to their parents, but Molly wasn't entirely sure he knew how to read them.

"The four of us might have been a family, but he chose her, he chose her family. He never chose us. Not once since they started dating, did he choose us."

Molly didn't know how to sit with that information. All this time she thought he was busy with work and working on his house. It never occurred to her that it was intentional. But she had assumed Ainsley's time away from her was, which she was right, but why didn't she think that about Jude? They were his family. They spent countless summers going to beaches and swimming and camping.

Why couldn't they all work it out? Most of them were adults, everyone but Molly. Surely, they were mature enough to have a conversation. Molly internally rolled her eyes at herself. She sounded like her mother. If she were here, she would do something about this. She'd probably force everyone to sit at the table and resolve whatever bad blood was between everyone. Molly doubted it would truly solve anything between Ainsley and Angela, but at least it would be laid out.

Molly didn't want to be the one to suggest

it. No way did she want Ainsley to call her out on sounding like their mother would. Instead, Molly sat quietly, listening to the beeps of the machines whilst Ainsley paced the room.

"I need to get back to the inn," Declan said after what felt like forever. "Both of you came with me, so..."

"All right, fine. But I will not be interacting with them." Ainsley huffed and walked out of the room.

Molly didn't know how she felt about Jude and Angela being around, mostly because they'd never come around before. She couldn't help but think that they were here for something. Angela was calculating, and never did anything without it benefiting her. At least that's what Ainsley used to say.

Molly didn't know what to say or do; she was mindlessly following Ainsley and Declan. She missed Jude, they used to have fun together, but seeing him again, she didn't know what the feeling inside of her was. A dull ache filled her chest, knowing they'd probably never be the same since Angela. She longed for her and all her siblings to be the same as they were when they were kids. But the likelihood of that happening was slim, especially where Ainsley was involved.

Chapter Twenty-Three
Declan

Declan could understand where Ainsley was coming from, Angela seemed to have a vendetta against her. But he couldn't turn away customers for the inn. Especially this time of year when the inn was usually full and he had three empty rooms.

"Ready to get checked in?" he asked, coming around the front desk.

"About time, we've been waiting for like two hours," Angela said.

Declan glanced her way, confused. "It was like forty-five minutes at most. You know how long the drive here from the hospital is."

"Whatever, do you have a room for us or not?"

"Yeah." Declan brought up the program to get them a room. "How long are you staying?"

"Does it matter?"

Declan sighed. "Yeah, because the room that I have is only available for three days. If you're staying longer I'd have to switch your room."

"Why can't we stay in the same room?"

"I don't make the rules, Mum did. How long are you staying?"

"How long is it going to take to get your

parents' will?" she came back.

A light went off in Declan's head, all the pieces clicked together. They wanted to know what they were getting. "I'll try to make accommodations for you, but I can't promise I'll have rooms available that long."

"Why can't we just stay at the house?"

"There is no room at the house. And I don't think Ainsley wants you there. Honestly, you're lucky she didn't ban you from the inn."

"She can do that?" Jude asked.

"No, she's not the owner. Only your parents can, and they're comatose," Angela spat, turning back to Declan.

He couldn't believe what he was hearing. Was she really that tone deaf? "Three nights for the king bed on short notice is going to be one hundred and thirty pounds per night."

"Is that with the family discount?" Angela asked.

"I don't have a family discount." Talking to her was exhausting. "Are you going to pay or are you going to go somewhere else? I have other things to do than argue with you."

"That's no way to treat a paying customer."

"Right now, you're not paying, are you?"

She pouted then pursed her lips, narrowing her eyes at Declan. "I don't think your website would like a negative review, would it?"

He rolled his eyes. "Jude, are you really not going to jump in here?"

Jude was standing back, hands in his jean pockets, his gut protruding out farther than their father's. *Man, what happened to him?* Did he really lose all senses?

"What is there to say? She's just asking questions."

"A hundred and thirty pounds per night. Take it or leave it."

"Fine, we'll take it." Angela pulled out a credit card and Declan put in her cost. He wasn't looking forward to cleaning her room. She'd probably use everything available to her, just to try to 'get her money's worth.'

"There's breakfast, lunch, and dinner served. Please let Albert know what meals you will be requiring so we don't waste food. There's a card you'll find in your room on the dresser, you can fill it out and hang it on the doorknob and I'll let him know to get it." Declan grabbed the key from the locked cabinet and passed it to Angela. "Room four-ten. Enjoy your stay." Declan smiled, though fake.

"I still can't believe you rented a room to them," Ainsley complained over dinner. She stabbed her fork into her fish. "You know she's going to ruin Christmas."

"Why do you say that?" Molly asked. "Maybe they're here to make things right, to apologize for alienating us."

"You really don't think she has an ulterior motive?"

"I'd think to think that."

"Then how come the three of us are in here

THE HOLLIDAY INN

having dinner together, and they are at the inn? If they were here to make amends they would be here, they'd be sincere, and she would not have a smug look on her stupid face."

"I think you need to chill," Declan said. "We don't know their intentions yet and you know what they say about assuming." But he knew their intentions. He couldn't bear to hear an 'I told you so' from Ainsley this early, so he reminded quiet.

"Fine. I'll chill, but I won't give her the benefit of the doubt."

"Okay. So, what do you think we should do?"

"We need to keep our guard up. I'll call the hospital and make sure they don't tell Jude or Angela anything. You treat them like you would any guest at the inn, and Molly, try not to get sucked into her charm. It's a facade that narcissists put on."

"I'm not stupid, I know she's manipulative," Molly said. Weirdly enough, she took the empty plates and brought them to the sink, rinsing them off. Ainsley and Declan looked at each other, confused and impressed.

"You guys do whatever you need to, I'll clean up tonight."

"Really?" Ainsley asked, doubting her. "Do you know how to clean a dish?"

"Just because I don't want to do it doesn't mean I don't know how. I think you guys have a lot going on, and I should pitch in more."

"I need to get back to the inn. Thanks, Molly."

"I'll go call the hospital." Ainsley left the table and Declan put on his coat.

"Molly, thank you. It's nice to see you growing up and taking initiative." One corner of her mouth turned up and she nodded, going back to her task, and Declan headed for the inn.

He wasn't particularly looking forward to interacting with Angela and Jude. Mostly Angela. Jude and Declan used to be best friends. Maybe they were forced to be friends because Jude was two years older, and they shared a room. Ainsley had gotten in Declan's head about never being chosen. Did everything they do as a family mean nothing to Jude?

They used to wake up on Saturday mornings and the entire house would have a Nerf war. They'd hide in cupboards, behind doors, and blast their parents with Nerf darts. Molly would run down the hall screaming and laughing that Jude and Declan were going to shoot her. Ainsley would sit on the couch watching her siblings; she'd laugh, but rarely participate. Was that the last time they chose to do something together? Declan never felt like they grew apart, but maybe Jude didn't think of family the same way.

Declan sat at the front desk filling out some paperwork. He still didn't understand anything, and to not be trained properly was right difficult. He knew that his parents would want the inn to stay in the family unless their will said otherwise. He didn't know what he wanted, he hadn't thought about receiving anything, yes this was going to be hard if he got to keep it. He'd have to learn how to run his own business with no prior knowledge, experience, or assistance. But if the inn went to someone else, or they were told to sell, he would fight. The inn was as much part of the family as any one of them were.

When Jude chose to run away with Angela and deny their mum a proper wedding, she was heartbroken. She tried to hide it, but they all knew. There were times she tried to talk about it like it was just an inconvenience. But then Declan would hear her talking to their dad asking what she did to make Jude think she didn't love him enough to be present at his wedding. At that point, he was the only one the Holliday kids thought would ever get married in her lifetime, and it seemed they were right.

Declan sighed heavily whilst creating a checklist for tomorrow, rooms that needed cleaning or touch-up, supplies needed, and put out a job listing for a cleaner.

"Hey." He looked up to see Jude. "What's up?" His voice was deeper than Declan remembered it. Then again, everything about him was different.

"Working."

"Right on."

"Is there something I can help you with?" Declan sat down his clipboard.

"Angel needs another pillow."

"I don't have any spares."

"Alright." He went back upstairs, Declan assumed, to his room.

Not a minute later, Angela was storming down the stairs in an expensive-looking robe. "Excuse me."

"Yes," Declan said with a sigh. He didn't know what was coming, but he felt it was going to be annoying.

"I need another pillow. You only gave the room two and I need two, but Jude needs one."

Declan blinked at her. "Did I not just tell Jude I don't have any spare to offer?"

"Can't you take one from an unoccupied room?"

"If there were any unoccupied rooms with pillows, but they are in the washing."

She slammed her hand on the desk. "You're doing this on purpose."

"Swear on my life I'm not. Something on purpose would be getting married without inviting the groom's entire family whilst yours is there." It was Declan's voice, but Ainsley's words.

She rolled her eyes and sighed. "Your family is really good at playing the victim, you know that? You guys aren't innocent in the exchange. I asked your mum to give up her plans for us one time and she said she couldn't. Something about being short notice or whatever."

"You got married at Christmas. The business is literally called the Holliday Inn, not just because our last name is Holliday, but because the holidays are our busiest time. You could've waited."

Declan was starting to sound like Ainsley. He didn't know he felt that way. He didn't think he did. He didn't care that he wasn't invited, but he cared that his mum wasn't, nor was his dad. He cared that they cared. It wasn't fair. How could they not realize that?

"You're overreacting, it was just a wedding. Can I get that pillow now?"

"No. Have a good night. The front desk is closing and there are no after-hours." Declan shut down the computer whilst Angela stood there with her mouth hanging open. "See you in the morning." Declan locked the money away in the safe in the office and then locked the office.

"So that's it? I thought if anyone was going to be reasonable in the family it was going to be you. But you're just as deluded as the lot of them. No wonder Jude doesn't come around anymore."

Declan stood at the door, watching her round the corner to go to her room. Did she say it was his fault that Jude didn't come around? That couldn't be it, they were best friends. At least he thought they used to be. Her words were like a knife in Declan's gut. How could that be true? The two boys used to ride their bikes along the path that their father made for them in the forest close to home. This didn't make sense. Ainsley was right about her. She was projecting, and she was manipulating Jude.

Could they make him see the truth in her?

"My shift is over at the bake sale, do you want to hang out?" Olive asked over the phone. Declan was sitting in the living room of the house. Molly was gone with Ainsley to the bake sale; though they did seem to be on better terms, Molly still favoured her friends.

"I've got the house to myself," he said, not totally trying to lure her over, but really wanting to see her. "We could watch a film, bake cookies, or something else if you want."

"Sounds fun, I'll see you in a bit." Her voice sounded cheerful. She was excited to see him, it made his chest warm.

He looked around the house to see if it needed a tidy before his company arrived; he could see pretty much everything, except inside the bedrooms that were in their own little hall. Everything looked decent, at least to him.

Maybe I should clean my room... not that he expected anything from her, but how often would they get to be alone again?

Not long after did she arrive at the house, letting herself in like it was her own home. "Hey," Declan said with a smile, pulling her by the waist into him. Her body pressed against his, sending an electric wave through him. Her hands stayed on his chest, and she giggled. "I can't describe to you how much I've missed this."

It wasn't that he missed having someone to be affectionate with, he had been with Jamie, but it was different with Olive. He could melt into her, he could be vulnerable. In fact, being around her made him feel vulnerable. He buried his face in the crook of her neck and kissed her. She returned the kiss to his neck.

She pulled away, taking his face in her hands, her eyes were glossy. "I'm so happy we get a second chance."

A light lit up inside him, he smiled at her. "Me too. You don't know how happy I am to hear you say that you want this again. I've been so worried."

Her face was soft, she gently stroked her thumb over his eyebrow. "You were made for me." She leaned in, lips parted, kissing him with a feeling he hadn't felt in a long time. *Love.*

It took everything in him not to utter those three words that he'd wanted to tell her from the beginning. So, instead, he kissed her back, hoping she'd know what he was saying.

Chapter Twenty-Four
Ainsley

Ainsley wanted to call Gavin and cancel, tell him something came up. She would've if she was the same person as when she first arrived. But it had been almost a month, and she was no longer the same. She wanted to see him, despite the anger rising in her body. Just having Angela around made Ainsley's body tense.

Molly didn't say much on the drive to town for the bake sale. She sat there texting. Ainsley guessed their talk from the other night didn't do either of them much good.

"Who are you texting?" Ainsley asked.

"Hilary and Amelia."

"Are you going to meet them at the bake sale?"

"Yeah."

Ainsley tried not to sigh. Apparently, if you show your frustration in front of the teen, it'll get sassy. "That's good. It's good to try to keep a normal life." She wanted to curl up in bed with all her blankets and ignore the world, but she didn't need Molly to know that.

"Are Jude and Angela staying?"

"I don't know." It was truthful, but Ainsley didn't want to worry Molly with her theories.

THE HOLLIDAY INN

"Is she going to do anything to sabotage us?" She put her phone away, she was invested in this conversation. Ainsley needed to share her thoughts with her. "Is she?"

"Molly, I know that it's confusing having Jude and Angela showing up like this." Honestly, Ainsley was surprised. Angela didn't seem like the type to care about anyone but herself, so this must have a chance at benefiting her.

"Do you think they're actually here for Mum and Dad?"

Ainsley chewed at her inner lip for a moment. "No." Did Ainsley know exactly why they were there? No. Did she wholeheartedly believe it was because Angela wanted the inn? Yes. Ainsley wished that they could've gotten an appointment with the lawyer sooner, they'd have the answers they needed, and they could've gotten rid of Angela and Jude.

"How did they hear about them anyway?" Molly asked. "I didn't tell him. I haven't talked to him in a year or more."

"Me neither, I haven't spoken to them since he slapped me and he and Angela tried to play the victim." Everything about this whole situation frustrated Ainsley. Angela could waltz herself into their grieving lives and assume they'd drop and cater to them? *I don't think so.*

"You get really defensive. Do you think your hostility towards her is a reason she's so rude too?"

"Me?" Ainsley knew she wasn't the problem. She'd been nothing but inviting in the beginning. Angela was to be their sister after all. It was important to welcome new family, but after the disrespect, Angela showed about caring to be part of their family, that's when things changed. Angela always liked the inn. When Ainsley, calmly, asked her about it, she sent Jude in and Jude slapped Ainsley across the face. Their parents sent him out immediately. They've not been the same since.

She never thought about what it'd be like to see Jude again, because she never thought she'd have to. Having him around worried her that they would try to do something else. Would he hurt her on his own? He was big enough to leave a worst impression than the first time.

"I'm just saying, you could ease up just a little."

Ainsley gripped the steering wheel tighter. "Are you going to need a ride home?" She parked on a side street. Main Street and the parking lot to the community centre was full.

"No, I'll get a ride."

"Text me when you leave," Ainsley called to Molly as she left the car to meet her friends. She had great friends, willing to drive a half hour out of town to bring her home. The kid had it pretty good.

Ainsley waited outside of the community centre, the cold air turning the inside of her nose to frost. She rubbed her hands together. People came in and out of the building. She could've sworn she waited nearly an hour. But the time on her phone assured her it was only twenty minutes, there was a message from him, telling her he'd be a bit late, and he'd explain when he arrived. She never thought to go inside, not until she saw him running through the parking lot. Thirty minutes late.

"I am so sorry," Gavin said, cupping her face kissing her lips quickly, as if they were a couple and kissing was normal for them. He paused a moment after, but let it go instead. "I got stuck with work. I thought an entire drive lost all my pictures from the week. But I recovered it."

"That's good," Ainsley said, not realizing how hurt she was in the beginning thinking he had stood her up. Molly would say something teasing about how her feelings for him were becoming real, but the thought scared her. Gavin and Ainsley both knew that as soon as her parents died, she would go back to New York. No matter how similar they wanted their lives to be, it wasn't in the cards for them. But a winter fling, that they could do.

"Did you go in?"

"No, I didn't want to go in without you." *God, if my friends in New York could see me now*, she thought to herself, *they'd wonder who the hell I was.* Waiting for a man before going in, out of the cold? Waiting a half hour for a man in general? But she knew Gavin, she knew he wouldn't have stood her up

Gavin took Ainsley's hand into his, lacing their fingers. He opened the door and the room looked completely different from the day before. Garland draped all around the top of the room, decorated with crystal snowflakes, fake poinsettias, and sparkling ribbon. Wreaths were hung on any door that was in the room, no matter where the door led to. And it smelled of homemade everything. Ainsley closed her eyes. Her family wasn't much into baking, but she imagined that it's what a stereotypical grandmother's house smelled like after baking all afternoon.

"I think they have pie." Gavin pointed to the first table.

"Maybe, but they look like they have cake." Her inner child started to come out, forgetting all about Jude and Angela, her parents. It all faded to the background.

"My mum helped with the decorating," Gavin said as they walked through the aisle. There were goodies everywhere, she couldn't decide, so they strolled through looking at everything first. "I think you two would get on well."

"Oh?" Ainsley tried not to let on that she certainly wasn't the right person to introduce to his mother. Had he ever introduced a woman to his mother before?

"She's right over there, with the scones."

Directly in their line of vision. She instinctively pulled her hand out of his. How would

THE HOLLIDAY INN

he introduce her to his mum?

"Hey, Mum," Gavin said. "This is Ainsley."

"Hello, darling," she said with a smile. She hoped his mum didn't expect anything to come of this. Did she fancy her son? Sure, he was a great guy. But this going too far. She looked like your typical grandmother with a grey perm and fun-rimmed glasses. She wore a Christmas-themed apron. "Are you in the market for scones, love?"

"I'd love some," Ainsley answered with a forced smile. "How much?"

"Oh, not a thing. I've got some set aside for Gavin, special." Her eyes twinkled. This was too weird.

"Are you sure? I don't mind paying for them. It goes toward the community." Ainsley dropped some loose change in the cup.

"Thank you." Gavin's mum smiled, her eyes crinkling the wider the grin.

"Now, I've got my eye on some cake back there. It was great to meet you..."

"Harriet."

Ainsley held her hand up in a wave and walked on.

"Was that too awkward?" Gavin asked.

"Awkward? What about that could've been awkward? The fact that you introduced me to your mum without warning me? Or that she insisted on me not paying her for her scones? Or was it the way she looked like I was going to be walking down a church aisle in a white gown and bearing your children soon?"

"You got all that from a look?" He chuckled.

"It's not funny!" She gently smacked his chest. "Why would you do that?"

He shrugged. "I wanted her to meet you."

As much as it worried her, she liked that he wanted her to meet his mother, she liked that he liked her. They did only exchange pleasantries after all.

Ainsley stopped at the cake table and bought a small vanilla cake. She was about to eat her stress. With the article due next week, with Jude and Angela showing up, with Gavin wanting her to meet his mother? This trip was getting out of hand. She had lost complete sight of why she was here. *Why was she here, anyway?* To help Molly? To get closure? She scoffed to herself, she wouldn't get closure, her parents weren't coming out of it, no matter how much the Holliday siblings wanted them to.

"Do you want to take a walk now?" Gavin asked heading for the main doors that had decorated garland around the frame and wreaths on the door.

"Sure." They dropped their food into their cars, his was only a couple cars up from hers.

Ainsley waited at her car, debating on running away from this, but he stopped in front of her before she could decide.

"Ready?" He held out his arm, which she looped hers through. "I'm sorry I ambushed you with my mum. I shouldn't have done that. I thought since I met your siblings it wouldn't be that big of a deal."

"I freaked out a bit, didn't I? Anyway, let's go check out Tree Light Drive."

They walked down Main Street, the streetlights were wrapped in garland and tinsel and big bows. Each store had their own decorations, but they coordinated so well it looked like one giant store.

Other couples walked around in the calm night, holding hands, leaning on each other, small kisses on foreheads. Butterflies filled Ainsley's chest. She leaned her head on Gavin's shoulder. "Are you still my date to Narine's house for dinner on Friday?"

"I wouldn't go for anyone else." He kissed the top of her head, despite her hat being there. She decided to go into this, whatever this was. *Just do it.* It would be over before they knew it and she wanted to enjoy herself.

"Tree Light Drive," he said, turning up the well-lit road. It was so bright it could be mistaken for daytime.

"Are you going to take pictures?" she asked, noticing his camera around his shoulder.

"If you don't mind."

"Not at all." She took her arm out of his and walked beside him, until she saw a display that looked like Santa's village. "Look!" Ainsley ran ahead of him. "Oh Gavin, this is gorgeous." She covered her mouth. "Oh look!" She pointed to elves that had hammers looking like they were making toys, even though there was no movement to them. "There's Santa!"

She pointed to the back of the village, by the house where Santa and Mrs. Claus were standing, watching over the village. They stood under a lit arch way. The path leading to the arch was lit too.

Ainsley turned to see if Gavin was looking at this beautiful display, but his face was behind his camera, pointed at her. Her body relaxed and she smiled for him.

Running over to him, her inner child was thriving, she'd never felt so happy. "Come look!" she shouted, slipping on ice, falling directly into Gavin. With a grunt they fell to the ground. "Oh my god, I'm so sorry." Ainsley start to get up, but he pulled her back down.

"I love seeing you so excited." He took his mitten off to touch her face with his bare hand. It was warm against her chilled cheek. She tried to keep an even breath, but he was so gentle, and they were lying on the ground, the wet snow probably seeping through his clothes.

Ainsley slowly leaned herself in, ready to kiss him with everything she had. As her eyes fluttered closed, a car honked its horn, driving by them. She jumped off Gavin, pulling him with her, falling back into the yard, into the actual snow. This time Gavin fell on her.

He was laughing. Ainsley laughed too, grabbed a little bit of snow in her hand, pressing it against his face. He gasped, laughing again. He leaned in, without hesitation, pressing his lips to hers. Desire filled her. She closed her eyes, only letting herself feel the moment, not what was to come, not what could be, or what will be. She only wanted to feel his lips on hers. She let herself, for the first time, admit that she had feelings for him, deeper than the surface.

She could stay in that little bubble forever, and the thought terrified her.

Chapter Twenty-Five
Molly

"I'm going to Hilary's house after school, so I don't need you to pick me up," Molly said to Ainsley on their way out the door. Declan was already going into the inn, waving at his sisters.

"That's great. I'm glad you're still enjoying yourself."

Molly shrugged. "It's depressing staying at the hospital. I like seeing them, but I hate seeing them just lying there."

"We'll go tomorrow. Just the three of us." Ainsley started the car and blasted the heat, waiting for the ice to melt from the windscreen.

"That'll be good. We could go for lunch. Pretend we're having a picnic." Molly looked out the window, *pretend our parents are just sleeping*. "Talk to them and remind them what they're leaving behind."

Ainsley nodded, but her face was cold. Molly didn't know if she believed they'd wake up, or maybe she didn't think they could hear them anymore. Whatever the case, it was too sad to think about.

Finally, the car was ready, and they left. "Are you going to see them today?"

"I am. I'm going to talk to the doctors before I start working. I'll make sure they know we all miss them."

"Are you going to tell them about Angela and Jude?"

"I don't know."

Molly sighed. "This whole thing is stupid, you know."

"I do know. I wish they'd stayed away, but they're here and we have to deal with it."

"I don't want to deal with it, that's why I'm going to Hilary's house."

Ainsley blew air out of her nose. "By that logic, maybe I should stay with Gavin and avoid them too." She winked at her little sister.

"You like him, don't you?" Molly teased.

Ainsley rubbed her lips together and gripped the steering wheel a little tighter. Molly raised her eyebrows at her sister.

"It's complicated."

"Oh my god, not the 'I live in New York' thing again." Molly rolled her eyes. "Grow up and let yourself have this," Molly said more forcefully than intended.

Ainsley looked at Molly, momentarily in disbelief, before turning her attention back to the road. "I'll have you know I'm plenty grown, thanks."

Molly muttered an agreement, turning back to the window. She didn't know how to properly process anything that was happening. It didn't feel like it was happening to her. It didn't feel like her parents were on the verge of death. It was like it was happening to someone else. Molly was convinced Angela didn't like the Holliday siblings and somehow turned Jude against them, even though Molly couldn't think of anything they've done wrong but love him and encourage him to do what he wanted...

Teagan found Molly at lunch, her and her friends joined Molly and hers. She thought that everyone was looking at her and Teagan, that everyone cared that Teagan was sitting with her, that Teagan had her arm around the back of Molly's chair. But they didn't. At least it didn't appear that way. No one looked at them, despite it feeling like the opposite.

"Do you want to see a film tonight?" Teagan asked Molly.

"I would, but I made plans with Hilary and Amelia. We're going to paint tonight. It's kind of our thing."

"I didn't know you painted." Teagan faced Molly more, learning more about Molly, her interests seemed to be exciting to Teagan. Molly smiled sheepishly, hiding her blushing face.

Molly shrugged. "I'm not good, but it's fun."

"Stop," Amelia said. "She's good, she's just being modest. Here." Amelia found a photo on her phone of one of their paint nights; Molly had painted a skeleton hand holding a monarch butterfly. "That's hers."

THE HOLLIDAY INN

"Bloody hell!" Teagan sat up, taking the phone from Amelia. "Seriously?" She looked at Molly in disbelief.

"Yeah. I free handed it." Heat rose into Molly cheeks, and she turned away whilst Teagan continued to ogle at her work.

"Babe, you're insanely talented."

"Babe?" Molly snapped her head toward Teagan, now drawing attention to her. Teagan's ears began to turn red, and she gave the phone back to Amelia. "Thank you," Molly said, trying not to draw the awkward moment out longer. "Actually, there's something I want to talk with you about. Mind going on a walk?"

"Sure." She got up and Molly gave Hilary and Amelia and wide-eyed look. "Sorry about the babe thing, it was a slip of the tongue."

"It's okay, I kind of liked it," Molly admitted.

"What did you want to talk about? Are you doing all right?"

"I don't know," Molly said honestly. "I feel guilty for spending time with Hilary and Amelia. Like I should be spending all my free time at the hospital."

"Yeah, I know the feeling."

"Am I selfish?"

"No. Who said that?"

Molly shrugged. "No one, I guess. It feels wrong to feel happy with my friends."

Teagan stopped, put her hands on Molly's shoulders, looking her in the eye. "It is not selfish to grieve the best way you can. If surrounding yourself with friends eases the pain, then no one has the right to tell you not to. They don't understand."

Molly pushed herself into Teagan, wrapping her arms around her waist. Teagan held her close.

"You grieve how you need to." Teagan gently patted Molly's hair.

"Thank you."

"You want to know what I did?"

Molly sniffed, pulling back. "What?"

"I spent all my time with my friends, I rarely saw my dad. He didn't say anything. He grieved by looking for the bottom of a bottle. Still hasn't found it." She chuckled lightly. But nothing about it was funny.

"I'm so sorry, Teagan." Molly touched her face. "Do you want to leave?"

"Won't you get in trouble?"

"Who are they going to call? My mum? Come on." Molly took Teagan's hand with a sly smile. "We're going to the library to look at comic books."

Teagan's face lit up. "I'll drive."

The town was packed, as usual, with tourists. They were shopping at boutiques, bookstores, hair salons, the cafe. No one in the town knew the girls, except for those that were working. But the streets were busy as Christmas was fast approaching; no one even had time to glance their way. Molly slid her hand casually into Teagan's. It felt nice being with her.

The wind had picked up and they burst through the doors to the library. The lady at the desk glared at them over the rims of her glasses. The girls muttered a half-assed apology and went back to find the comic books.

Teagan gasped. "This one is my favourite," she said, pulling a superhero comic book off the shelf. "I read it when I need some comfort."

Molly took it from her and flipped through the pages. "It looks a little murdery. Should I be worried?"

"No." She laughed. "I think that character is so dynamic and interesting."

"He looks like Spider-Man."

Her eyes lit up. "You know Spider-Man?"

Molly shrugged, handing the book back to Teagan. "My brother, Declan, liked the movies when we were kids, well, when he was kid. I always tried so hard to fit in with them, no matter what they were doing, I wanted to be part of it." Molly walked down the aisle of books, dragging her finger along the spines.

"Is it hard?"

"It wasn't. They wanted me around for a while, even if I was just a kid and they were teens. But I was eight when Ainsley first moved to New York. I was devastated. I thought we were best friends. And I was twelve when she stopped coming all together. It really messed with my head, thinking she didn't want to be around me anymore."

Molly paused for a moment; she didn't think Teagan would say anything; she was really good at just listening. Molly sank to the floor, leaning against the bookshelf. Teagan came over and sat beside her.

"I know now it wasn't me. But didn't she like me enough to come around?" Molly leaned her head on Teagan's shoulder. "And now I think I'm ditching my friends to be with you, and I never wanted to be that person."

"You're not. You turned me down for tonight because you had plans. If you were that person you would've cancelled on them."

"Why are you so nice to me?"

Teagan lay her head on Molly's. "Teenagers are assholes, but not to each other. I can't explain it. Also, I really like you."

"I really like you too," Molly said barely above a whisper.

Teagan dropped Molly off at Hilary's house. She made sure to let her friends know she was still going over. Hilary's mum was cooking a shepherd's pie. Hilary and Amelia were sitting at the counter, helping her cut up the potatoes.

"Hey," Molly said.

"Molly," Hilary's mum said with a sympathetic look. "How are you, love?"

"I'm all right. Getting by, y'know."

"Of course. You want to help the girls do up the potatoes?"

"Sure." Molly jumped on the chair beside Amelia, and Hilary's mum gave her a knife and some potatoes.

"If you need anything from us, you let me know. You're like a second daughter to us, a sister to Hilary."

"Thank you."

Molly never thought about all the support she had that wasn't family—or blood related family. In a way she thought of Hilary's family as her own too, and Amelia's. They'd been friends since they first started school. They had countless sleepover, their parents always made sure they were all taken care of.

"You guys are like family to me." Molly put her head on Amelia's shoulder for just a moment, as a hug, and went back to cutting potatoes.

"Thanks for your help, I'll call when it's finished."

The three girls went to Hilary's art room that used to be her brother's room, but he was gone to London for university. He always insisted that he'd never need his room again, but after his first semester he changed his mind.

"When is Travis coming home?" Amelia asked, jumping onto the couch that folded out into a bed.

Hilary and her mum were very crafty, so there was no hesitation when they got offered the chance to have an art room. When Travis changed his mind, that added a wardrobe for him and a couch that turned into a bed.

"He's on break now but staying with his girlfriend for a few days. He's coming home next week." Hilary set up the three easels and gave each one a canvas. "What do you want to paint?"

"I think I want to paint a gift for Teagan," Molly said before she could think it.

"Oh my god, that's so cute!" Amelia gushed. "What are you going to paint her?"

"A bookshelf with her favourite comics and anime shows and movies." Molly had already pulled out her phone to ask Teagan for all her favourites. Her cover was that she wanted to read them; maybe she would one day. She did love anime, and maybe she could learn to like comics. Teagan sent a large list, separating it out by comic, anime shows, and anime movies, and which ones were her top and which ones were good. Molly had her work cut out for her.

While Hilary and Amelia sat in the chairs looking at their phones for inspiration, Molly went to the desk and grabbed a notebook and a pencil. She made a sketch of how she wanted to lay out the picture, adding the titles to the spines, making sure to keep series together.

When she had finished her sketch on the paper, Hilary's mum had called them to dinner. The other two already had a sketch laid out on their canvas. They didn't care about eraser marks, and usually covered it up with white paint if on the blank canvas, which would be easier, and maybe Molly would start doing that so she wouldn't waste so much time.

Over dinner, everyone tried to avoid talking about Molly's parents. She didn't know what she preferred, them talking about it or avoiding it. Either way, they focused on Ainsley and Declan being home. She didn't want to mention Jude and Angela, because that felt like a private matter. Thankfully, the conversation turned to Amelia and what her plans were for the break, as it just started.

Usually, Amelia and her family went to Yorkshire to visit her grandparents, but as they were in assisted living facilities now, they were going to stay in Holly Grove.

Hilary's mum assured the girls that they could go back to painting. Molly thought she wanted her to stay as content as she could, and she knew that painting was something that really calmed her.

Maybe family was more than who you're related to after all.

Chapter Twenty-Six
Ainsley

Ainsley stared at herself in the bathroom mirror. Was it too much? Not enough? She finished curling her hair and added a touch of red lipstick. She didn't want Gavin to think she was trying too hard, and she really didn't want him to think there'd be more kissing. If she had lipstick on, maybe that would let him know she wouldn't be messing it up; even though it was kiss-proof.

"I'm going to dinner with Narine and her husband. I'm not sure when I'll be back," Ainsley said to Declan, who was sitting alone on the couch with a beer in his hand. Ainsley took in the image, thinking how much he reminded her of their father.

"All right."

"Molly is at Hilary's, if she needs a ride home get her to call me. She might only be coming home tomorrow." Ainsley tied a scarf around her neck. "And if that's so, then we can just pick her up on our way to the hospital."

"Around seven." His eyes were focused on the telly.

Ainsley rolled her eyes. "I'm going to spill that beer on your trousers."

"That's great."

THE HOLLIDAY INN

She huffed. "Declan, what's going on?" She stood in front of the telly. "Are you good?"

"I'm fine. You're in my way." He tried to see around her.

"I need to go, so if you could get over the fear of being vulnerable and talk to me, that'd be great."

"There's nothing," he insisted.

"Fine, but when you want to talk, I will be here for you." She lightly punched his arm and left.

Different scenarios of what could happen tonight ran through her mind. Would Gavin expect more from her after this? Would Narine think they were best friends again? Could they go back to the way things were before she left? There were too many ways that this could go.

Ainsley arrived at the address that Narine messaged to her earlier in the week. She sat in the car for a few moments, gathering her thoughts, trying not to have any expectations for the evening.

Gavin knocked on her window. She got out of the car. "Hello," she said.

"I pulled in just behind you, saw you sitting."

"Right. I wasn't sure if I was supposed to wait for you. I'm sure she thinks we were going to arrive together."

"We didn't."

"It didn't make sense to. She thinks we're together, you know."

He smirked. "We're not though."

"Oh. We're not. So, you introducing me to your mother was what...nothing? All the kissing we've done meant...what? Also, nothing?" She liked him, it was her fault for letting herself get involved.

His face fell. "I didn't know those things meant anything to you. You agreed with no strings."

She nodded. "You're right, I did. So, say goodbye to whatever string there was." She turned for the door, but he grabbed her wrist. "What?"

"We have to sit through hours of dinner, you don't want to sort this out?"

"What's there to sort? You told me exactly who you were, and I didn't take it at face value. I let myself like you. That's my fault." She had far more attitude in her voice than she intended, but her point was made. He stood back, watching her walk to the door. They still had to try to enjoy the night.

She knew she still had a couple more weeks, she had constantly reminded everyone she wouldn't be staying. The no strings was her idea. So why did she care that he was sticking to that?

"You made it!" Narine opened the door when Ainsley knocked. "Hi, Gavin!" She waved to Gavin, who was still standing by the car. He took that as his cue to come to the door. "Get inside, it's so cold."

The guests hung their coats and took of the

rest of their winter gear, following Narine through her simple home. The door led right into the kitchen. Which smelled of fish in the best way. Ainsley glanced over her shoulder at Gavin. He placed a hand on the small of her back as they followed Narine through the dining room and around the corner to the living room.

"Get your hand off me," Ainsley whispered. He removed his hand.

"Timothee, look who's here."

"Gavin!" he shouted, running over, and giving him a hug. "Mum's been talking about this dinner all week."

Narine blushed. "I'm excited to see my friends. I've missed you, Ainsley."

"Me too," Ainsley said. "You have a lovely home." Despite her living room overflowing with toys and barely any pictures on the walls, she knew they were happy here. "When's dinner?" she asked after her stomach settled from letting her know it was in survival mode.

"Shouldn't be long now. Ainsley, why don't you come help me? It'll give us a chance to catch up."

"Sure." She followed Narine back to the kitchen. "How's the pregnant life?"

"Hell, but that's not what I want to talk about. What's going on with Gavin?" she whispered as she poured wine into a glass for Ainsley and flavoured water into a wine glass for herself. Ainsley held back a sigh, did anyone enjoy anything that wasn't wine? "Just because I'm pregnant doesn't mean I can't pretend." She beamed. The women clinked their glasses. "So, Gavin? I thought you two were hitting it off."

"Oh please, we all knew that it wasn't going to last. He's so afraid of a little commitment that he can't even say that a fling is being together." She thought it'd be awkward being alone with Narine after all these years, but they fell right back into place. "I mean, just outside a few minutes ago, we're flirting, I think, and then he reminded me that all this was, was a fling. No strings." Ainsley sipped her wine but put the glass down. "Which I knew and agreed to. My life is in New York. But for a little bit it was fun to pretend that maybe it could work out and my life could be here."

"Wow," Narine said. What else could she say? It was a big deal that Ainsley thought she could come back after all the bad things that happened.

For a long time, Ainsley believed that this town wouldn't bring her anything other than potential heart ache, and she was right. She let herself get too close to Gavin, and there she was again, hurting.

"As soon as I meet with the lawyer and we read through the will, I'm out. I can't keep doing this."

"What about Molly?"

"She'll have Declan."

"You really think he's the best person to

take care of her?"

Ainsley groaned, tipping her head back to glare at the ceiling. Narine was right, Declan was practically a child himself. Yeah, he could take care of himself in London, but could he care for a kid too and the inn? It seemed like a lot to be adding to his plate.

"I can't move here and be reminded that Gavin doesn't want to be with me because he's afraid of committing to someone."

"So, don't come back for him. Come back for you, for Molly...for me."

"Aw." Ainsley wrapped her arms around Narine, getting blocked out mostly by her large pregnant belly.

"Is dinner ready?" Timothee asked, running around the corner with Patrick and Gavin behind him.

"Yes. Help your dad set the table." Narine went to the stove and started filling plates. Gavin and Ainsley took their seats next to each other at the dinner table.

"Can we talk?" he whispered to her.

"No," she said simply, smiling at Narine, who set a plate in front of her. "When this is over, fine."

"Come back to my place and we'll talk."

She had to hand it to him, for someone who didn't want anything to do with committing to her, he was pretty insistent on clearing things up. His maturity level was something rare for a man in their late twenties. Most of the ones she's encountered want nothing to do with a mature conversation.

"This meal looks delicious," Ainsley said to Narine, who took a seat at the head of the table, beside her, Timothee on the other side in a booster seat.

"Thank you."

It wasn't an extravagant meal that you see on telly when people have guests; it was a standard everyday meal. Ainsley thought that was more special. She was invited into Narine's home, feeding them like her family. Ainsley knew she chose well when picking her best friend.

They all ate mostly in silence with the occasional praise to Narine for the lovely meal. After they ate, she brought out dessert.

"Is that..." Ainsley started.

"Sticky toffee pudding. Your mother's recipe. She remembered how much I loved it as a child and gave it to me when I was pregnant with Timothee."

Tears stung Ainsley's eyes. "Wow. It looks exactly how she makes—made—it."

Narine put a scoop of vanilla ice cream in each bowl with the toffee pudding. "How are you holding up?"

"I'm staying strong. I feel like if I fall apart now, everything is going to come out."

"Everything?"

She sighed. "Jude and Angela are here. They're staying at the inn."

Narine scoffed. "Wow. They've got nerve."

It was comforting to know that she wasn't

alone in thinking that. Narine knew the story, the wedding, the hitting, but there was more. "They tried to hold a reception trying to mend the peace or some load of crap. But Angela cancelled it because her grandmother couldn't be there. Even though everyone else she invited could. Including Jude's side of the family. Which, we all remember, we weren't invited to the wedding. She held a reception that worked for her family, but because she didn't take us into account, we got overlooked, again."

"That's awful," Narine said.

Gavin put his hand on Ainsley's. "I know how you view your family, I'm so sorry this happened." Her heart fluttered, against her will.

"Have you talked to her since she arrived?"

"What would I say? 'I hope you have the life you deserve?' 'I hope Jude gets a working brain before you have children, so they don't suffer from your narcissistic personality?' 'I hope Jude finally gets a spine and stands up for himself and his siblings.' There's nothing I can say that would make the situation better."

"Invite her for tea and ask why she did those things. Trying to understand a person can go a long way."

"You've always been the voice of reason, Narine. But I don't know if I have the ability to do that. She burned the bridge between us. It's not my job to fix what she did."

"You're right. And you don't owe her

forgiveness for you to heal," Patrick said.

"Wow, that was surprisingly deep. Thanks." Ainsley looked down at the table, her hand still in Gavin's. "I know I can be strong-headed, defensive, and quick to react, but I don't believe what she did was right. I realise I could've handled seeing them at the hospital differently. It's just hard when you think you don't mean anything to someone and then they show up practically demanding to be included in the will reading after being excluded from everything they've done. Does that make sense?" She glanced up at Narine.

"It does. You don't owe anyone an explanation."

Everyone sat in silence for a moment, enjoying their last few bites of their pudding.

"Well, thank you for coming tonight, but we need to start Timothee's bedtime routine."

"Of course." Everyone stood from the table. "Do you need help cleaning up?" Ainsley offered.

"That would be so great..."

"Perfect. You and Patrick go do what you need, Gavin and I will clean up."

Her eyes glistened. "Thank you, so much." She and Patrick took Timothee upstairs. Ainsley didn't think it took two people to get a kid ready for bed, but Narine was also at the end of her pregnancy.

"You don't have to stay to help. No strings means no strings." Ainsley cleaned all the plates onto one and stacked them, bringing them to the kitchen.

Gavin grabbed all the utensils. "I'm not going to leave you to clean this up by yourself."

"Are you washing, or am I?" Ainsley held up a cloth.

"I'll wash." He took the cloth and started the water. "You know we have no idea where anything goes, right?"

"I'm going to do my best, that girl was like a sister to me, she deserves this."

"Of course." He started washing the dishes quietly. He was right, she knew where nothing went and before long the dishes were piling up in the sink faster than she could dry and put away.

"You know, what I said earlier about us not being together, I said that because that's what I thought you wanted to hear."

She leaned against the counter, back to him. "Why would I want to hear that you don't want to be with me?" She hated that this was what they became. Her only intention was to have fun with him—a fling—now there were feelings involved.

"It's not that I don't want to be with you. I do." The sound of the water stopped splashing. "There have only been two girls that I saw a life with, you're one of them." Ainsley turned around to that. He was watching her already. His face was hard like this was painful to talk about. "I couldn't hurt you the same way. I decided a long time ago that I wouldn't give myself the chance to hurt someone like my dad hurt my mum."

He wiped off the counter and folded the cloth, taking a moment before continuing.

"And then you waltz into the cafe with your sassy little attitude. I just knew you'd be fun. And you were—are. I've had more fun with you in the last week than I've had in a while."

"Why does it have to stop?" She started drying the dishes again. It seemed the distraction helped with the talking.

"Because you live in New York, and I live here. Neither of us wants to give up our life."

"Gavin, you and I literally want the same thing from life. What are the chances of ever finding that again?"

As she turned around to the sink, she crashed into him. His hands fell to her waist, her hands landed on his chest.

"I can see us having fun for a few months, maybe living together, then one day you're going to snap because I don't put my clothes with the dirty laundry but on the floor beside it. Or I'll be mad because you have too many hair products in the shower. We'll ignore it for a bit but after a year at most we'll end it, both cut deep."

"So put your clothes in the dirty laundry and I'll leave my hair products in a cabinet."

He smiled softly, touching her cheek gently. "You always have a solution."

"Except what I'd do for work if I did move back."

THE HOLLIDAY INN

"We don't need to think about that now." He pulled her closer, their bodies pressed together, and he, ever so slowly, lowered his lips to hers.

Chapter Twenty-Seven
Declan

Declan woke up Saturday morning with Olive sleeping beside him. He smiled brushing the tiny strands of hair out of her face. She wore one of his t-shirts and sweatpants. She stirred a little, rolling over to look at him. A tired moan escaped her mouth as she stretched.

"Morning," she mumbled.

"Hey," he said. "Thanks for spending the night." He left a kiss on her cheek.

"I had fun," she said. "When are you going to the hospital?"

He didn't want to think about it. He still couldn't fully wrap his head around the fact that the chances of him seeing his parents smiling again were non-existent. "After morning tea." Declan got out of bed and put on a shirt. "Did you hear Ainsley or Molly come home?"

She sat up and stretched again. "No, but I was out before the middle of the movie."

He remembered. He had turned off the movie when he realised she was sleeping. It wasn't long after that he'd fallen asleep too.

He left the room, followed by Olive, who made a stop to the bathroom. Ainsley's door was shut, and he didn't hear any signs of life.

THE HOLLIDAY INN

The kitchen and living room were both empty.

"Either they're still sleeping, or we've still got the house to ourselves," Olive said, wrapping her arms around Declan's waist from behind.

He turned around and touched her face. "I'm fine with that." He pressed his lips to hers. He couldn't think of a better way to wake up.

The clock read ten. It was practically time, yet no one seemed to be around. "I'll put a pot on and see if Ainsley is in her room. Molly probably slept over at Hilary's house."

It wasn't that he hated going to the hospital, but he wasn't excited to go either, it was more so he didn't want to face the truth about what was going to happen. Right now, he was in charge of the inn. But he never expected it to be a long-term thing. It was only until their parents got better. And going to the hospital was a reminder that they probably weren't going to get better, and he was the new innkeeper.

Declan knocked on Ainsley's door.

"What?" she grumbled.

"I didn't know if you were home. I've got tea on and then we'll go to the hospital?"

"Yeah."

He didn't wait for her to come out the room, but went back to Olive in the kitchen, who was pouring three cups of tea. She added a little bit of sugar to each and handed a cup to Declan.

"You spoil me," he said, kissing her cheek.

"Morning, Olive," Ainsley said joining them in the kitchen, taking a cup of tea. "What'd you guys get up to last night?"

"We watched a movie," Olive answered.

"No, I watched a movie, you fell asleep."

Olive giggled. "True." They all took a sip of their tea. A happy sigh came out of all of them. "How's work going?" she asked Ainsley.

"It's going fine. I can't for the life of me figure out how to write my article, let alone start it. It's due in less than a week."

"I'm sure you'll figure it out, you've always been good at that."

"Are you joining us at the hospital today?" Ainsley changed the subject.

Olive looked at Declan. "I don't think so. I think you guys should go alone. I can wait here for you."

"You should come," Declan said. He felt obligated to invite her, but he also wanted her there.

"I'm sorry, but I don't think I feel comfortable going. I need to get home to take care of Winston. Do you want to come over after?"

"Yeah, that sounds good." He kissed her quickly and she left, leaving only half her tea.

"Does it sound bad that I don't like hospital days?" Ainsley asked.

"No, I understand."

"Like I like seeing them, but I don't like seeing them like that." She looked at her tea. "I can't help but feel like if I'd been more present and not just assume that because we're a family everything is fine."

"I don't think it's your fault. The road was icy."

"I don't mean the accident. Everything with this family. Molly thinking I abandoned her, Jude and Angela." She sighed, rubbing her face. "I'm not sure how we went wrong there."

Declan didn't know what to say. She felt responsible for something that wasn't her fault, for something so out of their control, they never could have seen it coming.

She shook her head. "All right." She tapped her hands on the counter then stood. "I'm going to get Molly and meet you at the hospital."

She fluffed her short hair, adjusting her bangs. She had way less makeup on now than when she first arrived here. Weird of him to notice, but she looked like his big sister again, not someone trying to fit into a big city.

Before he went to hospital, Declan stopped by the inn to check on things. Albert had served breakfast and was rinsing dishes in the sink before putting them in the industrial dishwasher. He wiped his hands on his apron before turning to give Declan his attention.

"Are Angela and Jude here?"

"I haven't seen them. Do you want to give them a message?"

"No." There was nothing that could be said to them at this point. Declan was still trying to process why they were here after all this time.

"I'm running to town for a few hours, could you watch the inn?"

"Of course. Anything specific?"

"Not at the moment, just look after the front desk, I'll call if there's anything. Thanks." Declan left the inn and headed to the hospital.

Ainsley and Molly were just arriving to the room. "How was the night?" Ainsley asked Molly.

"Good. The painting was much needed."

The siblings all needed an outlet to release feelings. Declan still wasn't sure what his was.

"Do Dad's numbers look lower than they were last week?" Declan asked. It wasn't something he had really paid attention to, but they were different. There was something off about them.

"I think it's okay. If it was that drastic, the doctor would've called us to come in," Ainsley said.

Molly went over to his bedside, taking his hand in hers. "It's okay, the doctors are taking care of you. But we need you to pull through."

Ainsley went to their mum, taking her hand too. "You both have to wake up. We need you."

Declan bowed his head, listening.

Ainsley sniffed. "We're all just kids, no matter how long we've been away, we need you. Mum, Dad, *I* need you. Please."

There was a short moment of silence before one of the monitors started beeping faster. "What's that?" Molly asked, fear written all over her face whilst the older two looked at their father's monitor. Things were flashing, and it was beeping loudly.

"Move!" The doctors came running in. Ainsley pulled Molly into her. Then she held her hand out to Declan and took him in too.

His heart raced, Ainsley held the two of them, running her hand through their hair, despite them both being taller than her. The doctors did something to their father that made his monitor settle...*for now,* Declan thought.

"What's going on?" Ainsley asked, not letting her younger siblings go.

The doctor took in a deep breath. "There are some things we need talk about. Please, sit."

"No." Ainsley held Molly and Declan closer when they tried to move. It wasn't just about comforting them; it was to comfort her too. "What's happening to Dad?"

The doctor bowed his head for a moment then looked at the Holliday children. "He isn't getting better. Sorry." The doctor cleared his throat. "He's declining. There's nothing we can do to help him."

"What does that mean?" Ainsley asked.

"His organs are beginning to fail."

"He's dying?" Molly said, barely audible.

"He's brain activity has been decreasing slowly. His heart is failing, and he is going into multi-organ failure."

"So why did he go on the vent?" Ainsley asked. Declan couldn't tell if she was angry, frustrated, sad? He couldn't tell which one he was either.

"Because of the directive they asked for. They wanted a fighting chance. Thirty days."

"What do we do?" Declan asked.

"You have a choice to make. Pull the plug now or wait until the end of the month, if he'll make it that long, to go with your mum."

Ainsley's arms squeezed her siblings closer, her head lowered. Though Declan towered over her, her head fell to his upper arm.

"Ainsley, you're the one who claimed power of attorney. What do you choose?"

Molly and Declan looked at her.

"We need to end it," she whispered.

"No!" Molly shouted, pulling out of Ainsley's arms. "How can you say that?" A few tears slipped out of her eyes, but she didn't wipe them.

"Molly, he's dying, and he's probably in pain. It's not fair to him to prolong it."

"I'm not ready..."

"None of us are." Ainsley wrapped her arms around Molly, holding her tightly. "We're here together, we'll get through it that way too."

"He needs to know I'm sorry. I was so mad." Molly cried into Ainsley's chest. Watching them pulled at Declan's heart strings. He was watching a very intimate moment between his sisters, it felt wrong to watch, to listen. But Molly needed them.

"I wanted to go to Hilary's house; for what? I take it back." Molly sobbed. "I wish I could take it back."

"I know, love, I know." Ainsley rubbed her back. "Let's get the paperwork together."

The doctor nodded and left the room.

"Come here," Ainsley said to Declan. He engulfed his sisters.

"Should we call Jude?" he asked.

They all pulled out of the hug. He knew they each felt differently about the Jude situation, but he was still their brother, no matter how he treated them. They were a family, *right?*

"I don't have his number," Molly said wiping her eyes.

"Neither do I, and I'm blocked on socials by both of them. Probably Angela's doing, who are we kidding." Ainsley gently patted the tears away from under her eyes.

Declan checked his social media as well. "I'm blocked too."

Ainsley scoffed. "Typical."

"I can call the inn." Declan called, and Albert answered, he went up to check their room, but no one answered the door. "They're not at the inn," Declan said after ending the call.

"We've done all we can. If we can reach them…"Ainsley paused to take a breath. "I hate this. I hate to say it, but it's on them that they're missing this."

"Would we have tried if they didn't show up?" Molly asked.

Ainsley was the one to speak up honestly. "Probably not."

They stood in silence.

"Ready to sign?" The doctor came back into the room with a clipboard for Ainsley to sign.

She let out a long, heavy sigh. "Yeah."

They all knew it wasn't true.

She held her hand to the line, hesitating for a moment and signed it quickly, shoving the clipboard back at the doctor. "How does this work?"

"After I turn off the machines, he will be on his own until the end."

"Will he be in pain?" Molly asked, snuggling into Ainsley's side.

"No, we'll give him more medication for that."

"How long can it take for him to...die?" Declan asked.

"Hours...days... There's no exact time frame. Each person is different. But, in his case, I don't expect it to be long."

Ainsley pulled Declan back to her. "Okay. We're ready."

"Wait!" Molly shouted. "Can we push their beds together? I think Mum would want to say goodbye too."

Ainsley smiled with watery eyes. "I think that's a great idea." She looked at the doctor.

"Of course." He helped Ainsley push their parents' beds together.

Molly reached over, placing their mother's hand into their father's. "There."

"Beautiful."

Chapter Twenty-Eight
Molly

Declan pulled Ainsley and Molly into him this time. Molly used to hate being held. She thought hugging was some type of weakness. But as they watched the doctor turn off their father's monitor and remove his tubes and needles, she needed it. There was comfort here.

Their father looked like himself again. There were no tubes coming out of his face or arms. He was their dad. He really looked like he was sleeping now. Molly watched him, she couldn't miss his last breath.

The doctor moved to the back of the room. She wasn't sure if he was supposed to stay to have an accurate time of death or what the logistics were, but Molly was glad he moved to the back, so it felt like just the five of them.

Molly couldn't believe that Jude was going to miss it. He should be there; he should be with his family in their father's final moments. But they had no way to contact him. Angela made sure of that. Molly couldn't understand why her family was allowed to be so important, but her *husband's* wasn't. Was Jude really that easy to manipulate? He was always a calm person, but this felt like too much.

"Do you remember when we were kids," Ainsley started, "Dad would make a big breakfast every Sunday morning. The works, bacon, eggs, toast, crepes."

"He did that even when everyone was gone, and it was just me. He got creative when it was just me. We had chocolate crepes with bananas and strawberries a lot of the time because they were my favourite."

"He was a good man," Declan said. "We were lucky to have him as our father. We never went without anything."

"And Mum...they were so good to us; how did it take *this* for us to realise?" Ainsley asked.

"I feel like rubbish. They never knew that I felt so secure in them as parents that I became comfortable, I became expectant of them, and I rarely thanked them." Molly sighed and closed her eyes for a moment. "I'm sorry Dad, Mum."

Ainsley pulled out the hug. "His-his-his chest." She pointed frantically, stammering.

The doctor came over and listened with his stethoscope, then checked his watch. "Time of death two-thirty-four p.m."

"Oh god." Ainsley stepped further back, but Molly buried herself deeper into the hug Declan gave her.

"It's okay," he whispered, rubbing Molly back. Declan breathed slowly and controlled.

"I'll give you a few minutes before we take

THE HOLLIDAY INN

care of the rest." The doctor left.

"Take care of the rest?" Molly asked, pulling away from Declan.

"The body," Ainsley said. "He's dead. He's going to go to the morgue. We move onto funeral arrangements."

"Funeral arrangements?" The three of them turned to the door. Angela and Jude stood there. "Isn't that a bit premature?" Angela asked.

"No," Ainsley said bowing her head. "Dad is dead."

"*Excuse me?*" Angela came into the room. "What the hell happened? You didn't think that maybe his son might want to be here."

Ainsley sighed; this was the first time she looked exhausted. Dark circles showed under her eyes. Her messy bun had sprigs of hair giving away her sleepless night. "Angela, please. This isn't the time or place."

"Jude, close the door," Angela demanded. He obliged. "You have been against our relationship since the beginning, and I don't get it. I'm family now, I expect you start treating us with the same respect you show Molly and Declan."

"No. Jude is blood, but family? That ship sailed when the palm of his hand collided with my face."

Angela scoffed. "You're so—"

"Jude," Ainsley said calmly, stepped around Angela, who did *not* like that. Her hands flew to her hips in a record time. "Don't." Ainsley looked at Angela. "This isn't about you. Stop."

That was the thing about Angela, if something wasn't about her, she found a way to make it so. Molly always wanted to give her the benefit of the doubt, thinking that maybe she had some unhealthy attachment to her family, and bringing in someone else's was somehow a threat to hers. But this was something different. She was full of attitude and drama. Family didn't treat each other this way.

Angela's mouth fell open. "It's about me as much as him."

"God." Ainsley laughed sarcastically. "When will you give up? Jude, I'm sorry you missed this. We can let you say goodbye alone if you'd like."

Jude looked around at everyone. "It would've been nice to be included."

Yeah, we know the feeling, Molly wanted to say but kept her mouth shut. It wasn't her fight, and it definitely wasn't the time.

"See? You guys are so selfish for not including us."

Ainsley took in a deep breath, closing her eyes. Molly thought maybe she'd punch Angela; she wouldn't have blamed her. Anger rose in Molly's chest. But Ainsely turned her attention to Jude, ignoring Angela completely. "We wanted to, but none of us had your phone numbers. We tried you at the inn, but Albert said you weren't there. And we're all blocked from your social media."

"What?" Jude asked, looking at Angela. "You said they blocked us."

Angela rolled her eyes. "Does it really matter about the technicalities?"

"Do you want a moment alone with him before they come to collect his body?"

"Obviously we do."

"Jude?"

The fact that Ainsley was ignoring Angela making her angrier made Molly want to laugh. Apparently, it's hard for a narcissist not to be the centre of attention.

"Yeah, thanks."

"Okay." Ainsley patted Jude's back once on her way out of the room. Declan and Molly followed her actions, leaving him and Angela alone in the room.

"Is it smart to leave them alone in there?" Molly asked.

"What are they going to do? Unplug Mum?" Ainsley asked sarcastically, but none of them would put it past Angela at this point. She had a need to be on top.

"Hello?" Ainsley answered her phone. "Katherine, hi. Now's not—okay...It's going fine. It will be done by the deadline the end of day on the twenty-third...what? No, that's fine. Look, now's not a good time. We just..." She paused. "My dad just died, and I have to take care of everything. Can I call you on Tuesday? Great...oh, thank you."

Ainsley put her phone back in her pocket with a heavy sigh.

"My boss. This is the last thing I need, to be hounded to get an article out that I haven't even started."

Molly looked around the room. "I can't believe he's gone."

"Yeah," the other two agreed.

"I'm going to call Olive," Declan said. "You guys should call those you want to support you too. I mean other than us."

Molly nodded. Ainsley went to sit on the other side of the waiting room to call Gavin, Molly assumed. She pulled out her phone and sent a text to Hilary and Amelia with the news.

I'm so sorry! Do you want us to come to the hospital? **Hilary responded.**

No, I'll see you guys later. I'll come over later. Molly would get Ainsley to drop her off so she could see them in person, but now she wanted Teagan. Molly called her.

"Molly? Why are you calling? Don't we usually text?" she asked with a small laugh.

"Teagan..." She tried to keep her voice from cracking. She didn't even type out the words to her friends. All she said was 'dad's gone.' But Teagan, she needed to say it.

"What is it?"

"My dad is...dead." Molly fell into a chair and covered her face, her eyes stinging.

"Oh my god. Molly! What do you need from me?"

"Can you come to the hospital? I need you."

"Of course. Oh god...I'll be there in ten minutes, babe."

A few minutes later, Olive and Gavin came into the waiting room. Olive sat beside Declan, putting her hand on his. Gavin pulled Ainsley up from her chair and held her close to him, his hand in her hair.

Ainsley took Gavin's hand and pulled him over to Molly. "How are you doing? Did you call Hilary or Amelia?" She sat.

"I did, I told them I'd stop in to see them. They're still at Hilary's house." Molly looked at her hands clasped together in her lap. "I called Teagan to come."

"Molly..." She turned around, there stood Teagan. Her long black hair sat in a messy bun on top of her head, her face was practically makeup free except for some mascara. Molly's heart clenched. And she wore leggings and a nice jumper. "Hey, how are you?"

Tears pricked Molly's eyes again as Teagan sat beside her.

"We're doing as well as can be expected," Ainsley answered. "It was the outcome we all saw coming, but it doesn't make it any easier. You always have that little bit of hope that maybe they're the exception."

Teagan took Molly's hand and pressed it against her lips. "And your mum?"

"Hanging on," Molly whispered. "But..." She didn't want to say it. Not in front of everyone. It was a private thought that she would've shared if she and Teagan were alone.

"But what?" Declan asked.

"Why are we prolonging this?" Her voice

cracked, causing a few tears to break free. "We know this isn't going to end in our favour."

Everyone looked down. She was right, she hated it. Everyone was thinking it, they had to be. She saw how they looked at their mum when their dad was gone. He was gone and no longer in pain, suffering, forced to hang on when there was no end in which he'd come home and be himself again. Why were they putting their mother through it longer?

"I know," Ainsley said. "It sucks. But it was in their directive that they made with a sound mind."

"*You're* the power of attorney now. You have the right to do what you think is best for them, for Mum. And this, what she's going through in there, isn't fair to her or us."

Ainsley looked broken. Her eyes glistened. She shut them, maybe thinking Molly wouldn't notice. "I can't," she mouthed, sound not even coming out.

"What do you mean you can't?" Molly asked.

"We can't force her to do anything," Declan said.

"She's just lying there, probably in pain. Dad's not around anymore. We have an obligation to take care of her after all she's done for us."

"What's the commotion about?" Angela asked. "Who are all of you?" she asked with a scrunched nose.

THE HOLLIDAY INN

Ainsley, along with what looked like everyone else, was running out of patience for Angela. "I have a decision to make." Jude stood behind Angela like a lost dog. The poor guy; he had no guts to do anything or say anything to her.

"About?" Angela folded her arms. "Need I remind you we're still part of this?"

"I'm so tired of this, Angela." Ainsley melted. "I'm tired of your attitude, you feeling that you're entitled to make decisions that you are not part of, doing whatever you want and refusing to deal with the consequences. I'm done with it."

"What's *that* supposed to mean?"

"It means from here on out, you and Jude are welcome to visit Mum until it's her time, but I will not be talking to you, I will not be engaging in whatever little feud you're trying to win. And if I know my siblings, which I think I do, they'll stand by me. Except for you, Jude, I know you have a hard time seeing what's right in front of you or choosing your family."

"Is this still about the stupid wedding?" Angela rolled her eyes.

"If it's so stupid, why could you postpone it for your family, but not Jude's?" Declan asked.

Every one of them turned toward her, waiting for her response. It was a valid question. Why *could* she postpone for her family and not her *husband's* if it was just a stupid wedding?

"Well?" Ainsley asked.

"Oh my god!" Angela threw her hands in the air. "You guys are all overreacting. Jude even told me that you guys would act crazy like this if we came, but I insisted we come because family or whatever." She added an eye roll at the end, though tried to hide it by closing her eyes.

Molly gave Teagan's hand a squeeze. Molly didn't want Teagan to see this side of her family, how messy things really were. She felt like she was on the outside, like she was watching a film, and everything was just happening around her instead of to her.

"Wait a minute," Jude said. *Was she lying?* Molly wouldn't put it passed her to make herself look good, but this seemed like a new level of low, placing blame on Jude.

"The whole Holliday family is so sensitive," she said to the support friends. "You do one thing, and they hold it against your forever. Ainsley is a huge advocate for family, but she can't even let her own brother know what's going on with his parents."

"Now hold on." Gavin stood. "I won't sit here and hear you talk slander about the woman I—" Gavin sat back down, taking Ainsley's hand in his. "The woman I love."

"What?" Ainsley gasped.

"We can talk about it later," Gavin dismissed, turning his attention back to Angela, who had a scowl. "Ainsley has a lot to think about. She holds power of attorney and needs to make a tough decision, and she doesn't need to deal with your gaslighting, condescending fear tactics."

Angela scoffed with an eye roll. "Of course, she's power of attorney. Doesn't come around for seven years and gets to hold the fate of your parents in her hands," she said with an eye roll.

"What decision?" Jude asked.

"To end Mum's care early." Ainsley stared Angela in the eyes.

Chapter Twenty-Nine
Ainsley

"You can't end it until we talk to the lawyer." Angela was so persistent. It was as if Dorothy was worth more because she was near her time.

"I told you, I'm done with this, with you." Ainsley stood. "Gavin, would you like to get some lunch?"

Everyone watched Ainsley leave hand-in-hand with Gavin. Ainsley could feel Angela with her judging eyes. *How dare I go to lunch with a boy when my father just died.*

My father just died...

The elevator doors closed, and Ainsley fell into Gavin's chest and cried. Everything added up, the article that she was supposed to have written in less than a week that wasn't even started, Jude and his incredibly self-absorbed wife, her dad who was now dead, and she had to decide if now was the right time to call off care for her mum too. She was one person; she shouldn't have to deal with all of it. And she felt so alone. Declan was great for taking on the task of being the innkeeper, and she knew it wasn't easy for him. Molly was so strong, sitting up in the waiting room with Angela and her self-righteousness. Ainsley was glad she had Teagan.

Gavin held her close, rubbing her back, resting his head on hers. "It's okay."

"How is any of this okay?" Ainsley said between sobs. "None of this is okay." She pulled herself away from him, wiping her eyes.

"I didn't mean like that." He placed a hand on her face, wiping the leftover tears with his thumb. "It's alright to break down. You're going through a lot and honestly, none of your family seems to understand."

"They're going through it too. It's hard to support someone when you're going through the same thing. We each grieve differently, and I just know that Angela is up there judging me for getting food with you. I can't grieve with everyone watching me, wondering what I'm going to decide about Mum. It's too much. If they want to grieve by crying or telling funny stories or binge eating food with their favourite person, I don't care. I don't care how they process their feelings, as long as we can still agree to come together after this."

"You want to come together with Jude and Angela?"

"No, but I can't deny them access to the funeral or at least hear their opinions on what to do about Mum."

He nodded, not really understanding. Ainsley understood, after the way Angela constantly treated them, why should she give Angela's opinion any consideration at all?

Honestly, she didn't want to. Ainsley would be more than happy to tell her where she can shove her opinion, but she knew her mum would want her to be the bigger person, to do right by everyone.

What about right by me?

Ainsley and Gavin left the elevator and went into the cafeteria. There wasn't much, and what was there didn't look that appetising. She grabbed an orange juice and a chicken salad sandwich, paid at the register, and found a table. Gavin wasn't far behind her, with a ham and cheese sandwich and bottled water.

"So," she said, "you love me? Even after not wanting to be together?" She thought that it would freak her out. She thought that having a deep care for someone would make her want to run back to New York and not look back. But he sat there, across the table from her, eating his sandwich, at the hospital where they just said goodbye to her father, someone he didn't know all that well. He was here. He wanted the same things as her: freedom, travel, adventure, and most importantly he wanted it to be just the two of them.

Gavin choked on his sandwich. "That is what I said, yes." He picked at the bread, eating it as crumbs. "I know it's a lot, I think I said we weren't together to suppress the feelings I had for you. This is the last thing you need to be dealing with, but I want you to know that I care about you so much. At first it

THE HOLLIDAY INN

scared me; I had an idea of what I wanted from my life. I knew how my life was supposed to go. I thought I was supposed to be alone. But you, you're here, you want what I want, we have fun, and I find myself thinking about you all the time."

"Gavin," Ainsley said carefully.

"I don't expect you to say it. I didn't even mean to say it. We agreed that there were no strings. I tried to deny my feelings for you because of that, but I was only hurting myself. I'm pretty sure that I love you, never have I been so fully myself with anyone but you."

"That's a pretty big claim for only knowing me for three weeks." Ainsley bit into her sandwich. The thought of his love, his care for her, was comforting.

"You're right, but I also know that what we have with each other isn't something you can fake."

She nodded. She thought she hated him, for what, spilling coffee on her blouse? For the way that he always seemed to look at her with like he admired her? It wasn't long before that anger went away and she thought of him as a friend, she couldn't imagine hating him now. He'd easily become her best friend. Someone that she wanted to see every day, someone she wanted to tell everything to, someone she wanted to gossip with and wake up to watch the morning news or something that old people do. *That's* the thought that scared her. That she might reciprocate those feelings.

"I know you're going through a lot, and the last thing I want you to focus on is our relationship. But I want you to know, that I respect you and your work, and I would never ask you to stay if that wasn't something you wanted to consider."

"You wouldn't ask me to stay?" She had mixed feelings about that. She didn't want him to put her in that position, choosing her job, which she loved so much, or their relationship, which was still new and had potential. But if he truly loved her, wouldn't he want to do whatever it took to be together? Wouldn't he want to ask her to stay or to ask to go with her? Could she ask him to go with her?

Too many questions.

"Gavin, you are an incredible person. And you're right. I have a lot going on right now, with my parents. So, let's make a deal."

"I'm listening."

"Until New Year's, we keep going the way we are, and we will decide what happens then."

"New Year's," he said with a smile. Waiting until New Year's meant she would be staying an extra week. "I like it."

After they finished eating and putting their rubbish in the bin, they went back to the waiting room. Molly was still sitting there with Teagan and Declan.

"Where's Satan Spawn and Jude?" Ainsley asked.

"Gone to get something to eat, so she says," Molly said. "I don't know what her problem is. She was here saying that you had the audacity to go out and eat with your boyfriend whilst our father just passed, and then she complains that there's nothing good to eat in a hospital and needs to go get 'real food.'" Molly used air quotes.

Ainsley rolled her eyes. "She's so pretentious."

"What are you going to do?" Declan asked.

"Well, I was thinking that—"

"You were really going to talk about what *you* were going to do without us?" Angela's voice sent a chill up Ainsley's spine, similar to how nails on a chalkboard felt.

I cannot do this. Ainsley took in a breath. She said she was done, so she needed to prove it. "I'm going to listen to your opinions and make a decision based on what I think will suit us best."

"What suits us best isn't killing her," Angela said.

"She's already dead, Angie," Ainsley snapped, knowing Angela hated that nickname. "So, tell me what you think is best for us. Since you seem to know Jude's family *so fucking* well. Tell me. What is the best way to end the care of my already brain-dead mother?"

Angela pursed her lips and look down at her feet.

"That's what I thought. If anyone has

something productive to add, I'm more than happy to listen."

Everyone was quiet. Even those who weren't in the family, who were listening, avoided eye contact with Ainsley.

"Do you need to go for a walk?" Gavin whispered to her.

"You know what? I think we all need a break from this; from the hospital and each other." She sighed, rubbing her face. "I'm going to see Mum for a minute and then I'm leaving for the day, this has gotten way out of hand." She released her hand from Gavin's, making sure he knew not to follow her.

She closed the door behind her. The room was a lot bigger now that her father's bed was gone. Her mum was alone in the room, the way Ainsley felt alone in the decision.

"Mum." She kept her voice quiet. "I can't make this decision. Why was I made the power of attorney? Did you think it'd be easy for me to pull the plug on you?" Tears stung her eyes. "We fought and we didn't agree on much. We had very different views on how my life should have gone. But I can't...I can't do it." Ainsley closed her eyes and a tear escaped.

The machines beeped consistently, the slow rise and fall of her mum's chest as if she were breathing and the machine wasn't doing it for her. But there was no life to her. Ainsley knew she wasn't here, not really.

"I am so sorry, Mum. I wanted to be the daughter you could be proud of. I wanted so

THE HOLLIDAY INN

badly for your approval of everything, it nearly killed me. Why did you have to pressure me so much into doing what you wanted?"

Ainsley waited for her to answer, knowing it would never come. She was brave now. Now that her mother couldn't hear her or respond, now she could talk to her about everything she felt.

"I know that you wanted to be in our corner, but it was so hard to tell you anything. You were full of judgement, and we feared it. And maybe if this had happened at the peak of our fighting, I wouldn't have hesitated on ending the care, but now? I'd give anything for one more lecture on cleaning my room, or why I should have stayed home, or at the least moved to London instead. One more argument that leads to me rolling my eyes and stomping out."

Ainsley cried slow, quiet tears, leaning over the bed.

"I want to hear one more 'I love you.' I want to hug you and feel you hug me back. Just one more time." She couldn't even remember the last time she shared a hug with her mother. It had to have been years. "I'm so sorry, Mum. I didn't mean it when I said I hated you and this town and the inn. I was a teenager and stupid. God..." She leaned back in the chair. "This town is so beautiful and the inn? The inn is incredible."

Ainsley composed herself and cleaned up

her eyes. "I will make a decision. I'm sorry that it's come to this. I wish we had had more time." Ainsley touched her mother's hand gently. The first contact she'd made with either parent since being in the hospital. "I love you, Mum."

Before she could shed more tears, she left the room with the weight of the world on her shoulders.

"Ainsley, when you said a break from each other..." Molly stood.

"I mean," Ainsley held Molly's shoulders, "see your friends, hang out with your—Teagan. Take some you time and we will come back together for the tree lighting on Monday." Ainsley looked at Declan. "Is that okay?"

"Yes, we all grieve differently. I understand if you need time away."

"Thank you." Ainsley pulled Molly into a hug. "Just because I want some space right now doesn't mean I don't want to be there for you. If you need me, call."

"Where are you going?"

She locked eyes with Gavin, who had a sad look on his face and nodded. "Gavin's."

Chapter Thirty
Declan

Declan went back to the inn, after Molly assured Ainsley and him that she would be taken care of, she would call when she wanted them. He doubted she'd call him; he didn't have any experience when it came the touchy feely stuff. Ainsley and he laughed through the pain, usually. She'd cried a lot today; she probably thought they didn't notice, but her face was so red, it was hard not to.

Declan didn't know how he needed to cope. It's normal to want people around, people who love you. He should want Olive there, so why did he feel like he didn't care? He loved her, she was it for him. He'd never stopped loving her. But, as he sat at the front desk at the inn, staring at the door, he didn't care who walked through or what intention they had.

"Declan?"

He pulled himself out of his thoughts and looked at Albert. "Yeah?"

"Everything alright, son?"

His shoulders lowered, not realising how hunched he had been. "No. My dad died this afternoon, and we're debating on pulling the care from Mum too."

"That must be hard."

Declan wasn't the type to cry, he was the type to crack jokes and try to make people laugh in times of pain, no matter what was going on. But he couldn't think of anything. Dark humour was something he prided himself on, usually, but he was empty.

"Do you need anything from me?"

Probably, but I don't know what. "No, take the rest of the day."

"What about the dinner dishes?"

"They'll still be there tomorrow. I need to be with people. My people."

"Of course. If you don't mind, I'll watch the front desk for you until it usually closes."

"Thank you, Albert. I can see why my father hired you. You're not just a good employee, you're a great man." Declan shook Albert's hand. "Thank you."

"Go take care of yourself." Albert gave Declan a pat on the back and sent him on his way. Declan went into the house, calling Olive.

"I was wondering if I was going to hear from you. How are you?" Her gentle voice filled his ear, and his chest tightened. He missed her.

"Can I come over?" He hadn't intended his voice to be as desperate as it came out. But he was defeated. He needed someone to hold him.

"Of course. I'll see you in half an hour."

Relief washed over him. "I love you," he said after ending the call, throwing clothes into a bag. He thought saying it to her now would still be too soon. He thought back to

Gavin telling Ainsley; if his time here with his family taught him anything, it was that time is short, tell people you love them while you can.

Declan pulled into Olive's driveway. Her house was small and attached to another, like an apartment. He knocked on the door, she opened it and pulled him into her. "I am so sorry," she said, rubbing his back and closing the door with her foot.

The door led right into the living room, with a small closet for shoes and jackets, where she hung his.

"Thank you." He didn't want to feel useless, but he was comfortable enough that he didn't feel like he needed to put on a strong face.

"Have a seat, I've got something for you."

He sat on the couch, back to the kitchen that was also separated by a wall. She had a nice sectional couch placed in front of the telly.

"Where's Winston?" he asked.

"I let him out. He'll be in in a moment." She came into the living room with a big bowl of crisps and a side bowl of dip. "We're going to watch your favourite childhood movie and snuggle and eat food."

"That sounds great," he said. He couldn't express the feeling. Relaxed? He'd never felt so at peace than in that moment; when she let Winston in, she curled into Declan's side and Winston curled into her. She pressed play on the remote and the classic Disney castle appeared on the screen.

D. C. COOK

"What movie are we watching?"

"Do you really not know?" She looked at him. *"Treasure Planet."*

It was the best way to end the day. He still couldn't believe that he'd never see his father again, and the chances of hearing his mum's voice were so slim that they were considering ending her care early.

It made sense to him; their father was gone and there were no signs of her improving. If anything, he thought they waited too long. He thought as a man he was expected not to have emotions or something to that effect. But, truth was, he had so many different emotions coursing through him at that moment that it was all he could do not to cry.

Olive, of all people, was here, she loved him still. She loved him in a way he didn't know he needed. She may not have said the words, but he knew. She wouldn't have taken him again; she wouldn't be snuggled in his arms if she didn't. He pulled her closer, though she couldn't get any closer, and kissed the top of her head.

❄ ❄ ❄

Albert had gone in for Declan on Sunday too, whilst he stayed at Olive's. Ainsley was right, they needed some time apart. They'd grown so used to being apart that being together for so long, it was getting overwhelming. It was nice

THE HOLLIDAY INN

to take a break from everything going on to sit there with Olive. Was it wrong to pretend that everything was fine for a moment? For this moment in time, he was content, despite the fact that his father was gone, despite that his mum wouldn't be far behind him, despite having to completely learn a new job without any proper training and leaving the life he loved in London. He was happy to have found love again with Olive.

"I need to go back home tomorrow. The girls will be expecting me," he said. They sat on the couch eating breakfast.

"I need to go into the cafe tomorrow, and get payroll out before Christmas."

"That's right, it's Christmas week. Lord, everything is going to be busy. The inn is probably booked solid this week."

"Maybe you should go back today then." She glanced up at him over her spoonful of cereal.

"You're probably right, but I've enjoyed staying here." It was good to forget about all the bad going on right now, especially so close to Christmas. What he wouldn't give to have one more Christmas with his parents laughing, drinking egg nog. Declan was still on the fence about Jude's arrival, but he hadn't done anything wrong, it was all Angela. But he didn't do anything to defend his siblings either. It was all so stupid, they were a family, *why can't we move on and be together in this trying time?*

"I liked having you here too. But I think

Winston is a little jealous that he didn't get to sleep on the bed last night. Isn't that right, boy?" She scratched under the dog's chin. "You have me all to yourself tonight."

"I wonder if Ainsley made a decision yet."

Olive sat back against the couch. "Why are you all putting it on her? She shouldn't be doing this by herself, especially now."

"She says she'll consult us, but the decision is ultimately hers as power of attorney."

"What do you want to do?" She rested her arm against the back of the couch and leaned on her head, watching him.

"I don't know," he answered honestly. "Obviously I don't want my mum to die, but we know she isn't going to come out of it, so why prolong the inevitable?" It sucked to say, but it was true, and he was sure that that's how Ainsley felt. He probably knew the decision she was going to make before she did. He sighed. "How am I going from a person with two healthy parents, to a person with no parents? And Molly...will literally be an orphan. Am I an orphan? At what age are people not considered orphaned when their parents die?"

"Okay," she said, putting her hand on his. "You're spiralling. What can you do about it right now?"

"Nothing. I can't do anything. What could I possibly do?" *Nothing, right?*

"Right, so let's focus on the things you can do. You can be there for your sisters; you can take care of the inn. You can be with me."

He nodded. "I'm so glad we are here now." He took her hand to his lips, kissing the back of it gently. "I've loved you for so long."

"I know," she said, rubbing her thumb against his hand. "I've always wondered what would happen if we found each other again. I'm happy that we could pick up right where we left off. It's like no time has passed."

"I know. As much as I hated us being apart, I don't regret going to London. I know it sounds bad, but I think we needed to be apart to realize how much we really did love each other." He did love his time in London, his job, the friends, but he was miserable going home alone, without someone there, without Olive there to greet him, to talk about their days.

"Move into the house with me," he said.

"What?" She pulled her hand out of his, grabbing her glass of water, pretending it wasn't his statement that cause her to pull away.

"Move into the house with me. Ainsley will be going back to New York, and Molly loves you, and I just know she'll agree that this is a great idea." Excitement filled him, this was the one thing he knew would bring him so much happiness in this time when there was too much hurt.

"Declan," she said softly.

"Oh." He recoiled. "You don't want to."

"No, no it's not that. I just think it's a little fast."

"Waking up to you, falling asleep with you next to me has brought me so much comfort and I thought you and I were on the same page."

"We are. We want the same things, you and I together. We want marriage and kids, but we're only twenty-three."

"I didn't say anything about getting married or having kids, all I said was I want you to move in with me."

"You're right, that's all you said." She glanced at her dog. "It's a lot to think about. My business is in town, I'm close if something were to go wrong. I think we're going to have to settle on spending the night at each other's homes for now."

He tried to hide his disappointment, though he wasn't doing a good job.

"I think we should revisit the idea when you're not going through something so emotional. You should be present with your family, not thinking about me." He knew what she was really saying was that he'd moved too fast, that he was acting out of emotion.

"Will you come back to the house with me?"

"I don't want you hiding behind me. This is your family, your business. I don't want to impose."

He decided he wasn't going to let the small rejection ruin what they'd built back up. "You really think Ainsley isn't going to bring Gavin? Those two have basically been joined at the hip since she got here. I can't believe he said he loved her. She's made it so clear that she's going back to New York."

"Do you want her to stay?"

"I think so." The house was going to feel so empty when it was just him and Molly. Maybe that was why he wanted Olive to move in too because the house would be full again with another person there. And he knew he needed her by his side.

"I think you three should really sit down and talk about what it is you're expecting from each other. You don't want to grow to resent them like you all do Jude."

Declan sighed heavily. "Jude's case is different. I don't know, there's something about Angela that I don't like. I never really fancied myself the type to care about drama, but the way Angela holds herself, the way she talks to everyone, really boils my blood."

"Do you think she does it for attention? Do you really think she needs that kind of attention?"

He shrugged. "I haven't given it much thought. She's the only girl in her family, so I'm sure she's not lacking in the attention department."

"You guys should talk to her."

Declan let out a sarcastic laugh. "Yeah, I bet Ainsley would love to sit down with her and have a chat. At least come with me today, you can come back home later."

"All right." She kissed his cheek and went to the bathroom. "Can I bring Winston?" she called from behind the closed door.

"Of course, I can't say no to this fluffy little face." He patted the dog and his tail waved back and forth. At least he liked him, which meant that it would probably make it easier to move, whenever that day came. He wasn't going to pressure her.

When they got to the house, there was a new van parked in front. Declan got out of his car and looked around. No one was in or around the van. Maybe it was someone who knew Ainsley or dropping Molly off.

He opened the door and there stood someone he never thought he'd see again.

"Jamie?" he asked. She turned around, her blonde hair flicking over her shoulder as she smiled at him. "What are you doing here?" he asked, too stunned to move as she wrapped her arms around him.

"Jamie here claims to be your girlfriend," Ainsley said, sipping tea and leaning against the kitchen counter. She hated having her own drama, but she did love to be a viewer of everyone else's.

"Girlfriend?" Olive asked from beside Declan. "That's funny because I'm pretty sure *I'm* his girlfriend."

"I'm sorry?" Jamie asked a confused smile now on her face.

"Olive, this is Jamie, the girl I told you I went on a date with before I got the call. Jamie, you and I were never official, and definitely never exclusive. But Olive and I are,

THE HOLLIDAY INN

official and exclusive."

"Oh, no that's not what I was saying." Jamie cleared her throat. "I told your landlord that I was your girlfriend in order to get into your apartment and get some of the stuff I thought you would need. Since, you know, you won't be living in London anymore."

"You went into my apartment?" he asked. He blinked, trying to register what was going on. "Wait. You lied to my landlord, broke into my home, stole my stuff, and drove it four hours to give it to me?"

Ainsley tried not to laugh behind her cup. Jamie rolled her eyes. "When you say it like that, it sounds creepy. I was just trying to help you out. You literally said that I could do it."

Olive stood taller, though that didn't mean much. "Listen, lady. I don't care who you think you are in relation to Declan—"

"When?" Declan couldn't remember saying that she could do any of that.

"When you called me last week. I was literally just trying to help him out. I know you guys are going through a rough time and I thought this would save some headache, but I can see I was overstepping. I'm sorry." Jamie stepped passed Declan. "And I'm sorry about your parents." Then she left.

"What just happened?" Declan asked. "Was that real?"

Ainsley shrugged. "At least now you don't need to plan a trip to London. She put your stuff in your room and the furniture is at the flat still, she said you mentioned that it came with the flat?"

"It did. Okay, um..." He rubbed his hands together. "That was strange, right?"

"Extremely. You sure it was just one date?"

"I mean we...she came home with me, but it was literally the night I got the call to come here. There was no room to develop anything."

Olive nodded. "I'm going to pour some tea and forget that that ever happened." She circled her hand in the air in front of the door.

He ran outside, hoping Jamie was still there. She was. He knocked on the window and she rolled it down.

"Thank you," he said. "I know it seemed like I didn't appreciate it, or rather thought it was creepy, but truth was, you're the only one who's called to see how I was doing. Everyone else seemed to have forgotten I existed."

"She's the girl you told me about? The one you were hung up on?"

"Yeah, she is."

She sighed with a grin. "Don't be stupid this time."

He released a small chuckle. "I won't."

"It was good getting to know you, Declan."

"You too, Jamie. Take care." He waved as she pulled out onto the main road.

Declan went back into the house, where the three best girls were waiting for him. Maybe Ainsley wouldn't stay, but that made the rest of the visit that much more special. They were finally all in a place where they got along again.

Chapter Thirty-One
Molly

It was finally winter break from school. Molly didn't think she could've gone back after the weekend she had.

She understood their thinking when it came to their mother, she did. But it hurt so much that she couldn't express how much she wasn't ready to say goodbye. So, she tried to bury the thought down low, especially when Ainsley suggested they take the weekend to be apart. She thought people forced each other to be together in times like this, but not her family. She felt like Ainsley couldn't get away from her fast enough. But she remembered everyone grieved differently.

Hilary's mum brought Molly home on Sunday, after spending more time painting with Hilary and Amelia. No one mentioned what happened at the hospital, they didn't even ask how she was. She assumed they knew but didn't want to make a big deal about it. They knew she would talk when she was ready. Apparently, that time did not come.

"I'm going to be in my room most of the day. I have to finish Teagan's Christmas present," Molly said to Ainsley Monday morning over breakfast. "I don't need to talk," she said as

Ainsley sucked in a breath to speak.

"All right. I have a lot of work to do anyway."

"Are you going into town today?"

She rubbed her forehead. "I don't know. I get more done, but I just want to lay down for the next week."

"Why didn't you ask for time off?"

She sighed. "I'm afraid she'll fire me. She tells me all the time how great of an editor I am, but I know I'm replaceable."

"Do you like your job?"

"I do. I never thought I'd be stuck at a desk job though. I thought I'd get to travel and do the things I loved whilst still doing my job."

Molly nodded. "Adulthood seems complicated."

"You have no idea what you're in for." She turned to Molly. "You really like Teagan, don't you?" Ainsley asked, taking Molly off guard.

Molly rolled her eyes and cleaned out her dishes.

"Come on! You can talk to me about this stuff. I'm not Mum, I'm not going to tell you to stop seeing her."

"I do like her, but it's all new to me. The dating thing."

"You're fifteen, you'll figure it out."

"Can't you tell me? Give me a hint or something?"

"I could, but everyone is different, everyone dates differently."

"Like Gavin?" Molly teased.

Ainsley's turn to roll her eyes. "That's something that we don't need to get into."

"Oh, come on!" Molly said, repeating Ainsley's earlier words back to her. "He told you he loved you and you took him to lunch in a hospital cafeteria."

"It's for us to work out."

Molly sat back beside her. "Does this mean you're going to move back home?" This was her plan from the beginning, though she really gave up almost immediately, it'd be nice if it worked out on its own.

"I haven't decided yet. There's a lot to factor in, my job for one."

"Being apart from Gavin for two?" Molly wiggled her eyebrows.

"Stop it!" Ainsley laughed, pushing Molly away. Molly laughed too. "Our relationship is complicated. And at fifteen, you don't need to worry about complicated, you should only worry about being treated properly and having fun with them."

Molly nodded. "But why do you need worry about that? Why does being an adult mean your relationship is complicated? Doesn't Gavin treat you properly?"

"Well, yes." Ainsley hesitated.

"And don't you two have loads of fun together?"

"We do…"

The look on her face was something of a realization.

"And you both want the same things from

each other, so what is complicated about it?"

She sighed, giving into her grin. "You're right, there's nothing complicated about the relation-ship, it's everything else. But don't you worry, Molly. I am going to work on the everything else. Love you." She kissed the top of Molly's head and went into her room. Molly followed, turning into her room.

She didn't know if Teagan was going to get her anything for Christmas, nor was she expecting anything. But Molly wanted to show her appreciation for Teagan being around. Not only was she a great friend, being there, but she was under-standing in the relationship area, not rushing Molly into something that she wasn't ready for. She knew Teagan was going to love the painting, it was all her favourite comics and anime shows. And judging by the way she reacted to Molly's paintings that Amelia showed her, she was going to really love it.

Molly set her canvas on her easel, thinking of where she wanted to start again. She put on some Queen and got started with the painting. She could paint for hours and not realise how much time went by; that's exactly what happened when Ainsley knocked on the door, peeking her head inside the room.

"What?" Molly asked, not taking her eyes off the tiny details she was working on for the spines.

"Are you hungry? It's nearly dinner."

"Really?" Molly picked up her phone,

looking at the time. She had several missed messages from Amelia, Hilary, and Teagan. "Now that you mention it, yeah, I'm quite hungry. Teagan is asking if I want to go to dinner with her," Molly said, reading the message aloud.

"You want to go?"

Molly looked at Ainsley, a small smile hitting her lips. "Yeah, I think I do."

"Well, I was going into town to meet Gavin for the tree lighting."

"Is Declan coming?"

"I think he's taking a different car with Olive. And Angela and Jude are going, no doubt."

"Right..." Molly didn't want Ainsley's opinion of Angela and Jude to sway her, but she could feel herself sway to Ainsley's side the more she talked about Angela.

"Anyway, get ready. I'll take you in."

"Great."

Molly sent a message to Hilary and Amelia, letting them know that she was doing okay, that things with her siblings (minus Jude and Angela) were good. They were more attentive and caring than she thought they'd be. She wasn't ready to say goodbye to Ainsley. She hoped the month being here would be enough to convince her to stay, that she was enough for her to stay. But she wouldn't mind if Gavin helped.

Then Molly sent a message to Teagan telling her she'd love to have dinner with her, and she'd meet her at Denny's pub in thirty minutes.

A pub. It was a casual setting, fancy clothes were not required, but Molly still wanted to look nice. She wondered what Teagan would wear. Lately, she's been going easier on the makeup, it wasn't so black and thick.

Molly settled on Christmas-themed leggings and a plain beige cashmere-esque sweater. She tied her hair into a ponytail and added some mascara to her lashes, leaving the rest of her face bare to show off her freckles.

Ainsley didn't talk much on the drive, and Molly was too nervous to think of anything to say. This was her first official date with Teagan, her first official date ever. She took a deep breath when Ainsley parked.

"Where are you meeting Teagan?"

"Denny's."

"I'm meeting Gavin at Rudy's."

"Whoa. That's a nice place."

"I know," she said with a sigh, staring ahead. "Is it too fast? It feels like too much, but also, I don't want it to stop. And you and Declan, we've had so much fun getting together again. I don't want it to have to end."

"What are you saying?" Molly tried not to be too hopeful.

"I think I'm going to stay."

Hearing the words hit differently than wanting it. "Really?"

"I've loved being here this month, getting to know you again, hanging out with you and

Declan, being a family again. And what's going on with Gavin doesn't hurt either..." Ainsley sighed. "I don't want to stay for a boy, that feels too...too risky. I think if I continue to focus on us, it'll help reduce the risk of what happens if it doesn't work out with me and Gavin."

"So, what if you want to stay for a guy? Who cares?"

She shrugged. "I don't know, I guess it feels too anti-feminist. Remember how we'd roll our eyes at the girls who changed their life for a guy in the Hallmark movies? Here I am, living a Hallmark movie."

"Then it's only fitting you give in."

She nodded. "I guess I have a conversation to have with Katherine."

The girls left the car, Ainsley locked it behind her, and they split up, each going to their different restaurants.

Teagan was already sitting in a booth looking at a menu. Molly waved at Denny and slid into the seat across from Teagan.

"I don't know why I read the menu," she said without looking up. "I always order the same thing." Then she put the menu down and grinned at Molly. "You look beautiful."

"Oh. Thank you," she said, trying not to raise her voice an octave from being taken aback. "You look great too."

She really did. Molly liked her even when she had the thick black makeup and the black lipstick, but now she had a light smoky eye, with brown, and her lipstick was a neutral pink. Her black hair curled and all over one shoulder.

"Why did you stop wearing your black make-up?" Molly asked.

Teagan took her bottom lip between her teeth, trying to hide a smile. "Because you don't deserve the girl I am when I dress like that."

"What does that mean?"

She took in a sharp breath. "There's a lot you don't know about me, and you're so sweet and you deserve someone who isn't a mess. So, I'm trying not to be messy for you."

"I don't want you to change yourself for me. I like you. Mess and all."

"That's sweet, Molly, really. But it's for the best. My friends agree that since you and I started...that I've been happier, and I don't need to express myself in that way anymore."

"Okay, but...you could still wear the black lipstick?" Molly hadn't realised she almost preferred Teagan in the black lipstick.

The corners of her lips turned up and then spread wide. "Yeah, I can do that."

Denny came and took their order, then brought it back to the kitchen.

"Do you see Hilary and Amelia much?"

"Not during the holidays usually. I've seen them more this holiday than last year. Mum had me working a lot. I'm not sure how Declan is managing on his own."

She nodded. "Am I taking you away from

anything?"

"No. Ainsley is out with Gavin, and I assume Declan is with Olive. I'm not sure what Ainsley is going to do, but I think she wants to stay."

Teagan's eyes lit up, knowing that was exactly what Molly wanted. "That's great."

"You know." Molly looked at the table. "I thought a lot about you last year when your mum died."

Teagan's brows drew together. "You did?"

"Yeah, it was around when you started dressing in all black. And I thought it really sucked that you were going through that, and I couldn't imagine what I'd do."

They were silent for a moment.

"I still don't know what I'm going to do when Mum's officially gone, but I know that I will be able to go on because I have Ainsley and Declan, Hilary and Amelia, and you."

"I was so depressed that the one person who seemed to value me was gone. Dad was a wreck. He loved her so much and I don't think there was room for me because of her. I think he resented me a little because she loved me as well as him and not him alone."

"I'm sorry."

"I acted out. I wanted to be seen again. I didn't know how to get people to see me, so I went to the extreme." Teagan shrugged as if it were no big deal.

"Did you and your friends always play punk rock music or pop punk?"

"I think so. We loved Panic! At The Disco

and Fall Out Boy, My Chemical Romance. It just bled into our music."

The young women talked more, and Molly learned more about what it was like for Teagan without her mum, and that she was going to be okay. If Teagan could be okay without half the people Molly had, then there was no reason Molly wasn't going to make it through either. She just had to get through the rough part first, which was coming fast.

"Do you want to see the tree lighting? It should be happening soon," Teagan asked.

"Yes. I told Ainsley I'd meet her there so we could go home after."

"Great." Teagan went to the bar where Denny was shaking a cup, whilst Molly put on her coat, then she met her at the bar.

"What's my portion?" Molly asked.

"Nothing. All taken care of." Teagan's smile beamed.

"You didn't have to do that," Molly said.

"I asked you out, it's only fair I pay. Next time, you ask me out and you can pay."

"Deal," Molly said before realising that that meant they'd be going on a second date. But it wasn't something she was fearing now. In fact, she couldn't wait to go.

As soon as they left the pub, Teagan's hand found Molly's, lacing their fingers together. Molly relaxed into her. It was easy in a way she never thought it would be. They walked a moment before the snow started to float down around them.

"It's snowing!" Molly couldn't stop herself from shouting like a child. As if there wasn't enough snow on the ground already, but there was something magical about a snow-covered ground whilst it also floated out of the sky.

"You're so cute." Teagan chuckled. They stopped at the back of the crowd, around the tree in the centre of the town. "Do you want to get closer?" Teagan asked.

"I like it here," Molly said, turning to her. The mayor was making some type of speech that neither of them could hear.

"I like it here too." Her eyes met Molly's. She tried to hold Teagan's gaze but looked down at her feet. She tipped Molly's chin up. "Molly, I mean it."

"I know."

"I want to give us a real try. I know you and you said you weren't ready—"

"Yes," Molly breathed out, cutting Teagan off.

"Yeah?" Teagan asked with a smile.

"Yes," Molly answered in her normal voice, a slight laugh following.

As soon as the lights on the tree lit up, people clapped and Teagan pulled Molly into her, her stomach dropped as she anticipated what was coming next. Teagan held her as close as she could with their winter jackets and pressed their lips together.

Molly held Teagan's face, holding her close. This was the first kiss that Molly wanted to have with Teagan. A kiss that was sweet, not forced, not taunting. A kiss that left Molly knowing she'd be loved by Teagan.

Chapter Thirty-Two
Ainsley

Ainsley hadn't planned on telling Molly she was going to stay. She wasn't even sure if she was, but it felt right to talk to Molly about it, seeing as she was the one who was begging her older sister to stay in the beginning. The urge to stay hadn't come until they were parked outside before going to meet their dates. Ainsley knew she needed to have a talk with Katherine, and she wasn't ready to call her knowing she'd ask how the article was coming, even though it wasn't. Ainsley knew she was going to write about the town, it made the most sense, but what was the story? She wasn't a tourist here.

"What's on your mind?" Gavin asked.

Their meals were hot in front of them, the only difference was his was mostly gone and hers was still full. Ainsley thought she'd been eating, but her mind must have been focused on everything else.

"Sorry," she said. She took a bite, and suddenly she couldn't eat fast enough. "I've got a lot going on this week."

He nodded. "Have you decided what to do?"

"We're just going to do it, get it over with. We agreed that there's no sense in prolonging something we know is inevitable. No matter how shitty it's going to feel." It was the right thing to do, though Ainsley thought they'd let their parents go on too long. Despite knowing the outcome, it didn't make it any easier to deal with.

He nodded. "I'm sorry you're in this position."

"Me too. We're going tomorrow. I haven't been able to get in touch with Jude or Angela. Why show up here demanding to be included in this and then be out of touch until it's convenient for them, or rather for her."

"I can't begin to understand the level of complicated your family is, but wouldn't it be better for everyone if you guys talked it out? Figured out what the problem was and then moved on together?"

"You'd think." Ainsley huffed.

"No, I'm serious. You complain a lot about how she's a narcissist, but you don't seem willing to talk to her."

"Because there is no talking to her. You don't understand, so just stay out of it, okay?" She tried to say it as nicely as she could, but those words hardly left anyone's mouth without a rude, sinister tone.

"Of course." He turned his attention down to his plate.

Ainsley rubbed her forehead. "I'm sorry. I didn't mean to snap, it's just that there's so much going on and everyone is expecting a different level of attention from me, and I just don't have much more to give."

"I don't expect anything from you, other than your friendship."

Now that just made Ainsley feel bad. She was planning on staying, he had told her that he loved her and now all he wanted was her friendship?

"Look," he said, clasping his hands together. "You're going through a lot, it'd be wrong of me to demand you to feel the same, or even focus on us right now. But like I told you, I've never had anything serious, let alone something like what I feel for you this quickly."

She couldn't help the little laugh that escaped her mouth. "Me neither. You know, coming here, the last thing I expected was to fall for you. Especially after that coffee incident when we first met." She grinned from one corner of her mouth. "Gavin," she said, looking him in the eye. "I'm going to stay."

He took in a deep breath, what looked like fear flashed across his eyes before he settled into a smile. "Yeah?"

She nodded. "I'd be foolish to leave my siblings now, plus, I'd be lying if I said I wasn't interested to see where things with us go." She looked at her plate of food. He had told her that he doesn't do serious relationships for fear of ending up like his parents, but she couldn't help but feel like if she left before she saw it through, she'd always wonder *what if...*

"I'd be lying if I said I wasn't incredibly

scared to hurt you..."

Ainsley shrugged. "Then just don't be stupid." She grinned, winking at him. "We should probably go if we're going to make the tree lighting." They both rose and silently agreed to race each other to the till to see who got to pay for the date. He beat her. She thanked him for dinner, and they made it to the door, stopping to do up their coats.

"Awwww!" the restaurant chorused whilst looking at them.

"I'm sorry?" She looked at Gavin.

"Mistletoe!" Darla, the host, shouted, pointing above their heads.

Gavin grinned and pulled Ainsley into him by her waist. They'd kissed so many times before, but never with an audience. The way he lowered his mouth to hers was agonisingly slow. He tucked some loose hairs out of her face and settled one hand on her cheek, the other firmly around her waist. When his mouth finally met hers in a soft kiss, it felt different through her body. It felt like there was a possibility to their relationship. She allowed herself to melt into him, deepening the kiss. His mouth danced with hers, and she gave into the feeling below the pit of her stomach. She gave into him; she gave into everything. She kissed him like he held all the oxygen and she needed to breathe a little longer. His grip tightened on her hip, his other hand now in her hair.

She didn't know which one of them broke

apart first, but they were both breathless. He rested his forehead on hers, a small laugh escaping his mouth. He pressed his lips to her forehead before taking her hand and leading her outside into the wintery cold. The tree lighting wasn't far from Rudy's. Nothing was far from anything in the heart of town. They walked hand-in-hand down the pavement towards the crowd.

"There's Molly," Ainsley said, pointing ahead of them. She was standing with someone. And then she was kissing someone. "Oh."

Ainsley didn't know how to feel. She knew Molly liked Teagan; they had had that talk not too long ago about what she wanted to do. But seeing her now, her little sister, doing something teenagers do, was like a punch to the heart. Molly was growing up. She had grown up, and Ainsley had missed it. If there was anything that solidified her decision to stay, it was seeing her sister being grown. Molly wasn't the silly little toddler that used to chase her around the house or the kid who used to hang upside-down on the couch reading a kid-friendly chapter book. She was standing there, wrapping her arms around her girlfriend, resting her head on her girlfriend's shoulder, and looking at the newly lit Christmas tree.

Ainsley had completely missed the lighting, she dropped Gavin's hand. How was Molly old enough to be doing the same thing that Ainsley

THE HOLLIDAY INN

did with Gavin not three minutes ago?

Molly and Ainsley made eye contact, and Ainsley gave her a small wave. She said something to Teagan, and they started their way over.

"Hey!" Molly said above the buzz of the crowd, acting like she wasn't just snogging someone in public. Ainsley went along with it and pretended she hadn't seen Molly snogging someone in public.

"Hello," Declan answered from behind Ainsley. She and Gavin stepped aside so they could create a small circle for the six of them.

"Everyone this is Teagan...my girlfriend," Molly said. It must have been the first time they'd defined what they were because Teagan looked at Molly with a grin so wide and then laced their hands together. "Teagan, that's my brother Declan and his girlfriend Olive, and my sister Ainsley and her friend Gavin."

They all exchanged pleasantries. Ainsley was a little disheartened that Molly didn't introduce Gavin as her boyfriend but didn't say anything.

"So, when did this become official?" Ainsley asked, wagging a finger between Molly and Teagan.

Molly shrugged. "Since now, I guess."

It was great to see Molly comfortable with someone other than Hilary and Amelia, both of whom Ainsley swore she was attached to since starting school.

"Do you want me to come with you

tomorrow?" Gavin asked Ainsley. She didn't mind the silence with everyone, but it felt awkward, they all knew what everyone was thinking about, and Gavin was the only one willing to be the first to mention it.

"I would, but I think it should be the four of us. Me, Declan, Molly, and Jude," Ainsley clarified.

"You really think you can get Jude away from Angela?" Molly asked.

"You really think she's not going to throw a tantrum to be in that room?" Declan asked.

"None of our people are going, why should she get special treatment? She never once treated them like family."

"Because she's his wife and we're all just dating," Declan said. "I'm just saying," he said defensively when Ainsley glared at him. "You know she's going to throw you every reason she has to be there, regardless of if she wants to be there or not."

Ainsley sighed. "I know. Do we even know where they are?" She stood on her tiptoes looking through the crowd, but no one looked like Jude or Angela. "Are we going to be able to reach them tomorrow?"

"I can wait at the inn to see if they show up."

"Where do they even go during the day?" Molly asked. "I thought she said they were here for his parents."

Ainsley scoffed. "Please, you know they're here because they want a cut of whatever they left in the will."

Everyone murmured in agreement. You had to be blind not to see that that was the reason they were here. Just knowing they were around left a weight on Ainsley's shoulders, which she knew would only go away once they left town for good.

"What's going to happen if they do get a cut of the inn?" Declan asked.

"She'll try to sell it to us for way more than it's worth. She's got to know how much we don't like her around. That, or she'll try to convince us that she's the best fit to run the inn and that we should sell her our shares. And then she'll move here." Ainsley shuddered. "If the inn is even going to us," she added because for all they knew their parents could leave the inn to Albert, someone who actually liked working there and knew how to run it. "If she moves here, I'm not staying."

Everyone fell silent, she knew it wasn't the nicest thing to say, after telling them that she's decided to stay, but she couldn't if Angela was going to try to take the inn.

"Can we go over the plan for tomorrow again?" Molly asked. "I really want to be prepared for what's going to happen." Teagan pressed a soft kiss to Molly's temple.

"There's no way to prepare to say goodbye," Ainsley said. "But we're going to go in the morning. I'll sign the sheet that basically says I'm discontinuing care on Mum and then it'll take however long for her to pass on her own."

"Did I hear you correctly?"

The six of them snapped around to the voice.

"You're discontinuing care on your mother tomorrow?" Angela stood there, with her stupid white hat with a pom-pom and holding a hot beverage in her hand. Strange that Jude was nowhere to be seen; he usually followed her like a lost dog.

"We are," Ainsley said. "It would be great if Jude could come. It'll be happening around ten."

"Just Jude?" she asked, raising her eyebrows.

"Yes," Ainsley said firmly. "We'd really like it to just be the four of us. But you're welcome to wait in the waiting room."

"I'll be in that room," she said as if it was a fact.

"Angela," Declan started. "This really isn't about you. Can you, for once, just think about Jude and *his* family?"

She sighed with a dramatic eye roll. "Whatever."

"Wait," Ainsley said. "Say it with me. Ten o'clock in the morning."

Angela rolled her eyes. "Ten o'clock in the morning, I'm not stupid."

Ainsley had a feeling that they would not be seeing Jude tomorrow at the hospital.

Chapter Thirty-Three
Declan

The next morning everyone was quiet. Olive had gone back to her house, saying it was important for the Holliday siblings to be present with each other today. Ainsley made tea with a permanently neutral face. Molly didn't even greet her older siblings when she came into the kitchen and poured herself a bowl of cereal.

They ate their individually made breakfasts in heavy silence, knowing what the day was to bring them. Declan had never felt his chest so heavy. He never thought he could feel the weight of something that was yet to come. His sisters were going to need him, he needed to stay stoic if he wanted to make it through the day. He needed to not talk; to not talk about *it* if he wanted to make it through the day without shedding a tear.

Without discussion, the three of them cleared their dishes simultaneously and got ready for the day. What did a person wear to the unplugging of their mother? Nothing felt appropriate. He held up his long sleeved pink shirt with the grim reaper on the back standing over a coffin saying, 'wish you were here.' He cringed. Definitely *not* appropriate, though if you had the right sense of humour...no. He put it away and settled on black jeans with a black and white plaid shirt.

He knocked on Ainsley's door, letting her know he needed to go to the inn before going to the hospital. She said she'd text him when they were ready.

At the inn, Albert sat at the front desk. "Mr Holliday," he greeted Declan with a smile.

"Hello, Albert. How's it going?"

"Been busy but going well. How are you all holding up?"

Declan shrugged. "It's hard, but we're together and I think that helps, especially for Molly."

He nodded.

Declan sighed, assuming he already knew the answer to the question he was about to ask. "Is Jude or Angela in?"

"They left not too long ago. I didn't ask where, but assumed they were going to meet you at the hospital."

"Good. Thanks, Albert." Declan nodded and was ready to leave when his phone chimed with a text from Ainsley saying she had warmed up the car and they were ready to go.

Here goes nothing.

"Was Jude coming?" Ainsley asked, beginning the drive to the hospital.

"No, but Albert said that they had left already."

She nodded. Molly sat in the back, watching all the trees pass by as they drove down the

THE HOLLIDAY INN

road. The road had a fresh thin blanket of snow that had yet to be ploughed. The trees were all dusted with fresh snow. Though it did look nice on the pine trees, Declan really liked how the snow looks on the dead ones. He held in a laugh, he supposed that was the theme of the day. He tried to shake the dark humour out of him, he didn't know how the girls would react if he said everything he was thinking. On a normal day he was sure they would laugh along with him, but this...this wasn't something they should joke about.

Ainsley found parking and they stalked solemnly into the building up to their mother's room. Declan couldn't believe they were there. The half-hour drive felt like three minutes. He stood at the foot of the bed, looking at his mum. Her skin was sinking into itself, dark circles sat under her eyes, and they all knew the only reason she was breathing was because of the vent. He sighed, bowing his head.

"It's all right. We'll get through it together," Ainsley said, rubbing his back gently. "Should we wait for Jude?"

Ainsley glanced at the clock. It was only just ten now.

"Let's give him ten or fifteen minutes. You know how she likes to make an entrance," Declan said.

"Of course. I need to talk with the doctor. I'll be back." She left the room, leaving him and Molly alone.

She sat beside their mother but pulled out her phone. He wasn't mad, they all handled these things differently, but how could she be scrolling at a time like this? Was texting her girlfriend more important than being present with her siblings? Was scrolling on her social media more important than sitting in silence with him?

"Here it is," she said, sliding her chair closer to him. "This picture was from when Mum took me sledging a few years back." She turned her phone towards him, and he felt like a dick. He'd just assumed what she was doing.

In the picture, their mum was holding Molly on the sledge, Molly in the front. Their father must have taken the picture. Molly was dressed head to toe in her winter clothes. She even wore sunglasses, so the only part of her face that showed was her toothy grin. She hadn't grown into her teeth yet. Her face was so young, but her adult teeth, especially the front two were large. She had to be at least ten in the picture.

Their mum on the other hand, though only five years ago, was looking her age. Through her smile, her eyes were tired, her wrinkles were adding up, and even her mouth wasn't in full smile. Still, she held a thumbs-up to the camera.

"Here's the video." Molly swiped to the next photo, but it was, indeed, a video.

The video started with them in the same position as the photo. Dad's voice boomed from behind the camera, "Ready?"

"Yeah!" tiny Molly shouted. She thrust her body forward, but the sledge didn't move until their mum began pushing through the snow with her feet. The hill wasn't big, Declan wasn't sure either of their parents could've handled a large hill, but it was still big enough that Molly didn't know better.

Her little voice giggled the whole ride down, but they hit a bump and flipped over. Molly screeched and their mum laughed, laying on her back. Their father chuckled, watching the girls.

Declan pressed his lips together, holding back tears. Molly, beside him, didn't bother to hold them back.

"We haven't gone sledging since. The bump caused her to have a hip problem and she couldn't sledge comfortably. She said she'd take me so I could go on my own, but it never happened." Tears slipped silently down her cheeks. If he wasn't watching her, he wouldn't have known she was crying. He wrapped an arm around her, and she leaned into his shoulder, replaying the video.

"Have Jude and—what's going on?" Ainsley asked, coming into the room.

He cleared his throat and Molly sat up, putting the phone away. "Is it time?"

"Jude and Angela still aren't here?" She checked the time on her phone. "It's twenty after ten, we can't wait any longer."

Declan nodded. He didn't agree with not

waiting until Jude was here, but the hospital had guidelines to follow. They had stalled them long enough; they had reminisced and it was time for Mum to join Dad.

"You know the drill from your dad, it may take minutes or could take hours," the doctor said, reading the chart. Declan wondered how many of these he had to do in the span of a week. "Did you say your goodbyes?"

"I'd like to if you don't mind." Declan stepped forward. "Mum. I'm—I'm sorry that I didn't come home as much. I know now that time together is as important as time apart. I also learned that just because we're biologically family, it doesn't mean the same to everyone. But the three of us here...we feel the same. I'm so sorry Jude isn't here. He should be." Declan stepped back to the chair he was in before. None of them were able to contact either Jude or Angela. They were always gone, nowhere to be found. They had specifically told Angela what time it was when she ran into them because they knew she would blame them for Jude—her—not being there. Declan had a feeling she'd be the first one to the lawyer meeting.

Molly took her bottom lip between her teeth, probably debating if she wanted to speak. Declan wanted to say he felt better after talking to her, but he didn't. It was still her end, and she didn't hear him.

"I'm not going to apologize for not being the perfect daughter," Ainsley started, looking at the ground. "I wasn't and we all know that. You had some dreams for me and that's great, but I'm not sorry for the path that I took." She paused, closing her eyes. Declan couldn't imagine how she felt. "I am sorry that you didn't approve of how I wanted to live my life. I'm sorry that it came between us, and I felt no other option than to stop visiting. That wasn't fair to Molly, and the way you had treated me wasn't fair to me."

Ainsley wouldn't have dared to say that if their mum was conscious. None of them would. As they'd gotten older, they felt braver voicing their opinions, but she wasn't always warm to talk to. She was always on the defence, and quick to play the victim. The release that Ainsley must have felt...her shoulders relaxed, and she stood a little taller.

"I'm sorry I was a brat that night," Molly whispered. That was all she said. It was a word their mother would have used to describe Molly's behaviour.

Once they were all quiet for a short time, standing at the foot of their mum's bed, the doctor began the process for the second time in less than three days. Declan wasn't ready for what was about to happen. It all felt surreal. He never had to process something like this before, let alone twice in the same week.

Ainsley came between Molly and Declan and keep their hands in hers. Declan wondered if they were thinking the same as him—feeling the same as him. Their family was coming to an end; it was only the siblings now. They had to keep it going. It was harder than their mother ever made it look.

The machine beeped faster until it flatlined, which meant Mum was unhooked. The doctor turned off the machine and they all watched their mum, each squeezing the other's hand. They stood there, probably holding their own breaths, for what felt like hours. He was almost positive they had passed lunch and dinner and it was completely dark outside. But when their mother's chest stopped moving, they all relaxed, tears slipping softly down their cheeks, he saw the clock that said barely an hour had passed.

"I'm going to call the lawyer," Ainsley said. She gave Declan a hug, wrapping her arms around his waist, squeezing harder than normal. He held her close, comforted by it. Then she turned and did the same to Molly, holding on longer than with him. The two were glued together; Molly's shoulders shaking as she cried into Ainsley's chest.

Finally, Molly let Ainsley go. "Tell the doctor to take her to the morgue with Dad, and I'll handle the funeral arrangements," Ainsley said before leaving the room.

"I guess I'll find the doctor."

Chapter Thirty-Four
Ainsley

Ainsley didn't want to let go of Molly, she held onto her little sister until she was the one to let go first. Ainsley needed to call the lawyer, maybe they could get the will reading done sooner and get the funeral out of the way before Christmas.

She sighed out a laugh, leaning her head against the wall of the elevator. The chill air outside was like a slap to the face, knocking the breath out of her. Her tear-stained cheeks froze.

"What's going on?" Jude asked, standing right in front of her. "You...you didn't wait for me?"

"Wait for you?" She wiped the tiny frozen tears from her face. "We told Angela ten, we even waiting until ten-thirty for you."

He squinted his eyes at her. "No, you didn't."

"Excuse me?" Ainsley held a hand to her chest.

Angela walked up beside Jude with a cup from Oli's Cart in her hand. "What's up?" she asked nonchalantly, tossing half her hair over her shoulder.

"Did you tell Jude to come for noon?"

"Obviously. As you can see, we're here early."

Ainsley couldn't help but laugh. "What is your problem with this family? We agreed on ten. You even said that you weren't stupid, yet here we are."

She gaped at Ainsley. "How *dare* you. We come all the way here from Yorkshire and *this* is how we are treated?" She turned to Jude. "I told you they don't respect you or me."

"Actually, we don't respect you, we feel sorry for him," Declan said from behind Ainsley. She turned to see him and Molly. Her arms were wrapped around her jacket, holding it tight to keep the cold air out.

"We don't need this. Call us when it's time for the will reading." She turned around, expecting Jude to follow her. When he didn't, she stopped and glared at him. "Hey, Jude. Are you coming?"

He looked between her and his siblings. Water filled his eyes when he looked at his oldest sister. "Can I see her?"

"They just took her down, you'll have to wait for the funeral," Declan answered.

Jude's whole body shrunk into itself, his shoulders hunched, and Ainsley saw a single tear fall out of his eye onto the cleared pavement.

"Come on," Angela demanded.

"Hey," Ainsley said softly, putting a hand on Jude's shoulder. "I'm here for you. I will never be here for her, but if you need your big sister,

I'm willing to give you a second chance. If you can promise me you won't hit me again, I will be here for you. I'm your big sister, regardless of if you're taller." Ainsley added that last bit to hopefully ease the tension.

Jude opened his mouth, but Angela pushed him aside getting in Ainsley's face. "*He* isn't the one that should be asking for a second chance."

"He is, actually. The pair of you should be begging us to continue to include you, but I'm not going to hold my breath. If you want to come to the reading of the will, fine. Thursday at eleven, but I assume you'll be early for that."

Angela narrowed her eyes at Ainsley. "What are you implying?"

"I'm *insinuating* that you're only here to argue about what you think 'Jude' is entitled to."

Angela scoffed and rolled her eyes. "Whatever. We'll see you Thursday at eleven." This time she didn't give Jude the chance to follow, she grabbed his arm and pulled him along with her.

"Wow," Molly said. "She's a special kind of person."

Declan and Ainsley shook their heads in agreement, watching the two of them walk away.

Ainsley never hated Jude, she hated how he treated his siblings when he got with Angela. Suddenly they were never good enough for him, only her family was. Her family was all he was allowed to see. Ainsley didn't even know if he had friends that weren't her brothers or people he worked with. If he worked. Ainsley's heart ached for her family, not even the passing of their parents could bring them all back together. It was time to accept that they would never be good enough for Angela, and worst of all, they didn't know why.

Ainsley could live with Angela not liking her, she didn't care. Angela was way too dramatic and full of herself for Ainsley to ever consider welcoming her into their lives, but what have they done to make her treat them so terribly in the first place?

"I'm going to call Olive, I'm sure she's going crazy wondering how we're all doing."

"I'll do the same with Gavin. And I should probably talk to Narine. I haven't talked to her since dinner at her place."

"I'm going to call my friends," Molly said. They went back inside, this time staying in the lobby, but sitting far enough apart that they couldn't get distracted by the others' phone calls.

"Hey," Gavin answered, his voice soft. "How is everyone?"

"We're all a little sad, obviously, but we're together and I think that helps." Ainsley's voice cracked, tears filling her eyes. All she wanted was Gavin to wrap his arms around her, holding her tightly, squeezing the sadness away.

"If you need anything...actually, would you mind if I stayed with you guys for a few days? I can help keep the house together whilst you three work out the details of the funeral and the lawyer."

Ainsley nodded, even though he couldn't see her. "That'd be really great, I think they'd appreciate it." She sniffed, not realising the tears were still coming.

She was upset about her mum, about her dad, but she thought she was also upset about what happened with Jude and Angela. Her heart literally ached in her chest when she thought about what had happened just outside the hospital. Angela had completely disregarded them as Jude's family, his siblings, and as people. How could she expect them to be the ones to ask her for forgiveness?

"Hey," Declan said coming to sit beside Ainsley, Molly had already come to her other side. "So, Olive offered to come stay with us for a few days to help keep the house together while we worked through everything."

The corner of Ainsley's mouth twitched upward. "Gavin offered too."

"I said yes."

"So, did I. Is it going to be too many people?"

"No," Molly said. "I think we need them around, especially if they are going to continue to be in our lives; they should be here for the hard stuff too."

Ainsley turned to her little sister. "Are you sure you're okay with two extra people staying with us?"

She nodded. "I like them both and I know how happy they make you."

"What about you?" Ainsley asked. "Shouldn't you have someone here for you?"

"I have you guys. It's Christmas, and I don't want to take Amelia and Hilary away from their families."

Ainsley pulled Molly into a big hug. "When did you become so grown up?" Ainsley couldn't believe how mature Molly was being. This didn't feel like the same Molly from the beginning of her visit. She was stronger, sure of herself now. Ainsley loved her sister even more.

"You're squishing me," she mumbled against Ainsley's chest.

"Oh, sorry." She pulled back. "I just can't get over how big you're getting."

Back at the house, Olive and Gavin had arrived before the three siblings, each waiting in their own car that was still running. As soon as Ainsley parked the car, Gavin was at her door, Olive to Declan's; she pulled Declan and Molly into a tight hug, and Gavin embraced Ainsley. He rubbed her back, though she could barely feel it through her thick jacket. It was comforting. She didn't have to be so strong in front of him. Gavin wouldn't judge her for falling apart. She never felt she needed to hide

THE HOLLIDAY INN

her feelings around him. She was so mean to him in the beginning, and he was still around. She couldn't lose him now.

"Let's get them inside," Gavin said above her head to Olive. She must've silently agreed because they started moving toward that house, with Gavin's hand still on her back.

"You go sit in the living room and we'll make tea," Olive said once they were inside. She nearly pushed Ainsley into the living room because she was going to help them with the tea.

"It's nice to have them here," she said, sitting on the couch at the opposite end as Molly, and Declan curled himself on the chair. "Though I feel like I should be the one in the kitchen and they should be here comforting you."

"Why? They didn't lose a parent today."

"Molly," Declan said. "Be nice."

"I'm just saying that Ainsley lost her mum and dad, she shouldn't have to do anything for anyone."

She was right, Ainsley knew that deep down, but who was she to sit there and expect to be taken care of by people whom she's spent barely a month with?

"Here," Olive said, placing a full tray onto the coffee table. She curled into Declan, resting her head on his shoulder.

Molly took a cup, added sugar, and sat back.

Ainsley watched Gavin enter the room. He carried a bowl of crisps, setting it on the table beside the tea. "Come," he said, holding his hand out to Ainsley. She took it and he led her down the hall to her room. "I know you like to be alone when big things happen."

Her room was cleaned, the suitcase that she had on one side of the bed was picked up and rolled against the wall, the bed was made and on it was a set of pyjamas and a throw blanket. He added candles to the bedside table that were waiting to be lit. Her laptop sat closed on the bed, charging ready for her to work.

Everything about this was perfect. It had been barely a month since they first started seeing each other, and here he was knowing her so well. She wrapped her arms around his neck. "This is perfect. It doesn't even feel like my room." She buried her face in the crook of his neck. He held her tightly like if he let go she'd crumble into a million pieces. And maybe she would, but he had her.

She pulled back a little, so she could see him. "Truly, thank you for doing this, but I think I'd like to sit out there for a bit."

"Of course. I'll let you change and meet you out there."

She kissed his cheek. "You're something special, you know."

He smiled and gently pressed his lips to her forehead before closing the door behind him. She changed into her pyjamas. She wrapped the thick, soft blanket around her shoulders and went back to the living room.

"...forced me into a dress when I clearly

hated it," Molly was telling a story whilst Ainsley came in quietly sitting on the couch, leaning into Gavin. He draped his arm around her. "So, she'd yell at me all the time for yelling because I didn't want to wear dresses, but she constantly put me in them."

"Oh yeah!" Ainsley said. "You were what, six? And the school was putting on a Christmas show, and she had the dress from when I was six and wanted you to wear it."

"Yeah!" Molly laughed. "It was so ugly, no offence, but it had those puffy sleeves you see on wedding dresses from like the eighties. And I think it was like a baby poop green with red, because Christmas colours." She rolled her eyes, laughing.

Ainsley laughed too. "Oh my god, yes. It was so bad! And Molly threw the biggest fit."

"How'd she get out of wearing it?" Olive asked with a grin.

"Oh." Molly sat her tea on the table and clapped her hands. "I found a jar of pickles in the fridge and dumped the juice all over the dress."

"At least the smell matched the look," Ainsley said, causing more laughter. This sound was perfect. She could imagine their mum there either laughing with them or scolding them as they continued to talk about all the times she tried to dictate their lives and they'd lashed back. There was nothing Ainsley would change about that moment. She snuggled deeper into Gavin, whilst Molly

D. C. COOK

scrolled through her phone, looking for a picture to prove it was the ugliest dress to disgrace the face of the earth.

Chapter Thirty-Five
Declan

Olive's hand traced little circles in Declan's hair whilst the siblings all told stories about their parents. He held her close to him. He was determined to make it last, to keep her around for the rest of time; he couldn't stand to lose another person.

"What's that story about the bath?" Declan asked Ainsley, knowingly with an evil grin.

"No!" She covered her face with her blanket and giggled. "Don't." She peeked her head out and glared at him.

"Oh, come on, Gavin needs to hear it. It's so funny!" Molly joined in.

Ainsley groaned heavily. "Fine," she huffed. "Okay, so I was like four, a mere child. Barely a child, still a young lass, a tot if you will—"

"Get on with it!" Molly said.

"Fine. So, I don't know what I was doing, playing maybe. Anyway, Mum declared it was time for a bath. But my sweet young soul had no interest, so I said no and continued what I was doing. Well, Mum did not like being told no, especially by a child. Now, instead of giving a time limit, like a good parent would do, I got an ultimatum...remind you I am four. What four-year-old knows how to handle an ultimatum?"

"You're dragging it out and making it less funny," Declan said.

"Fine!" Ainsley shouted, exasperated. "Mum threw me in the tub with all my clothes on because I had told her I didn't want a bath."

"All your clothes?" Gavin held back a laugh.

"Yes. Socks, underwear, pants, shirt, the whole lot."

"What was it that Mum would say after telling that story?" Declan grinned again, knowing.

Ainsley rolled her eyes. "I never told her no to a bath again."

This is what caused everyone to laugh.

"Poor baby Ainsley." Olive touched her heart like it was breaking for a younger Ainsley.

"It could have traumatized me. I don't take baths, now. Ever."

"Mum would've rolled her eyes so hard to that. Traumatize," Molly sighed. "We could never be traumatized. She gave us everything, what would we have to be traumatized about?"

"Of course," Ainsley agreed. The room fell into some kind of silence. Declan didn't know what anyone else was thinking of, but he couldn't stop thinking that he was glad these were his people. They didn't have to tell only happy stories about their childhood to honour their parents, they honoured them by remembering all parts of their childhood, the good and the bad. It felt right. He'd feel like a fraud if they were only telling the good stuff, because not all of it was good, and that's okay. They were never a perfect family, and he couldn't imagine pretending to be one now that their parents were gone. All of those experiences made the siblings who they were now.

"How different is this Christmas now compared to when we were little." Declan sighed, pulling Olive closer. She continued her circles in his hair, kissing the top of his head. He rested his head on her chest.

"Yeah," Ainsley said, blowing out a long breath. "I feel like a visitor now, not like this is my home."

"Molly said you were thinking of staying?"

She nodded. "It just makes sense. I've had a good time, other than all the hospital stuff. I've loved getting to know you guys again and meeting Gavin. I really think it's the best thing for me, for us as a family."

Declan nodded in agreement. He missed his sister. They could go ages without talking, but everyone came together it was as if no time had passed. He didn't think he could handle her leaving again, losing another person.

"Wait." She shot up. "That's it. That's what I'm going to write my article about." She paused, looking at Declan and Molly who just looked confused.

"Go!" he said. "Go write, it's your job. We're all good here."

"I'm going to get dinner started." Gavin stood as Ainsley left for her room.

"I need to finish Teagan's Christmas gift." Molly stood and went off to her room too.

"And then there were two," Declan said.

"You think she's okay? Molly, I mean," Olive asked. "She's got no one here, whilst you and your sister have your partners."

He never thought of that. He was sure she was okay with it; they had touched on it whilst in the hospital when they arranged for Olive and Gavin to come over. She said she was fine with it, was she lying?

"Should we call someone for her?"

"I don't know her friends' phone numbers."

"Her phone is right there." Olive pointed to the table.

"If you think I know her passcode you're delusional." He chuckled, pulling her face down to give her a kiss. "I can't believe we're here—you're here. It feels like a dream to be in your arms."

"Well, I am. I thought for sure I'd never let myself love you again, but the truth was I never stopped. I saw you and everything came flooding back like time never passed. I tried to move on from you, but you're...you're Declan, you're my love. My one great and true love." She planted kisses on his face. "You're nerdy and silly and loving and sexy," she said the last one as a whisper in his ear, sending a shiver up his spine.

They all spent dinner apart, Ainsley and

THE HOLLIDAY INN

Gavin in her room as she worked on the article that she couldn't lose her train of thought on. Molly stayed in her room, painting her portrait for Teagan for Christmas. Olive and Declan sat at the table.

Gavin had prepared a great dish of bangers and mash. Declan was surprised he had found sausages in the fridge, or maybe the freezer. The most surprising was that their potatoes were still good. They'd been served with gravy and peas. It was a basic meal, but delicious. Declan, too, would've opted for an easy meal, though the clean-up wasn't going to be easy, He hated dishes. He thought every person in his family did.

"Don't worry about the dishes," Olive said.

"What?" Declan turned his attention back to her.

"I see you watching the dishes willing them to clean themselves like something from *Beauty and the Beast*. I'll take care of it."

"You're truly the best part of me." He reached beside him to hold her hand.

Declan didn't see Ainsley most of the day on Wednesday because her article was due on Thursday morning, the same day they were to meet the lawyer. She claimed that it was going well but they were not allowed to read it until it was published. Declan couldn't lie, he was excited to see how she turned the article into something good that didn't make her seem like a tourist in a town she was only just getting to know again. Her original idea was something like what happens in the town at Christmas, which he thought would've been fine, but she said this was much better. She'd been digging through old boxes from the back of her mum's closet.

It wasn't until Thursday at eleven in the living room that she finally emerged from her room. Just as she suspected, Jude and Angela were early.

"Should they really be here?" Angela asked about Gavin and Olive. Ainsley was nestled into Gavin, who had his arm around her protectively. Olive was sat on Declan's lap, and he held her like a comfort teddy bear.

"Why shouldn't they? You're here," Ainsley said, turning her attention to the lawyer. "Let's get this done."

"You guys are *barely* dating. Jude and I are *married*. There's a difference."

"You don't get to dictate who we have here as our support people," Declan said.

Molly came into the room wrapped in her favourite yellow blanket from when she was a kid. Declan hadn't seen her use it in years, but that didn't mean she didn't use it behind closed doors. She took the empty seat beside Ainsley and leaned into her.

"All right, now that we've settled," George, the lawyer, said. "We are here for the reading of the will of Dorothy and Edward Holliday. Present we have their children Ainsley, Jude Declan, and Molly."

"Please remember this is a legal document, whatever is written here is not the fault of anyone sitting before us now."

Declan wondered if anyone else thought he was directing his comment toward Angela. The lawyer hadn't been here for ten minutes before she was on her regular bullshit complaining that Ainsley was late, even though she came into the living room exactly when the meeting was supposed to start.

"The car, Dorothy's car, goes to Molly June Holliday on her sixteenth birthday. If that day has passed the car goes right to Molly," George read. "That wasn't the one in the accident, was it?"

"No. They were in Dad's truck," Molly said, a grin spreading across her mouth. "I can't believe they trusted me with their new car."

Declan nodded, impressed. They had just bought the car a few months before last Christmas; he remembered commenting on it.

"The house goes to the child whom you all feel should have it." George narrowed his eyes, but said nothing else, so that must be what is stated, or at least paraphrased.

"I think—" Angela started, but Declan quickly interjected.

"Jude and Angela already bought a house in Yorkshire, so I think it should go to either me or Ainsley."

"It should go to you," Ainsley said. "You're the one already running the inn. It only makes sense that you own the house that goes with it."

"We don't know who gets the inn yet," Angela said. "Let's settle down."

Declan hated it, but she was right. They didn't know who got the inn and that could change who they thought would get the house. He instinctively held Olive closer, nervous about what George was going to say about the inn.

"They leave everything in the house to the four of you, letting you decide what to do with it, whether to throw it or keep it. They thought you all would know best and want to make the house your own."

Declan couldn't tell if George was reading and paraphrasing or remembering a conversation he had with their parents. He was relaxed like he did this all the time. He probably did. *Wow, that's depressing.*

"And what you've all gathered for: the inn." He flipped the page, nodding as his eyes skimmed the words. "The inn is left to Ainsley Mae Holliday, Declan Allan Holliday, and Molly June Holliday."

"Wait." Molly sat up straight. "I get a share of the inn?"

"I *don't?*" Angela asked. "We," she corrected when everyone glared at her, but it wasn't any better. If either of them should get a share, it should be Jude not the both of them.

"Yup, there's always something," George muttered to himself. Declan couldn't believe that he knew this was going to happen.

THE HOLLIDAY INN

"What's written is legally binding. If any of the other three want to sell you their share then they can, but it needs to be done legally. I would recommend going through me as I've known your parents since we were in high school, but whatever you choose is up to you, Ainsley, Declan, and Molly."

"Wait, wait, wait." Angela shook her head, holding her hands up.

Ainsley rolled her eyes. Olive shifted in Declan's lap. He couldn't blame her for not liking Angela, he couldn't wait for her to leave.

"Let me try to understand this. Molly, a fifteen-year-old, has a share in the inn and Jude, a grown man, does not?"

"That appears to be what is written." George closed the will. "You guys can read over it yourselves, I'm here to read the big stuff and make sure it goes smoothly."

"There's nothing smooth about this. Jude is their son, he deserves at *least* a quarter of the inn."

"Why do you care?" Ainsley asked. "You've never bothered to come help when they had a flood in the basement six years ago, you never bothered to get to know any of us and completely shut us all out since dating Jude. What makes you think he deserves anything from them? He shut them out, so they did the same. It's not right, but it's their decision."

Declan silently agreed, it wasn't right, Jude was still their son. But he understood. If they left something to Jude, they were also leaving it to Angela, and no way were any of them going to leave something as special as the inn to her.

"You're just going to sit there and take this?" Angela asked Jude. "God, you're terrible." She huffed and stormed into the kitchen. Jude followed her immediately.

"Okay, so if that's everything, I'm going to go now." George packed his things and left.

"All right, so we are the owners of the inn now," Ainsley said. "What do we do with that?"

"Well, I was thinking of hiring more staff. Someone to clean, specifically."

Molly nodded slowly like there was a beat that one else could hear. "So, I'm fifteen, what can I even do? Is it even legal for me to own a business?"

Declan shrugged. "It's in the will and George didn't say anything else about it, so it must be."

"Should we talk to them?" Ainsley asked. "I mean, I don't want to sell them my share, because lord knows what she would do, but we could try to like lessen the...pain?"

Declan nodded, gently pushing Olive to stand.

"Maybe you two should stay here, this feels like a sibling plus Angela thing," Ainsley said putting her hand on Gavin's arms.

"Of course," he said. He kissed her forehead, and she closed her eyes until he pulled away.

THE HOLLIDAY INN

Declan kissed Olive's cheek, sliding his hand around her waist before leaving for the kitchen. Molly trailed behind her older siblings. This wasn't her battle, regardless of her holding shares, she shouldn't have to deal with Angela's bullshit.

"So, that was a lot of information," Ainsley said, trying to be nonchalant. "How are you guys holding up?"

Angela narrowed her eyes as if to ask *how the f—you think?* "We're fine, thanks." She smiled sarcastically.

"I'm sorry you, *Jude*, didn't get anything. It's not completely fair. So, if there's anything you want from the house, I think it's pretty reasonable to let you have something."

"Yes, anything you want," Declan quickly agreed. It wasn't as big as getting a portion to the inn, but at least he would have something of their parents'.

"We don't need your charity. I know you don't like me, and you don't have to. Frankly, I don't like any one of you either, but he is still a Holliday; he should have a part of that inn."

Declan nodded as if finally understanding. "You don't care about a memento of our parents. You want the inn. You know how popular it is, how much money it makes in a year. But that inn is a *family* possession. It took me a while to realise what the definition of family is."

"Just look it up, it's like parents and their kids. He is their kid."

"Maybe so, but family is more than a definition, it's a feeling, it's treatment, it's security. None of us have a good time when you're around. You suck the joy out of everything, you're only in it for you. That's not family, that's narcissism.

"Family is sacrificing things for others. Ainsley gave up her life in New York to stay with us and help run the inn." He didn't know if the last part was true, but she didn't correct him. They were a united front when it came to Angela. "I dropped a job I loved, a flat that had a great view of the city to help Molly through this time."

Angela crossed her arms over her chest with a dramatic eye roll.

"My first thought when Molly called me was about her and how she was going to handle this. Not about me. You came here to know what you got from our *dead* parents. We are not the same. You are not family. You're greedy."

"Are you going to stand there or are you going to stick up for me?" Angela accused Jude.

Unexpectedly, Jude let out a laugh. "How can I defend you?"

"Excuse me?"

"Oop." Ainsley covered her mouth.

Chapter Thirty-Six
Molly

Ainsley had slapped a hand over her mouth when Jude began to stand up for himself. Molly almost couldn't believe it was happening. He was so easy to walk over, Angela could manipulate him into anything. Molly hated the way he acted like he didn't care about anything. But this was the final straw, he was finally doing something about it, finally acting like an adult and not an immature teenager, and Molly should know what those are like.

"Angela, Declan is right. You came here demanding to know what they left us, they're dead. I didn't get to say goodbye to my dad, and you sabotaged me saying goodbye to my mum." His voice cracked at the end. Molly felt so bad, if she hadn't had the chance to say goodbye or apologize, she'd never have had the closure she did. She knew her mother was safe now, she was with their father and they would be together forever. "They got to grieve to say goodbye." Jude gestured toward Ainsley, Declan, and Molly. "And I got to wait for the lawyer to learn what we get?"

"Because you deserve everything, babe." Angela reached for his face. "I want you to get everything you deserve. These people are keeping it from you."

Jude pushed her away. It was like watching a movie but in real life. Or maybe more like a train wreck, Molly couldn't quite decide.

"The only one keeping me from it is you. All I wanted was to say goodbye to my parents, to see them go, and you gave me the wrong times, so we'd miss it."

"This is the most I've ever heard him talk," Ainsley whispered. Molly stifled a giggle, but she was right. The whole time they'd been here Angela was the one talking or dictating.

Jude glanced their way, but he didn't stop. "I don't know why you don't like my family, but we used to have the best times together until we grew up and..."

Please say: and then I met you.

"And we grew apart. You convinced me I didn't need them because Ainsley left for New York. She was the piece that held this family together. She's the eldest. But what did any of them do to convince you that they weren't worth being at our wedding or worth coming to visit for the holidays? Hell, I slapped Ainsley for you and she's still willing to be there for me. Christ."

Angela couldn't answer. There was no answer. They had welcomed her in, and she was the one who burned the bridge.

"I think you need to leave," Ainsley spoke up. "Jude, you're welcome to stay, there's a lot we need to talk about, but Angela. You are not welcome into our home anymore."

"You can't do that; I'm his wife. Legally—"

Ainsley chuckled. "You're such a drama queen. Go. You have a room at the inn. And might I suggest making a new reservation elsewhere as soon as possible, because I know the owners, and well, let's just say they don't really like your attitude."

Angela narrowed her eyes and pursed her lips. "This isn't the end of this." She watched Jude the entire time she got ready to face the outside, but he didn't move. He was either too scared to be alone with her or he genuinely wanted to talk with his siblings.

"Tea?" Ainsley asked, she started the kettle anyway. Jude sat at the table, ready to have it. "You know what you did back then was wrong."

"I know." He bowed his head, clasping his hands in front of him on the table.

"I don't care that we weren't there if it was truly only going to be you two. But the fact that her family was there, and no one thought to ask about us?" Ainsley turned to him. "What the hell, Jude?"

He shrugged. "I don't know what to tell you. She made all the plans and I just showed up."

"*That's* the problem, Jude. You didn't do any-thing. You can't sit in there and expect to get anything after literally doing nothing at all to defend your family. If it were up to me alone, neither of you would've been allowed at that reading."

Molly tried to stay neutral, but she agreed. He treated them all like dirt and came in expecting something? Even if it was mostly Angela, he was with her.

"What do you want from us?" Ainsley asked.

Declan sat at the table across from Jude, but Molly made herself comfortable sitting on the floor, against the fridge.

"I don't know."

"Do you want to be part of this again? Or are you happy with her in your little bubble that seems to only include her family?"

Jude shrugged.

Ainsley's hands clenched slowly into fists. "If you're going to sit here and shrug and continue with the 'I don't knows' then you can go. There's nothing that we can do for you at this point. You're just as bad as she is." Ainsley turned back to the tea.

Jude shot his head up. "No, I'm not."

"You could possibly be worse because at least she shows how narcissistic she is. You just hide behind her. You don't really want to be here, you don't really care about us, do you?"

"I don't know what you want me to say, Ainsley. You didn't come to my wedding, I'm sorry? Is that what you want?" Jude's words came out snarky, only making Ainsley angry.

"No. I don't care about your fucking wedding, Jude! I care about *you* not treating *us* with the damned respect that we deserve!"

THE HOLLIDAY INN

Her face turned red; her words flew out quickly with force. No one knew how to respond.

Jude didn't say anything. Molly didn't know what Ainsley expected from him, but she huffed and turned to the tea kettle.

What could someone say to that? Molly didn't know how she would respond; she didn't think anything he said could change what he'd done. All he could do now was move forward and be better; that was all any of them could do.

"Molly?" Ainsley's voice came out soft.

"Huh?" Molly snapped her head toward Ainsley, who was holding up a spoon of tea over a cup.

"No, thank you, I need to keep working on Teagan's Christmas gift."

She rose from the floor, pulling the blanket a little tighter around her, and trailed off to her room. She didn't even know if she was going to see Teagan until after Christmas, but painting her gift was the only distraction from whatever was going on in the kitchen. She synced her earbuds to her phone and turned up the music.

She paid attention to every detail, the colours, the designs on the spins; she did her best to make it look accurate. She was nearly finished. But it was missing something. Something personal. *What can I add?* Teagan had told her about a voicemail she kept on her phone, from her mum. It was the last time she'd ever heard her mum say 'I love you.' Molly painted a piece of paper that looked tacked onto the edge of the shelf and wrote 'I love you - Mum' in the nicest cursive she could manage. It took a long time.

But it still felt like it needed something, something personal from Molly. In the top corner of the shelf, she made it look like they etched their initials in it. It was subtle, she doubted Teagan would even notice if she didn't tell her, but it made Molly's heart soar.

Molly remembered back when she realised she was attracted to women and not boys, she thought her entire family would leave her. But her mum pulled her close, stroked her hair, placed a kiss to the top of her head and said, "You're still our little girl."

Molly took her bottom lip between her teeth, trying to hold back tears. They never once thought of her any differently. They never treated her differently. Her parents were her biggest support-ters. They even let her decide if she called her siblings or not. She did. Except for Jude, she never knew how Angela would twist it around. But looking at her initials carved into the bookshelf inside of a heart with Teagan's confirmed that she was who she was, and she loved who she was. And she really liked Teagan.

Molly thought her mum would like Teagan. Mum would've welcomed her with open arms, despite having personal judgements on how Teagan looked with her grunge appearance.

THE HOLLIDAY INN

She could almost picture them interacting together. Her chest tightened and she stumbled back onto the floor. She pulled her knees up to her chest and let the tears come.

"Molly, you have—oh."

Molly looked up at Ainsley in her door frame.

"You have a visitor," she said, stepping a half step to the side to reveal Teagan.

"This could not be a worse time." Molly laughed, wiping her eyes.

"I can come back." Teagan slowly came into Molly's room and Ainsley shut the door, walking away.

"It's okay. Um..."

"Is that..." Teagan went closer to the easel with her painting on it. "Those are all my favourites."

"It's supposed to be for Christmas." Molly sniffed.

"Is it done?"

Molly sniffed again and nodded.

Teagan awed over the painting for what felt like ten excruciatingly long minutes. But, according to Molly's clock, it was just two.

"Molly, this is incredible." Teagan snapped her head toward her. "That's our initials in a heart."

Molly's eyes widened. "Yeah. You saw it?"

Molly moved to her bed and leaned against the wall, embarrassed now that she made the heart.

"I love it. I can't believe you painted that for

me." She sat beside Molly, their shoulders touching. "That might be the most thoughtful gift anyone has ever given me."

Molly laid down so her head was in Teagan's lap, and she grabbed the blanket Molly was previously wrapped in, and wrapped her in it, rubbing her arm.

"Thank you. The note on it was a perfect touch." Molly glance up at Teagan, tears were pooling in her eyes. "I miss her so much."

Molly snuggled in. "I know. I was just thinking how mine would never get to meet you." The tears that threatened to come made Molly's nose sting. "She would've loved you, once she finally got over the things you wore. She is—was—a bit judge-mental."

Looking at Teagan now, her hair in long French braids and barely any eye makeup on, you'd never think she was the rock band girl from earlier this month.

"Why did you stop wearing so much makeup?" Her clothes were different too. She wore a white, blue, and purple plaid shirt and light blue ripped jeans. She's never looked hotter...but still. "And your clothes."

Teagan tipped her head back against the wall, at this angle Molly could only see under her chin. A scoff of a laugh escaped Teagan. She tipped her head back down to meet Molly's eyes. "You know how I wanted to be seen. When I met you, and you wanted to be with me, despite what people were saying, I didn't need their attention. I had yours. *You* see me and I don't need anyone else to."

"Oh, Teagan..." Molly reached up and touched her cheek. Then, thinking she must look stupid, she sat up and rested their foreheads together. "You're an incredible person."

Teagan's eyes fell to Molly's mouth, and she broke the tension by pressing her lips to Teagan's. She held Molly close. Every emotion filled her body as they shed their tears and kissed. Molly couldn't believe how happy she was to have someone like Teagan have feelings for her, she understood Molly completely. She was a mess and Teagan didn't care. She didn't know who she was as a whole yet, and Teagan was right beside her anyway. Molly was happy that her siblings have decided to stay, to help each other through this, to keep the inn in the family name. She was incredibly sad that her parents would never be there to meet Teagan, to see her graduate, to see Ainsley happy in a relationship, to see Declan taking initiative and responsibility without being asked.

But a little part of her found comfort in thinking that wherever they were, they were watching their children. And maybe the kids wouldn't be okay for a long time, but it was in that moment, where Teagan was looking at Molly with such hope and love in her eyes, the way Ainsley brought two cups of tea into the room with a protective-like instinct, or the way that Declan was sitting in the kitchen with Jude and she could hear them talking about all the snowball fights, and laser tag games, and Nerf gun fights they all used to have as kids. Jude was laughing. Ainsley was smiling.

It didn't matter what Angela did, or what she tried to say. It wouldn't matter because the three of them were a united front. They might not have their parents anymore, but Molly knew they would be happy that in their final days, they brought *all* of their children back together.

Epilogue

Molly woke up on Christmas morning with little to no expectations. The four of them had stayed up late on Christmas Eve to watch a movie, and though none of them fell asleep in the living room, she was happy the tradition lived on.

She left her room; Ainsley was already in the kitchen making tea and breakfast. Declan sat in the living room with Jude, who was planning to return to Yorkshire with Angela that morning. There were small boxes covered in Christmas wrapping.

"What are those?" Molly gestured to the pile, unsure of when any of them had time to go shopping, let alone wrap gifts.

"We got you a little something," Ainsley said following Molly to the living room.

"I didn't get you guys anything, I didn't think that we were doing that." Molly felt bad for not thinking of getting her siblings something. There was so much more going on, it didn't even cross her mind that they would be exchanging gifts.

"No worries." Ainsley smiled.

Molly sat on the floor starting with the biggest. She unwrapped six new canvases for her to paint on. In the smaller boxes were new paints and a new set of brushes.

"I've seen your brushes. You're welcome," Ainsley said.

"Thank you. I love it." Molly closed her eyes, taking it in.

Almost immediately, it was time for Jude to leave. They didn't know when they'd see him again, but they didn't mind, he had an open invitation. The four Holliday siblings still had a lot of work to do, especially with Angela, but they weren't giving up on each other. Ainsley wasn't giving up on the family she had left.

Ainsley hugged her brother. "Thank you for coming home. Next time, don't wait for a traumatic event, huh?"

"I won't, promise."

Ainsley, Declan, and Molly stood on the front step waving goodbye to Jude. They didn't hold onto hope that they'd see him soon, but it was Christmas time, and the feeling in the air was enough to ease them.

"Bye Angela. Happy Christmas," Ainsley said, non-sarcastically, taking Declan and Molly by surprise. She put her arms around her younger siblings and watched Jude and Angela pull away. "I love you, guys."

Acknowledgements

I know that I thank the same people over and over, but it wouldn't be possible to write without my husband. He's so supportive. Nothing would get done without him.

Thank you to my critique partners and beta readers. You guys are what helps get the story looking its best.

A big thank you to my siblings—my family. I love you guys. Thank you for being the lowkey inspiration for this book. As the oldest sibling I care for all my younger siblings so deeply. You guys are my best friends. Some have strayed over the years, but what is family if not people willing to love you despite your flaws? I hope that it was articulated through this book that I hope we always have a strong connection.

Thank you to my ARC team. I've loved growing it this year, and am always looking to grow my team. If you're interested you can email me, dccookbooks@gmail.com

From the East Coast of Canada, D. C. Cook is a YA and NA romance author. She's been writing romances for over twelve years. Over the years she's taken the craft seriously and became a proofreader for other authors. D. C. Cook loves meeting readers and writers of all types.

For inquiries please email: dccookbooks@gmail.com

Or visit her website: www.abooksnook.ca

Made in the USA
Middletown, DE
06 October 2022